ROSEVEAN WAS A HOUSE OF SECRETS, MENACE AND JEALOUSY -- AND ITS EVIL SLOWLY REACHED OUT TO STRANGLE ANN FORRESTER.

As personal assistant to the wealthy and elderly Mrs. Pendine of Rosevean, Ann Forrester thought her duties would be routine. It wasn't long, though, before she realized that there was more to Rosevean than met the eye. Somewhere in the past of the forbidding Gothic mansion lurked a terrible secret.

Now something strange was going on at Rosevean, and Ann was deeply involved. Soon she found she could trust no one in the sinister house with her love—or her life!

A Paperback Library Gothic

This is a genuine Paperback Library Gothic.

ROSEVEAN

A Paperback Library Gothic by

Iris Bromige

PAPERBACK LIBRARY, Inc.

New York

CHAPTER I

ANN FORRESTER looked across the desk at Mr Cardew's thin, parchment-coloured face, and found it hard to visualize him outside the dam, dusty, file-crammed offices of Cardew & Pakes, solicitors, so well attuned was he to his surroundings. His limp, grey hair, pale eyes and narrow, colourless lips seemed to have had the life drained out of them by the legal documents he worked with. Even his voice suggested the thin, dry rustle of papers. He was the executor of her father's will, and they had just cleared up the last of the points arising from it. As he shuffled some papers together, Ann drew on her gloves.

'By the way, Miss Forrester, you were telling me that you hoped to find a new post far away from London and the—er—sad reminders of your loss.'

'Yes, Mr Cardew. I haven't found anything suitable yet, but I've only just started looking, and the house is mine for another month.'

'Quite so. I raise the matter because a client of mine, a Mrs Pendine, who lives in Cornwall, is looking for a personal assistant, whose duties she only vaguely indicates in her letter, and has asked me if I know of any young woman of good family whom I could personally recommend. It occurred to me that you might be interested.'

'A personal assistant. That could mean anything,' said Ann slowly.

'Well, let me tell you a little about my client. She is a widow, not far off eighty, if I remember rightly, and very wealthy. She lives in a huge old house in Cornwall with her niece and granddaughter. She is, if I may say so, a somewhat formidable old lady who has not moved with the times and prefers to ignore the world as we know it today. In fact,' he added with the ghost of a smile, 'she will not even avail herself of a motor car, although at her age and in that place, it would indeed be valuable, preferring to keep a pony and trap and refusing to allow cars to enter the drive of Rosevean. I thought,' he added with a little more sensitivity than she had credited him with, 'that might appeal to you.'

'Yes.' Ann looked down at her hands and wondered how long it would be before even an oblique reference to the car accident which had killed her parents two months ago would not penetrate like a cold dagger. 'It sounds interesting, although I would naturally want to know a good deal more about it.'

'Quite so. Mrs Pendine has asked me to let her know by the end of the week whether or not I can help her, as she intends to send an advertisement to the personal column of *The Times* next week if a private recommendation is not forthcoming. If you would like to write for more particulars, I will give you her address and write her a note commending you as a young lady of good family.'

His dry tone drew a little smile from Ann. Mr Cardew was not, after all, quite lacking in humour.

'Thank you. I'll certainly write to her. I had thought of going abroad, but perhaps Cornwall will be far enough.'

Mr Cardew leaned back in his chair, placed his finger-tips together and looked over them at the pale, composed face of the young woman whom he had come to like during their recent interviews. He had known her father for many years, on a business footing only, and recognized in his daughter the same flavour of steadfastness that Jim Forrester had possessed. In his experience, bereaved persons could be a great nuisance, expecting him to solve their personal problems as well as their financial ones, telephoning him over all kind of trivialities and using him as a kind of universal aunt. This young woman had neither wept nor complained, but had shown admirable self-control and common sense. If there was one thing he detested, it was being bathed in women's emotions, and he accorded Ann Forrester full marks for her restraint.

She had looked shocking when he first saw her, after her discharge from hospital. Miraculously, her injuries had proved of a minor nature, but she had worn a look of numbed pain that was all the more marked for her reserve. He doubted whether she had grasped much at their first interview, but subsequently she had taken a grip on things, and had earned his approval. A terrible experience for the girl. He had been surprised that Forrester had left so little. Still, the architectural profession was a tricky one where small practices were concerned. He cleared his throat and said,

'I should, perhaps, warn you that Rosevean is very isolated

and may not offer you quite the distraction you seek. You won't meet many people there.'

'You can feel awfully lonely in a crowd. The peace and beauty of the country might be a greater help.'

'Very true. Well, here's the address. Worth investigating, anyway. I'll write a note to Mrs Pendine this afternoon. Now if there are any financial matters that you're not quite clear about, I am always at your disposal.'

'Thank you, Mr Cardew. You've been most kind.'

'A pity the house was so heavily mortgaged, but the little capital remaining should tide you over any emergencies.'

'I'm not worried about money. That's the least of it,' she said as she stood up and leaned on the desk for a moment as though she was tired.

It was always the same, he thought. Those who wept and wailed the loudest found quick consolation in the money, and those who kept their grief hidden often had an indifference to money which made it seem quite irrelevant. To youth, anyhow, he supposed, it was never so important. Time had not corrupted them to a worship of money. Middle-aged legatees, he had found, were worst. Rapacious was a word which unhappily often occurred to him in such connections.

'Well, my dear young lady, a new life in different surroundings will help you to put all this behind you. You're young. The best of luck to you.'

As she took his hand, he thought that the best thing that could happen to her would be to fall in love with a decent young man. She was not unattractive, he considered. An interesting face, with those dark brown eyes set wide apart, and the unusually sensitive mouth which, though too wide for conventional beauty, seemed to him beautifully expressive. Beneath the close-fitting, helmet-shaped hat, smooth fair hair framed the oval face with a narrow, curving rim. She was a good height, but too thin, he thought. Although he was not a man given to paying much attention to the looks of the opposite sex, it yet occurred to him to be glad that the small scar across the top of her forehead was the only visible damage from the accident.

After he had escorted her to the door, he returned to his desk and picked up Mrs Pendine's letter. Perfect copperplate writing. Why did she want an assistant who could type? It didn't seem to fit in with Mrs Pendine's way of life. An uncompromising autocrat, she would be no easy employer. He wondered whether, perhaps, he had done Miss Forrester no favour by putting her in touch with the owner of Rosevean. Then he shrugged his shoulders. At twenty-five, with a good head on her shoulders, Ann Forrester was well able to judge for herself whether the post would suit her or not, and he had too much to do to give any more thought to it. He drew a pile of letters towards him, placed Mrs Pendine's on the top, and rang for his secretary.

.   .   .

The reply to Ann's letter came by return, giving her no particulars of the position to be filled but asking her to come to Rosevean for an interview. Full details of the journey were given. The night train from Paddington would be met at Truro, and she would be driven to Rosevean for breakfast. They would discuss all that was necessary during the morning, and she would be driven back to Truro in time to catch the early afternoon train. Her expenses would, of course, be paid.

Ann propped the letter against the coffee pot and reflected that it was a long way to go for an interview when she knew so little about the post. The inertia which had overtaken her in these last weeks made it difficult to face the effort involved. It was as though all her capacity for feeling had been exhausted, and nothing seemed to matter any more. But, somehow, she had to make a new life for herself and this offered novelty, if nothing else. If she stayed here much longer, in this quiet empty house with only ghosts for company, she would drown in her own desolation. She posted her reply that morning and booked her sleeper on the train.

She left London on a cold, wet night, and to her surprise slept well throughout the journey. Sleepless nights had been so frequent since the accident that she could not believe it when the porter thrust in a tray of tea and told her that she had half an hour. When she lifted the blind, she saw the first pink light of the sun above some woods on the horizon. As the sky reddened, the branches of the bare trees in the fields stood out sharp and black against it, and, for the first time since the accident, beauty stirred her senses again and her heart seemed painfully to come to life so that tears blurred her eyes. With little time to linger, however, she brushed them aside, and had a sketchy wash in the swaying compartment as the train thundered on.

The pony and trap awaited her at the station, attended by a good-humoured looking man with grey hair and a ruddy face, who greeted her with a smile which did credit to him at that early hour.

8

'You'll be Miss Forrester, I guess.'

'Yes.'

'Good morning. I hope you had a comfortable journey.'

'Very, thank you. I'm sorry to have been the cause of bringing you out so early.'

'That's all right, miss. As a matter of fact, we enjoyed it, Sambo and I. The sun came up just as we left, and although it's a bit nippy, the morning air is grand. I'm Hilary. Frank Hilary, Mrs Pendine's gardener and general factotum, you might say. Let me have the case, miss. You'll need both those rugs.'

Ann never forgot the drive through the winding lanes to Rosevean on that early morning in February. The air, although chilly, held a softness in it which did not seem to belong to winter, and as the sun rose in the sky, it touched her face with the warmth of spring. The hedgerows, which in some places almost brushed them as they passed, were showing signs of the yielding of winter, too, for she saw hazel catkins gold with pollen and dogwood red with the rising sap. At the foot of a bank where the lane curved, some celandines were in flower. Where the hedges had grown tall and trees overhung them, they formed a shadowy tunnel; in summer, when the leaves would form a canopy, the enclosure would be complete. Sitting behind Hilary's broad back, snug beneath the tartan rugs, Ann looked around at the new morning world with delight, while the sweet, clean air caressed her face and the steady clip clop of the pony formed a pleasant accompaniment to the snatches of birdsong.

Hilary passed an occasional remark over his shoulder about the country they were passing through, but addressed himself more often to the pony, who, by the responsive pricking of his ears, appeared to enjoy this communion. Nearly an hour had gone by when Sambo picked up speed and had to be restrained as they swayed round a bend in the narrow lane.

'He always hurries when he gets near home,' observed Hilary. 'At this next bend, if you look to the right, you can just get a glimpse of the sea, miss.'

It was only a brief glimpse of the sea, far below, breaking in a tiny cove, but it excited her as though she were a small child again, seeing the sea for the first time. Perhaps it was because she had felt so dead in spirit since the accident that this sense of awakening, which had begun in the train and was now flooding through her veins, seemed so wonderful. She had thought that happiness would never stir in her again, that it died in the wreckage of the car with her parents, but that morning she felt it breaking through the wintry landscape of her heart as surely as the sap was rising in the hedgerows. She felt interested again, involved with life, so that she looked around her with eager curiosity as they swung off the lane between two stone pillars into a drive. Just inside the entrance, to one side, was a small circular clearing, on which stood a car. For the rest, there was nothing to be seen but woods on each side of them as Sambo trotted along with determined vigour, refreshment now close at hand.

The long straight drive emerged from the woods into a circular sweep round a lawn with a battered sundial in the middle of it, and behind the lawn rose the gaunt stone Gothic structure of Rosevean, backed by tall elm trees, and flanked on one side by a river which flowed quite close to the turret at the corner of the house, giving it a moated appearance. It was both imposing and forbidding, and Ann wondered how anybody of this age could still live in what more nearly resembled a castle than a house. It seemed to belong to a legendary past. As she gazed at the grey stone walls against their backcloth of bare trees, and at the corner turret overlooking the dark, silently flowing river, she thought of Camelot and the knights of the round table and the Lady of Shalott.

Hilary helped her out of the trap, led her to the huge oak door, studded so thickly that the wood was scarcely discernible, and pulled a bell at the side. Ann, in a state of high imagination by now, would not have been surprised if two bloodhounds had leapt through the door at her, but the woman who invited her in had a pleasant, safe-looking face and a matter-of-fact welcome for her.

'Glad to see you, Miss Forrester. I'm Mrs Pendine's niece, Madge Trent. Come along in. You must be starving.'

'I am,' said Ann, smiling.

'Breakfast is all ready for you. We're having it alone together. Mrs Pendine will be seeing you afterwards. Here's a cloakroom where you can leave your things. While you're tidying up, I'll tell the housekeeper to dish up the bacon and eggs, so don't be long. That door opposite is the dining-room. I'll see you there."

The dining-room was large enough to accommodate a banquet, but their breakfast was served at a smaller table in the window bay. Bacon and eggs had never before smelt so delicious, Ann decided, and proceeded to enjoy a breakfast which normally would have been quite beyond her appetite. There was a lot to be said for an early morning drive across country in a pony trap.

'Do you know this part of the country at all?' asked her companion as she poured the coffee.

'No. Somerset and Devon, but not Cornwall. I once stayed for a few days at St Ives, but that was when I was very young and I've only the haziest recollection of it.'

'As you'll have seen for yourself, we're very isolated here. The village is half a mile down the lane, and that's all. After London, it could be deadly.'

'I like the country, though I've never lived in it.'

'Well, I'll not try to influence you one way or the other. Personally, I think it's pretty grim,' said Miss Trent cheerfully, 'but it has its compensations, I suppose. I came here eight years ago from a London hospital, and the contrast between being a nurse there and looking after Aunt Alice here was a bit much to swallow. Still, after her fall, the old lady needed me, and I was glad to come to her rescue. Can't get any sort of staff down here, you know. Not surprising. Who would want to work in this gloomy great place? Not that I want to put you off,' she concluded, laughing.

She had the same cheerful, bluff manner as the nurse who had attended Ann in hospital. Her large, round face with its bright blue eyes was innocent of make-up, and she wore her dark hair so short that it was almost an Eton crop. She was heavily built and the arm which lifted the coffee pot looked strong enough to lift a sack of potatoes. Ann supposed her to be about forty and found her forthright manner reassuring. But if Miss Trent was Mrs Pendine's nurse and companion, what would her personal assistant have to do?

'I want a complete change from London. I had thought of going abroad, but this sounded interesting.'

'What have you done up to now? What sort of a job, I mean?'

'I was a secretary in an oil company.'

'Like it? Help yourself to toast.'

'Thank you. Yes, it was pleasant enough. Not altogether satisfying, though.'

'You're not there now?'

'No. I decided that I needed a change,' said Ann, not wishing to embark on her private history. There was something about those bold, inquisitive eyes which sent her back into her shell. She still could not discuss the accident with strangers.

'Well, my aunt is a strict employer, but fair enough. I'm fond of her, and she appreciates my services, I know. For my sake, I hope you'll take the job, Miss Forrester. We can do with a few fresh faces round here. But don't think it'll be cushy. My aunt expects good value for her money.'

'I should try to give it.'

'You know, you puzzle me a little. A young person like you thinking of burying herself down here. I told my aunt that she'd never get anybody, unless it was some poor old frump at the end of her tether.'

The words jarred a little, and perhaps something in Ann's face revealed it, for before she could reply, Miss Trent went on cheerfully,

'You mustn't mind my blunt tongue. I just say what I think and don't dress it up.'

'Is Mrs Pendine's health not good? You mentioned a fall.'

'Yes. She fell in the garden. It was year ago. Silly thing, really. Tripped over some hose. But she broke her leg and it's never been quite right since. She was nearly seventy then, and old bones are brittle. Don't mend too well. She's got a bit of cardiac trouble we have to keep an eye on, too. But she's a remarkably well preserved woman for seventy-eight, although a very bad patient, I may say.'

'It sounds as though you have a difficult job.'

'Oh, I get round it all right.' She glanced at her watch. 'Half-past nine. Mrs. Pendine will see you in the study at ten. Would you like to have a walk round the grounds with me until then? I usually take a constitutional after breakfast. Mrs Pendine always has her breakfast in bed. That dates from her fall. Really, she considers it a slack habit, but the doctor backed me up and between us we managed to get her to accept it after a long, running battle.'

Ann fetched her coat and joined Miss Trent in the hall. The latter scorned a coat and wound a thick woolen scarf round her neck instead. Ann found that her companion was not the ideal guide, for Miss Trent marched her round at a brisk pace, for all the world as though they were on a route march. As the sun was pleasantly warm, the only reason could be that she considered the exercise beneficial. Across the lawn at the back of the house they strode, and plunged down a path through the elm trees which led them round to the river bank. Turning right sharply as soon as they reached the river, Miss Trent led the way along the bank, past the turret, and through the woods which flanked the front drive. By the time they arrived back at the house again, Ann was slightly breathless, having gathered only a fleeting impression of grounds that had been left in their natural state for the most part, although carefully tended so that paths were kept clear and the woods were free of undergrowth. The only cultivated part she had seen was at the back of the house between the terrace and the elm trees, where a formal garden was laid out.

Miss Trent, cheeks glowing, eyes bright, strode into the hall, rubbing her hands.

'That's better. Nothing like a brisk walk to tune you up for the day. Now if you'll wait in the study, Miss Forrester, I'll see if Mrs Pendine needs any help from me.'

Waiting in the study, a gloomy, oak-panelled room, Ann's curiosity was mingled with a little apprehension. Mrs. Pendine sounded a formidable person. The room was cold, inadequately heated by a gas fire which she guessed had only recently been lighted, and the leather chairs were not inviting. It was very silent in there, so that she jumped at a sudden tapping on the window, which turned out to be no more than the bare twigs of a tree moving in the breeze. The woods on this side of the house grew close to it, shutting out the sky. She heard the grandfather clock in the hall strike ten, and wondered why this moment should seem so pregnant with foreboding. It was probably the effect of the gloomy study. After all, she had only to refuse the post if it did not appeal to her. She was quite free. Why, then, did she feel as though Rosevean was casting a spell over her? A spell that was dangerous. She had felt happy and confident up to now, rejoicing in her newly awakened interest in life. This sudden uneasiness was probably an effect of nerves made unstable by the accident. She felt herself stiffen as, on the last stroke of the clock, the door opened and Mrs Pendine stood there.

CHAPTER II

ANN remembered her father once saying that the really significant moments in our lives were never recognized until long afterwards, that apparently trivial things could change the course of a life, which made it all seem rather senseless, but, as her eyes met Mrs Pendine's, Ann knew with certainty that this was a significant moment in her life, that far more than a job of work was involved. She could give no reason; it was

purely intuitive, for Mrs Pendine's manner was kind and gracious, and far too autocratic to suggest that personal issues might
be involved. First, she dismissed Miss Trent, who had drawn a
high-backed chair up to the desk for her.

'Thank you, Madge, dear. Leave us now. Tell Mrs Vincent
that we should like coffee in the drawing-room at eleven
o'clock, and lunch at twelve-fifteen, so that Miss Forrester has
comfortable time for her train.'

After Madge had left them, Mrs Pendine drew a sheet of
paper from the desk and opened the silver ink stand. She had
beautiful white hands with long fingers. Ann's first impression
had been of a classically beautiful, but hard, face. Mrs Pendine
was tall and thin, unbowed in spite of her age and the slight
limp which had been noticeable as she walked to the desk. Her
white hair was beautifully dressed, high above her forehead,
revealing the sharp bonework of her long, narrow face. She
had fine dark blue eyes, a straight nose and firm mouth. She
wore a soft grey dress with tight, wrist-length sleeves, which
was unfashionably long but which seemed exactly right for
Mrs Pendine, and round her neck she wore three rows of
pearls. The rings on her hand were heavily jewelled, but the
effect she created was one of austere elegance.

'Now, Miss Forrester, tell me something of yourself before
we start. I would like to know what your background has been,
and what experience you have had in employment. Mr Cardew
has told me that you lost your parents in an accident a few
months ago, and that you are seeking a fresh environment.
Could you tell me something of the old one? I don't wish to
stir up painful memories, but you must appreciate that this
aspect is important when employing somebody who will be a
member of my household.'

Prodded skilfully when she hesitated, Ann found herself giving Mrs Pendine particulars of her education, her father's profession, her mother's family, her own business experience. An
odd imp of humour popped up in her when Mrs Pendine
showed her approval of the professional classes. She had a
wild impulse to declare all kinds of undesirable characters as
her forbears, for Mrs Pendine's class-consciousness seemed to
belong to Jane Austen's generation. However, levity and Mrs
Pendine were not compatible, and Ann composed her face and
gave the information in a sober manner.

'Yes, well, that all sounds very satisfactory from my point of
view. You can no doubt furnish business and personal references if we decide that you are the right person for the post.
Now it's my turn to give you some information. This is a job

14

which calls for some degree of versatility, Miss Forrester. You see, it will have three different departments.'

'That sounds interesting,' said Ann, as Mrs Pendine paused and appeared to reflect on her words.

'First and foremost, your duties to me. Purely business letters, which I have always hitherto written, I should like you to type. I do not like type-written letters, but concede their convenience. I suffer from slight arthritis in my hand which makes writing a little more laborious than it was. I shall have to confine it to personal letters only, and have letters to my bank manager, lawyer, tradesmen, and so on, typed in future. That will not prove very arduous for you. The only other major task is to re-catalogue the library for me. Do you read much, Miss Forrester?'

'Yes. We were a bookish family.'

'You have a nice voice. I should like you to read to me in the evenings sometimes. My eyes get a little tired towards the end of the day. My niece, a good soul, reads like a child of ten and her voice is not melodious. She has the broad vowels of her Australian father, and I would sooner listen to a parrot. Now I come to the second department of your duties. My grand-daughter, Gemma. I had hoped you would have met her at breakfast, but Madge tells me that she left a note saying that she would not be in to breakfast. Apparently she took advantage of Hilary's early departure this morning to be dropped off at the lane leading down to the cove, where she intended going out with a fisherman to some lobster pots.'

'What fun!'

'Yes. But I find my grand-daughter's unpredictable habits a little trying. I hope she will be back soon, however, so that you can meet her. She is eighteen, and since she left boarding school last summer, she has been running wild here. I did think of sending her to a finishing school in Switzerland, but she was unwilling to go, and I love having her here. She is all I have now. The last of the Pendines.'

Mrs Pendine paused, looking down at the sheet of paper on which she had jotted notes of Ann's disclosures, but obviously not seeing them. When she looked up, she spoke more briskly.

'My son married an Italian girl, and they were both killed in an aeroplane crash flying home from a holiday in Italy. Gemma was five. Mercifully, they had left her here with me that time, although they usually took her everywhere with them. Since then, Rosevean has been her home. She's a dear girl. High spirited, a little wilful. I feel it's lonely for her here, though, and I thought that someone older than herself but young enough to be a good companion would be a great asset to Gemma just now. You seem a responsible young woman, Miss Forrester, and I think you would provide just the stabilizing influence needed. She takes a little handling, of course. She does not get on very well with my niece, I'm afraid.'

'What would my duties be where your grand-daughter is concerned, then, Mrs Pendine?'

'Oh, no specific duties, but you will have a good many free afternoons, and if you could spend some of them with Gemma I think you would be good company for each other. I would expect you to exert a little restraining influence on her. If she likes you, that won't be difficult. Gemma is very warm-hearted.'

'And the third department?'

'That is more specific. My god-son, Rex Vernon, has just returned to this country after a long assignment abroad on a bridge-constructing job. He is a civil engineer. Whilst there, he contracted an illness which left him very weak. He resigned from his firm after the job was completed, for reasons which I need not go into, and has decided to set up in practice as a consulting engineer, but his health needs building up and I am trying to persuade him to spend the summer at Rosevean, where he can have a complete rest. He is considering it. I know he wants to finish a text book for his particular sphere of engineering, and write some papers for his Institution. He is a brilliant young man in his field. If I can add the extra inducement of a typist here at Rosevean, I think that will settle it. I should put you at his disposal when he needed you.'

Ann, feeling like a pawn on Mrs Pendine's chess-board, nevertheless perceived that the post offered great variety, and that whatever else it might prove to be, it could not be boring. Once again, she felt excitement stirring in her, swamping the odd scruples which had laid a cold hand on her heart while she had waited for Mrs Pendine. She could not imagine a greater contrast to her old job in London, and that was what she wanted. Something completely different. Another world. From being a small cog in a huge machine she would become an individual, involved with other individuals, in a setting as wild and lovely as any she had seen. It seemed to her that it was life that was challenging her, and she knew that she could not resist the challenge.

'The post sounds a very interesting one, Mrs Pendine. I think I should like it, although it will be a very different life from the one I'm used to.'

Mrs Pendine went on to give her details of salary, a generous one, and was in the middle of a description of Rosevean's situation in relation to the village and transport facilities, which seemed scanty almost to vanishing point, when the door burst open and a girl in bright blue slacks and a red sweater dashed in.

'Grandma, Rex is here. I saw his car. Where is he? When did he come?'

'Gemma, please. Where are your manners? I have a visitor. Allow me to introduce her. Miss Forrester, my grand-daughter, Gemma.'

The girl turned to Ann with a polite smile and outstretched hand. She was small and slender, with a heart-shaped little face of striking beauty. Its white skin was petal smooth, and framed by shoulder length cloudy black hair. She had the same striking dark blue eyes as her grandmother, fringed with long black lashes, beneath finely arched black brows. Her greeting was as brief as politeness allowed, and she turned back with barely concealed impatience to her grandmother.

'It is Rex's car, isn't it, down by the gates?'

'Yes, Gemma.'

'Then where is he? I expected to find him with you. I'm longing to see him. Dear old Rex. It's such an age. I thought he wasn't coming until tomorrow. Did you know he was coming today, Grandma? Why didn't you tell me?'

It was at this stage that Ann first saw Mrs Pendine assert her will in the manner which was to become familiar to her in the future. Her voice was cool and incisive, and her face implacable as she said,

'I will not have you interrupting me in this violent, uncouth manner, Gemma, and firing questions at me as though I'm on trial. Now sit down on that chair and keep quiet while I finish the discussion I was having with Miss Forrester. Afterwards, I will explain about Rex. You will stay here, Gemma, please," she concluded as her grand-daughter turned towards the door, and there was no ignoring the tone in which those final words were spoken.

Gemma sat down on the chair and studied her hands with compressed lips and an air of holding herself in only with the greatest difficulty. With calm deliberation, Mrs Pendine continued to give Ann such information about life at Rosevean as she deemed relevant. She took quite a long time over it, concluding with,

'You would no doubt like to think about it a little while before giving me your decision, Miss Forrester. For myself, I have decided that you are very suitable, and, subject to favourable references, of course, the post is yours to accept or refuse. I would like a decision before you leave today.'

'There is one point I'm not quite clear on, Mrs Pendine. Is this a permanent post, or do you have in mind a limited term of employment? I ask this because some of the duties you have mentioned would seem to be only temporary.'

'As my personal assistant, it is permanent, as long as I am permanent,' said Mrs Pendine with a slight smile. 'You will appreciate, however, that I am not immortal. I need a personal assistant. There will be other services you can render when the immediate ones are no longer needed. If we do not work together as smoothly as I anticipate, a month's notice on either side can terminate it, but I am a pretty good judge of people, Miss Forrester, and I anticipate no trouble. But don't be rushed. Take more time to consider it if you have any doubts.'

Gemma twisted her legs round those of the chair in an agony of impatience as Ann smiled and said,

'I accept the post, Mrs Pendine, and I hope I'll fill it to your satisfaction.'

'I'm very pleased. Now, if you will wait just a few moments while I put my grand-daughter out of her misery, we can go and have our coffee. Now, Gemma. One question at a time, please.'

'Where is Rex?'

'In bed. He is not to be disturbed. He drove down yesterday evening and arrived here just after two o'clock this morning.'

'Did you know he was coming down last night, then?'

'He telephoned yesterday evening. He had cleared up his business affairs and was tired of London noise and dirt. You would have been told had you not gone to bed early with a book to avoid the company of Dr Lloyd. Rex telephoned just before Dr Lloyd left.'

'He's such an old bore,' said Gemma. 'I wish I'd known. About Rex, I mean. I'd have waited up for him.'

'Oh no you wouldn't. I did that. He looked very tired, and I hope he'll spend the day in bed, although he said he would be down to lunch.'

'Shall I take him up some coffee?'

'No, dear. Let him sleep on. I should have told you of his arrival this morning if you had been available, but this is the first time I have set eyes on you today, remember. Did you enjoy your visit to the lobster pots?'

Gemma's cheeks dimpled at her grandmother's dry tones.

'Lovely. The sea was calm and pearly. But there was only one lobster.'

'And have you had any breakfast?'

"Yes. I had some with Jim when we got back. Mrs Dakers cooks a lovely sausage. They were super.'

'I wish you wouldn't use the Dakers' cottage as a snack bar whenever it suits you. However, we won't keep Miss Forrester from her coffee any longer. If you're going to join us, Gemma, you had better change those trousers. They are not suitable for the drawing-room and moreover they are wet.'

'I know. I didn't roll them up high enough when I helped Jim to haul the boat in. Salt water takes an age to dry. Shan't be long. I'll ask Vinny if she can find some cake for me. I'm hungry again.'

'Gemma, keep away from the turret. I've placed those rooms at Rex's disposal. While he is here, they will be his private quarters, not to be invaded except by invitation. He's a sick man still. You understand, dear.'

'Right you are. Grandma, have you persuaded him to stay the whole summer?'

'My dear child, the early hours of the morning are not for discussions of that sort. He will be staying for some time. I hope until the autumn. He needs a long period of rest and quietness. But nothing has been finally decided.'

"He will. We'll both get to work on him. Do you know it's more than two years since we saw him? *Do* keep him as long as you can, Grandma.'

'Run along with you. We'll do our best.'

After Gemma had gone, Mrs Pendine turned to Ann with a little smile.

'Gemma is devoted to Rex, as you will have gathered.'

'She's a very attractive young girl.'

'Yes. A great responsibility, too. You see what I mean by a restraining influence being beneficial. Now come along and have your coffee, Miss Forrester.'

After coffee, Gemma was asked to show Ann the library and the room above it, which would be her room. She was given to understand that the study would be her office. Wandering round the library shelves, sampling books at random, Ann felt that here was one sector of her work which would be engrossing, for she saw enough to recognize that this was a library of wide literary taste. It was difficult to concentrate on the books, however, with Gemma's lively tongue claiming her attention.

'You know, I'm awfully relieved that you're young and not frumpish. I'd expected a bossy, middle-aged type like Madge,

19

because, although Grandma said she was looking for a personal assistant, I had a hunch that she was using that as a cloak for a kind of governess for me. Grandma is frightfully old-fashioned, you know. She still thinks in terms of chaperones. She wants someone to keep an eye on me.'

Ann smiled, thinking that young Miss Pendine was not quite as ingenuous as she seemed. She shared her grandmother's shrewdness.

'That would be quite a task, I imagine.'

'That's what I love about this place. You can get away on your own where nobody can find you. I simply hated school. Did you?'

'No. I rather enjoyed it, but I didn't go to a boarding school, and my parents gave me plenty of freedom. Tell me what you do with yourself here, Gemma. Apart from going out to lobster pots.'

'Oh, boating and riding and exploring. I read a lot, and I'm supposed to practice my singing, but I've got to feel in the mood for that. Anyway, Grandma can't play the piano much now, because of her arthritis, so there's nobody to play for me. Can you play the piano?'

'Yes, but not very well.'

"Now Rex is here, it won't matter, anyway. He's a jolly good pianist. He thought I ought to have my voice properly trained, but Grandma wasn't keen.'

'Are you keen?'

'Not really. Of course, I shan't stay here at Rosevean always. But Grandma hates the thought of me living anywhere else, and I'm happy enough here for the time being, especially,' she added, jumping off the library steps on which she had been perching, "if Rex is here. He'll liven things up no end. Now we'd better go and inspect your room. It's rather nice, with a view over the river.'

It was a handsome room, large enough to hold a party, with the same lofty ceiling and Gothic arched windows which characterized the whole house. Below flowed the river, dark beneath the overhanging trees, and from the window she could see the rounded wall of the turret curving out to the right and blocking the view that way. The red carpet, the large four-poster bed with its white counterpane, and the low, broad blue couch, made the room look warm and inviting in spite of its size. The red velvet curtains were looped back with gold cords from which hung long tassels. Another world, thought Ann comparing this with her small, contemporary bedroom at home. She felt that she was being whisked back in time to the

20

nineteenth century. She had wanted a change, and she was certainly going to get it. How her father would have delighted in this picturesque anachronism, she thought with a little stab, and then found that her companion was skipping about impatiently by the door. Following her down the broad twisting staircase, it occurred to Ann that Gemma suggested a ballet dancer rather than a singer. She had changed into a short, full green skirt and a matching sweater which hugged her slight figure and emphasized her slender waist as the skirt billowed out in her flight down the stairs. All her movements were quick and light as a bird's, and she was seldom still. Through the open front door, the sunshine streamed into the hall, and Ann saw the back of a man standing on the gravel drive outside. Gemma let out a joyful cry of 'Rex', jumped the last three stairs and flew out to him. He turned at the sound of her voice, and held out his hands with a smile.

'Mia Gemma. And how is my girl?'

She flung herself into his arms, laughing and breathless.

'How lovely to have you here at last, Rex! Do you feel better now? It's more than two years since you were here. Poor dear.' Gemma stood away from him and looked at him with wide eyes. 'You do look yellow. And thinner. It must have been a beastly bug.'

'It was. And you look as lively and blooming as ever. Quite grown up now, too. Definitely a good sight for a sick old man. Introduce me, sweetheart,' he added as he came into the hall with his arm round Gemma's shoulders.

'This is Miss Forrester, who is coming here as Grandma's personal assistant.'

'You've only done half the job, Gemma,' broke in her grandmother who had just emerged from the dining-room. 'This is Mr Vernon, Miss Forrester.'

Ann shook hands with him, aware of a pair of penetrating dark eyes in a swarthy face. He had an attractive, slightly husky voice, and he held her hand a moment as he turned with a quizzical smile to Mrs Pendine.

"So this is part of your bait, Madrina, is it?'

'Behave yourself, and come into lunch, all of you, or Miss Forrester will miss her train.'

Ann sat opposite Rex Vernon at lunch, and found it difficult to decided whether she liked him or not, but quite impossible not to be deeply aware of him. In spite of the yellow tinge of his complexion which Gemma had mentioned and the dark shadows under his eyes, he gave no impression of weakness after illness. Rather the reverse. His alert face and lively tongue seemed to indicate a mental and physical vigour above average. Watching him, her eyes dropped when he turned suddenly and caught her scrutiny. Although she concentrated on her plate for the next few minutes, she knew that he was studying her, and felt like the proverbial toad beneath the harrow.

'And what do you think of Rosevean?' he asked, without speaking her name, as though fully aware of her attention.

When she looked up, she found an odd little smile on his lips.

'Its impact is quite breathtaking. I feel that I've stepped into another age. I live in London in a house designed by my father only five years ago,' she explained.

'All glass and flat as a pancake outside,' said Madge, helping herself liberally to butter. 'I know. I've seen some.'

'Picture windows. I like them,' said Gemma. 'We had them in our new wing at school. Have you brought loads of photographs back with you, Rex? I hope so. India is a country I'd love to go to.'

Glad of Gemma's grasshopper mind which switched the conversation to India, Ann relaxed and listened. Rex was a good talker, graphic and incisive. Gemma's hero-worshipping attitude was understandable, for there was no denying the personal magnetism of this man. To a teen-ager, his appeal would be strong. Ann supposed him to be well into his thirties, but she could not imagine him ever looking immature. He looked as though he had been born knowing it all, she thought, a little irritated without knowing why. Far from good-looking in any conventional sense, there was an attractive oddity about his looks, and the teasing affection which he revealed for Gemma would have had any young girl at his feet. A little uneasy, conscious of straining against his charm, Ann said little. Had Rex Vernon detracted from the appeal of the post she had accepted or added to it? She found it difficult to answer and postponed her verdict until she could think about it quietly alone.

CHAPTER III

'Now, Rex, while we have coffee, are there any questions you would like to ask Miss Forrester about her qualifications? She'll be working for you even more than for me, after all.'

'You've decided that I'm here for the summer, then, have you, Madrina?' asked Rex, lounging back in an armchair, and regarding Mrs Pendine through half closed eyes.

'My dear boy, I naturally leave the decision to you, but it seems such a sensible arrangement for all of us. You need a long rest before you embark on a new business and a new home.'

'What a pity you gave up that lovely flat when you went abroad, Rex,' said Gemma, perched on a hassock at his feet.

'M'm. A bit expensive to keep empty for two years, though. I thought of living in a hotel for the time being.'

'Gemma, dear, don't keep interrupting,' said her grandmother, 'or we shall never get anything settled. You're not well, Rex dear. Here you can have peace and quiet, you can finish your book, and give us a great deal of pleasure in having you. By the end of the summer, you'll feel strong again and able to tackle your new business venture. I can't see any argument against it. I promise you that you shall be quite undisturbed in the turret, and see as little or as much of us as you please.'

Ann saw Mrs Pendine flash a glance at Madge while Rex turned away to reach an ashtray. Immediately, as though on cue, Madge said,

'Be sensible, Rex. The doctor said you'd need six months to get over these recurrent bouts of fever. I'll be glad to keep an eye on you.'

'Bless your heart, there's nothing to do except sweat them out.'

'I bet they leave you feeling pretty grim,' said Madge.

'Weak as a kitten. But it passes. You know, you girls are really ganging up on me, aren't you? I don't have a leg to stand on.'

'Do, do stay, Rex darling,' urged Gemma.

Ann saw his eyes meet Mrs Pendine's over Gemma's head. She sensed in him a strong reluctance to yield. Mrs Pendine smiled and said quietly,

'I don't want to make it difficult for you to refuse if you want to, Rex, but I shan't see many more summers here. It would give me great joy to have you here for this one.'

And Rex, ruffling Gemma's black hair, capitulated with a little shrug.

'So be it. Thank you, Madrina, for your hospitality. I appreciate your kindness. If I seem a little reluctant, it's because six or seven months seems a long time to be out of action.'

'But the time won't be wasted, with Miss Forrester here to type your book and any other work you have for her.'

'Which is where we came in,' said Rex, smiling a little grimly, Ann thought, as he turned to her. 'And I take it that you can spell and punctuate properly as well as type.'

'Of course,' replied Ann.

'It doesn't always follow, I assure you. Shorthand?'

'Yes.'

'Good. I'll be glad of your services.'

'That's splendid,' said Mrs Pendine. 'I'm sure we shall all work very well together. Now I don't want to rush you, Miss Forrester, but if you've finished your coffee, I think it's time we had Hilary round with the trap.'

'Can I run Miss Forrester into Truro? It will be much quicker in the car, and she can then stay for another cup of coffee,' said Rex, passing his cup to Mrs Pendine for a refill.

'After all that driving last night, Rex,' began Mrs Pendine, a little doubtfully, and as she paused to fill his coffee cup, Ann said quickly,

'It's kind of you to offer, Mr Vernon, but I would sooner go in the trap. Thank you, all the same.'

'Sensible girl,' said Mrs Pendine approvingly. 'Abominations, cars. The motor car has ruined our countryside. I think it a great pity that the eternal combustion engine was ever invented. Run down to the cottage and tell Hilary that Miss Forrester will be ready in five minutes, Gemma. She'll come down to the gates, so tell him to wait there.'

Ann had said goodbye to the others and was half way down the drive with Gemma, who had been deputed to see her off, when she discovered that she had left her scarf behind. Sensing that Gemma, who had been glancing at her watch, was eager to get away, Ann said,

24

'Don't worry about waiting to see me off, Gemma. I'll run back for my scarf.'

'Do you mind? You see, I'm going out fishing with Jim Dakers this afternoon and I promised I'd be down there by two. If I'd known Rex was here, I wouldn't have arranged it. Are you sure you don't mind if I slip off? I go the back way, through the woods.'

'Quite sure, Gemma. Goodbye. And enjoy your fishing.'

Gemma flashed her a smile and ran off down a path through the woods, her duffel coat swinging loosely from her shoulders. She had changed back into slacks during the few minutes that Ann had needed to fetch her coat and say goodbye, and as her bright blue legs disappeared into the gloom of the trees, Ann reflected that it would need the skill of a detective and the speed of a greyhound to keep up with young Gemma Pendine, let alone restrain her. She was like quicksilver. Here one moment, gone the next.

The front door stood open when she arrived back, but the hall was empty and silent. She slipped into the cloakroom and found her scarf on the floor in a dark corner. It must have fallen off the peg and she hadn't noticed it.

'Well, what do you think of our Miss Forrester?'

It was Madge's voice in the hall, and Rex Vernon replied.

'Seems a pleasant enough young woman. Wonder if she realizes what she's taking on.'

'Aunt Alice, you mean? Oh, she's all right if you don't cross her. The girl has the right idea there, I guess.'

Ann, behind the half open door of the cloakroom, pressed herself against the wall, unwilling to embarrass them by disclosing her presence. Their steps had moved past her to the front door, but she could still hear their voices.

'Yes. I doubt whether she's quite as submissive as she looks, though . . . What a grand afternoon! Spring has certainly arrived here in Cornwall.'

'It was a good line to refuse the car and take the trap. Nothing endears people to Aunt Alice more than to have them condemn the modern way of life. Was it your face Miss Forrester didn't like, Rex, or was it syrup for Aunt Alice?'

'Your guess is as good as mine. She's scared of something, you know. Wonder why she wants to bury herself here.'

'Well, Aunt Alice is known to be a wealthy old woman, you know. This girl was recommended by Cardew. He'll have set her wise about that, no doubt, and some females make a habit of cultivating rich old people."

'She didn't look the mercenary type.'

25

'Be your age, Rex. When did looks tell all the story? Still, maybe I'm too suspicious. I've seen so many vultures after the old lady's money, including our distant relations who turn up hopefully every now and again, that I'm probably prejudiced.'

'You're a good sort, Madge, to have stuck this as you have. I don't know what Madrina would have done if you hadn't come to her rescue after that fall. She'd have died rather than leave Rosevean and go into a nursing home.'

'You're telling me! No mule could be as obstinate as Aunt Alice.'

'And what a dictator! I'm very fond of her, but I've no illusions about what you have to put up with. How you keep so good-humoured about it all is beyond me.'

'Oh, what's the use of getting in a stew about things? And Aunt Alice did a lot for Mother and me after Dad died. I admire her, too, although her autocratic ways are a bit much sometimes.'

'What's she cooking up for me this summer, Madge? She's dead keen to have me netted down here, and although I know her concern is genuine, I have a feeling that she's plotting something. And you're a blackleg, you know, helping to close the net.'

'Go on with you. Do you good to vegetate for a bit.'

Ann clasped her hands, wondering how long she was going to be kept a prisoner here. She realized, too late, that she should have disclosed her presence straight away and made her escape.

'Vegetate!' exclaimed Rex. 'One poor male surrounded by you females, like a dog trapped in a hot-house. I shall have to go up to London now and again to get a cool draught of male company.'

'You'll have Uncle Barney, and Hilary. His son is coming back here next month, too, to help his father. Did you know?'

'No. Wasn't the boy studying for some diploma in horticulture?'

'That's right. He's got his diploma now. Hilary's frightfully proud of him. You know, I like that family. Trouble is, Aunt Alice is such a snob that we're expected to keep them in their place and not mix socially. She doesn't realize that the world's changed. That you can't treat people like that any longer. Isolated as we are here, it's ridiculous. I wonder the Hilarys put up with it, but they've been here so long now, and I suppose they, too, have expectations.'

'M'm. A decent lad, young John, I used to think.'

'Well, I don't know if you're thinking of propping up that door post all the afternoon, Rex, but I'm going for a constitutional. Why not come along, too? Do you good.'

'Don't start nursing me yet, my girl. You always did like managing me when we met here in the school holidays. Or trying to manage me.'

'That's more like it. Those holidays when I had to keep an eye on you weren't all jam. At ten years old, you were the wickedest boy I'd ever come across.'

'And you were just about to start training as a nurse and felt yourself a person in authority already.'

'Pity we weren't more an age and we could have enjoyed begin together. Eight years difference was too much. You were a tiresome, horrid little boy and I was grown up enough not to want to be saddled with you. Not that I ever did see much of you, but I was the one who got the blame for losing track of you.'

'Poor old Madge. Always the unlucky one. But what a marvelous place this was for kids! I used to revel in it. Pure magic. Now, it gives me the jitters. It's still lovely, in its gloomy, haunted way, but there's something unhealthy about it.'

'What, bad drains, you mean?'

'No, chump. The atmosphere. Too intense, bottled up. Can't explain it, but I feel it. I wonder if Miss Brown Eyes will find the air quite as fresh as she expects.'

'Probably be a nine days wonder. Don't think I'll need a scarf. Are you coming, Rex? I thought of walking along the river.'

'All right, but at my pace, please, which is a leisurely one. None of your race-track training excursions for me.'

'Soft, my boy. But I'll humour you as you're a sick man.'

'Are we supposed to leave this door open for Gemma?'

'Don't think so. She said she was going off fishing. Looks as though she went straight off. Irresponsible young baggage. Did you know that Doc Lloyd . . .'

The door closed and after giving them a minute to get clear, Ann cautiously opened it again. She saw their backs disappearing round the bend of the river past the turret, and ran down the drive to Hilary, patiently waiting with the trap. She apologized for the delay, but he assured her that they had reasonable time, and whipped up the pony, a different one this time, to a smart trot.

So much seemed to have happened to her since they had come that way a few hours ago that it seemed impossible to believe that it was still the same day. Her head was awhirl with the vivid impressions of that strange, almost mediæval house, and the impact of people with such strong personalities that she felt battered. She had hitherto led a quiet, sheltered life among pleasant, ordinary people. Here, in these beautiful, wild surroundings, Rosevean had held for her at odd moments the vaguely threatening, pent-up atmosphere which Rex Vernon had tried to describe. The conversation she had overheard, too, had been disturbing with its undercurrents. And yet, the place and the people drew her in a queer way. She wanted to know more of them. She wanted to live in that gloomy old castle with the silent river twisting along below its walls and learn all about it. Her curiosity was deeply aroused, and would not be put off at any cost. If she backed out of the job because of these indefinable fears, she would always be plagued with conjecture about it.

She saw little of the countryside on the way back, for Rosevean and its inhabitants filled her thoughts and would not let her go. She caught her train with only a few minutes to spare, but again saw little of the counties through which the train ran on that long journey to London, and gave up all efforts to read her book after she had read one page twice over and still could not say what she had read, for across the pages jolted the cold face of Mrs Pendine, the vivid smile of her grand-daughter and the swarthy disconcerting countenance of Rex Vernon. His husky voice, too, kept haunting her. Madrina. Why did he call Mrs Pendine that? It sounded Italian. Of course. God-mother. The dictator. But they were all, in their different ways, dictators, she thought. Mrs Pendine, Gemma, Madge and Rex. A formidable quartet to live with. Rex Vernon's words echoed in her mind: Not quite as submissive as she looks . . . I wonder if she realizes what she's taking on . . . Ann stirred uneasily as recollections of all that had been said that morning went through her mind. Whatever Rosevean held in store for her, it had penetrated the cold inertia which had settled on her like a fog, blanketing her from the world, after the first desolation of grief. She had come out into the world again. Rosevean beckoned her with an enticing finger to investigate its sombre landscape, and she obeyed it with a little fear, a certain excitement and an intense curiosity.

CHAPTER IV

'ANN?'

'Hullo, Gemma. I thought you'd gone riding.'

'I changed my mind. Would you like me to show you the way down to the cove? We've plenty of time before dinner.'

Ann looked down from her perch on top of the library steps and smiled as she replied,

'I'd like it very much. I've been here a week and haven't seen the sea.'

'Goody. I'll wait for you in the drive.'

Gemma had proved the brightest spot of that first week. She had dispensed with all formality on the second day, and had offered her friendship frankly and warmly from then on. After the cool formality of Mrs Pendine's attitude to her new assistant, Gemma's was doubly welcome. Ann had seen little of Rex Vernon, who had been confined to his rooms with another bout of fever. In spite of that, she had been kept unexpectedly busy by Mrs Pendine, and she welcomed Gemma's invitation on that Friday afternoon.

The path through the woods behind the house soon started to drop steeply in hairpin bends, and they stopped to rest on a fallen tree trunk half way down. It was a blustery March day after a week of grey days and much rain, and Ann welcomed the fresher air. The wind made music in the treetops and set the wood anemones dancing. She was admiring their white fragility when two men came into view round the bend. She recognized Hilary, but not the tall, fair young man with him.

'Can that be John?' asked Gemma a little incredulously. 'It must be. Madge said he was due today.'

'Good afternoon, Miss Gemma, Miss Forrester,' said Hilary, giving them a little salute as he passed by, but Gemma called him back.

'Introduce me, Hilary,' she commanded with a mischievous smile. 'I don't recognize him.'

'Young Gemma,' said John Hilary, smiling and holding out his hand. 'You've grown up since I left here.'

29

'And so have you.' Gemma's tone left no doubt that she considered the years had brought great improvement. 'Ann, may I introduce John Hilary, horticultural expert? This is Miss Forrester, Grandma's new assistant, John, and I don't suppose she'll mind if you call her Ann, because we all like to get away from Grandma's formality when we can.'

As Ann shook hands with the young man, she wondered whether Gemma had sensed his discomfort at his father's attitude of servility, as she had, and was showing unusual tact, or whether she was merely being her own natural self, for Gemma had no respect for the conventions.

'And how do you like it here?' he asked Ann, ignoring his father's shuffling feet.

'I've only been here a week, so it's a little early to judge. The country is beautiful. Gemma's just showing me the way down to the cove.'

'Yes, it is lovely. And it never changes. I've been away for six years, and it's not changed by a twig, I do declare. Only Gemma reminds me that time has passed. At twelve, she was such a funny little shrimp.'

'I won't tell Ann what you were. It wouldn't be polite. It's good to see you back again, though. Are you here for good?'

'I doubt it. I've other ideas.'

'Now don't talk like that, John, in front of Miss Gemma. You're going to give Rosevean a trial for a year, anyway. We can certainly do with some help here, and with your qualifications, we shall expect a lot.'

Again Ann saw him pinch his lips at his father's words, but he smiled as he put his hand on his father's shoulder.

'Come along, Dad. Mother will have tea ready for us.'

He topped his father by several inches and apart from his blue eyes, bore little resemblance to him. Nor did his good looks come from his mother, except for the fair, wavy hair, for Mrs Hilary was a pleasant but nondescript little woman whose features were hard to recollect in her absence.

Gemma watched the two men until they disappeared. Then she said in an amazed voice,

'Well, what do you know? Who would have imagined that gangly, pimply youth growing into such a dream-man? He left here when he was sixteen or seventeen, you know. I used to think he was an awful drip. All he ever seemed to be doing when I was home was wheeling wheelbarrows of rubbish to the compost heaps. His shirt was always hanging out and he shuffled along as though his gum boots were too large for him. I just can't believe the transformation.'

'Where has he been since?'

'Worked at some horticultural institution for a time and then took a Diploma course at a college of agriculture in Surrey. He's certainly changed,' concluded Gemma.

"Are you going to show me the sea today or not? You know we'll be in trouble if we're late for dinner.'

'And if we don't change. I wonder Grandma doesn't insist on evening dress. Really, she has an obsession about keeping up proper standards, as she calls them. Do you know, she won't let me appear at dinner in a jumper and skirt? It must be a dress. Isn't it silly in a place like Rosevean when it's only ourselves to dinner? I just don't see the sense of it.'

'It's good training in self-discipline, I suppose. How lovely!' Ann exclaimed, stopping as a clearing revealed the little cove below, its pale sand smooth and unbroken lying like an oyster shell between the steeply wooded slopes, open only to the sea which ran over its sand with boisterous surf, for the wind was behind the tide.

'This is the only way you can get to it unless the tide is low, but nobody ever comes here but us. It's fine for bathing as long as the tide is coming in. It's dangerous otherwise,' said Gemma, and skipped ahead down the last stretch of the path, from which a jump landed her on the beach.

They walked along the fringe of the waves, the wind blowing their hair, the sand unexpectedly firm beneath their feet. The sea was flecked with white horses and was prancing vigorously in the March sunshine. With that vast expanse of sea and sky in front of her, Ann was transported into that rare state of happiness which is nature's reward to those who respond to her beauty. Personal affairs were dwarfed and forgotten, her ego ceased to be aware of itself, as she was caught up in some bigger and more glorious purpose. It was in this state of reflected glory that she climbed up the wooded slopes again to Rosevean, where her mood was quickly shattered.

Mrs Pendine called her into the drawing-room as soon as she heard her come in. Ann found Rex there, looking sallow and washed out as he lounged back in the arm-chair, but his eyes were as lively as ever when he assured her, in response to her inquiry, that he was quite well again now.

'Where have you been, Miss Forrester?' asked Mrs Pendine, resuming her chair and taking up the piece of embroidery on which she had been engaged.

'Down to the cove with Gemma, Mrs Pendine.'

'What time did you leave here?'

'Oh, soon after four, I think.'

'I wish you had told me. We arranged that your hours of duty were from nine-thirty until five-thirty. During those hours, I should know where you are and what you are doing.'

'I'm sorry, Mrs Pendine,' said Ann, with scarlet cheeks, aware of Rex Vernon's amused expression, 'but I thought that spending some time with Gemma was part of my duties.'

'Quite so. I am not disputing your right to go with her, my dear. Only the fact that you disappeared without telling me where you had gone, or asking me if I needed you in any other capacity. As it happened, Mr Vernon wanted a letter typed in time to catch this evening's post.'

'I'm sorry,' said Ann, addressing the remark to Rex but fixing her eyes on a space above his head. She felt angry at being stood up here like a naughty schoolgirl and lectured in front of him.

'That's all right. It wasn't all that important. Tomorrow will do,' he said imperturbably.

'Another time, Miss Forrester, please remember what your hours of duty are. What you choose to do with the time outside those hours, is, of course, your affair. You may think I am making a fuss about this, but for your sake as well as ours, I think it best to be quite clear about your working hours. During them, I have jurisdiction over your activities. That is what every employer is entitled to, I am sure you will agree.'

'Yes, Mrs Pendine. I understand. It was just thoughtlessness on my part.'

Mrs Pendine smiled and inclined her head graciously. Now that she had cracked the whip, she was willing to relent.

'That's all right, my dear. You're doing very well. I'm pleased with your work. There are bound to be a few points to be settled as we go along. Now that Mr Vernon is better, I've arranged that you shall report to him every morning at half-past nine to see if he has any work for you. I will come to the study at eleven, since he assures me that he will never keep you later than that, and deal with my affairs then. Is that quite clear?'

'Yes, Mrs Pendine.'

'Now you had better run along and change for dinner. I hope you enjoyed the walk with Gemma.'

'Yes. It was lovely.'

'Rosevean has much to offer you, Miss Forrester. I am sure you will be very happy here, once you have settled down.'

Ann managed a small smile and escaped. It was so long since anybody had treated her like a naughty child that incredulity mixed with her anger. She was twenty-five years old, and had been treated like Gemma. She was to find that age made no difference to Mrs Pendine if anybody thwarted her will, and was often to be an unwilling witness while Madge was dressed down in the same way, for all her forty-odd years.

Outwardly composed, she was still smarting from the humiliation when she went down to dinner, and she escaped directly afterwards by going for a walk along the river. The moon was full and the wind had fallen light, so that no clouds came to obscure it and make her way difficult. Where the woods closed in, however, the aspect became a little sinister and she turned back and sat on a roughly made seat on the river bank, not far from the house. It was chilly and she turned up the collar of her tweed coat, reluctant to go in. She had been there for about ten minutes, feeling just about the loneliest person in the world, when she heard footsteps and looked up to see Rex Vernon approaching. She looked away, hoping he would pass by with a formal greeting, for she had no wish to talk to him.

'Hullo, there. Mind if I join you?'

'Not at all.'

'Said in icy tones meaning the reverse. Sorry, but this is the only seat for miles, and I want a peaceful smoke without exertion.'

'I was just going, anyway, so I'll leave you in peace.'

He caught her arm as she got up and pulled her back again. He was surprisingly strong, and she sat down with a bump.

'Come on. Get it off your chest. I knew that you were seething all through dinner. Frightfully bad for the digestion.'

'I don't think I'm going to like this job.'

'Because of Madrina's little whipping party this evening?'

'Partly. You seemed to find it amusing, Mr Vernon.'

'That's my unfortunate face, perhaps. It has what Gemma calls a permanently irreverent expression. If you stay here, Miss Forrester, you'll have to be prepared to do exactly as you're told. My godmother is a stern disciplinarian. She has been accustomed to wielding power over others for so long now that she has become an absolute dictator.'

'Do you do as you're told? I doubt it.'

'I am the exception. She has no power over me. Don't misunderstand me. I am fond of her. She has many good qualities. But the power her money has given her has made her a dangerous autocrat. According to her lights, she is just and generous, and is convinced that she manages people for their own good. I didn't think you were the right type for this job when I first saw you.'

'Why not?'

'Because you have a sensitive face and a light in your eyes that means you have some spirit in spite of a deceptively composed manner. Both of those attributes are, I assure you, deadly handicaps where Mrs Pendine is concerned. If I were you, I'd look for another job. You won't be happy here unless you can knuckle under. From what I saw tonight, I think you'll find that difficult.'

'I shall give it a fair trial. The country here is so lovely, and I don't want a routine job in an office. This one offers variety.'

'Is that really why you came here?'

'Yes. Isn't that a good enough reason?'

'Perhaps. If I diagnosed a love affair that had gone wrong, would I be off mark?'

'Miles off. What made you think of that?'

'Because I think you're running away from something.' Ann said nothing, amazed at his perspicacity. Everything he had said about her had been true, and yet they had spent no more than a few hours in each other's company. 'Oh, well,' he went on, 'no business of mine, but if you're running away from trouble, you've come to a fine retreat, believe me. About as soothing as a wasp's nest.'

'You're not very encouraging, Mr Vernon.'

'Put it down to the lowering effects of my fever. I'm doing myself a disservice by sowing doubts, anyway. I've got a stack of typing waiting for you. It's an amazing thing, but when I get these attacks, I find my mind works with great clarity and I've made a lot of progress these past few days in bed. I hope your eyesight is good. My writing is never very clear, and in bed it's decidedly dodgy.'

'I'll do my best.'

'Don't be late in the morning, then, Miss Forrester. You will find that in my own way, I am every bit as much of a tyrant as Mrs Pendine.'

'You are not the only one who can draw penetrating conclusions about people, Mr Vernon,' said Ann, a little smile in her voice, as she got up from the seat.

He chuckled then, a throaty, husky chuckle, and threw his cigarette into the river.

'Remind me to ask you about them some time. Shall we go back?'

Gemma, bored with her book, looked up with a smile when they went into the drawing-room.

34

'Oh, there you are. Rex, be an angel and come and play table tennis with me. You come, too, Ann, and then Rex can have a rest if he gets tired.'

'What a restless imp you are!' said Rex. 'Going to put any money on it?'

As Ann followed them to the door, Mrs Pendine called her back.

'I wonder, dear, whether you would be kind enough to read to me for a little while. My eyes are tired, and I'm sure the two young people will be happy enough on their own. Trollope is so soothing.'

It was difficult to refuse, and Ann found herself sitting in a chair opposite Mrs Pendine with a copy of *Barchester Towers* in her hand. Madge picked up her knitting and said,

'There's a programme I want to look at on television, Aunt Alice, so I'll leave you to it, if you don't mind.'

'Very well, dear, but Trollope would be much better company for you, I am sure.'

'Not my cup of tea, I'm afraid,' said Madge, and strode out, taking an apple from the fruit dish as she went.

Mrs Pendine sighed as she picked up her embroidery.

'Dear Madge is sadly lacking in culture, but I'm grateful for her practical qualities, and one mustn't expect everything. She takes after her father.'

'I didn't know there was a television set in the house,' said Ann.

'I allowed Madge to have one in her own room. Hideous things. I wouldn't have one in my sight. Symbol of this vulgar, pleasure-loving, moronic age. I concede some value to wireless sets, which have brought music into many homes, although people would be better off making their own music, in my opinion. However, my husband installed it here and I do occasionally listen to concerts.'

A peal of laughter rang out from the game room, and Ann found herself wishing that she was there. As though divining her thought, Mrs Pendine said,

'Gemma is always so happy with Rex. Madge left the door ajar, dear. I wonder if you would be kind enough to close it before you start.'

Ann closed the door on the laughter and returned to her chair. Mrs Pendine's observation earlier that evening that Ann was free to do as she pleased in her leisure time seemed to be open to a very loose interpretation. She read for an hour, after which she was asked to play the piano. At ten o'clock, Mrs Pendine said good-night and went to bed. Ann stayed on at the piano, playing softly, drifting from one piece to another, wishing she could feel less homesick for the old, safe life when her parents were alive. The clock was striking the half-hour when Madge came in.

'Oh, you're still here. I've just seen Aunt Alice safely tucked up. She sat up later than usual tonight. You've done your penance, have you?'

'For what?'

'Running off this afternoon. I hear she tore a strip off you.'

'More or less.'

'She always follows it up with a little session of penance, to make sure you're docile again. I know. I've had some.' Madge flopped on the sofa, put her legs up and lit a cigarette, all of which would have been frowned upon by her aunt, Ann thought. 'Lord, I'm tired. The old lady does take a lot of running after. By the way, want a tip?'

'I'll be glad of any help.'

'Don't tag on to Gemma and Rex. If you do, Aunt Alice will head you off with some ghastly chore. She wants them to be alone together. Savez?'

'You mean? . . .'

'She's set her heart on Gemma marrying Rex. That's why she was so anxious to get him down here. Why you were roped in, too. That stopped his plea of work as an excuse to make his visit short.'

'But Rex is years older than Gemma.'

'Sixteen years older, to be exact. Doesn't signify. Aunt Alice adores Rex and thinks he would be the perfect husband for Gemma and the Pendine money. She was nuts about his father, you know.'

This sounded so incredible that Ann's eyes widened. She could not imagine Mrs Pendine being nuts about anybody.

'Really?'

'M'm. All very hush-hush, of course. I shouldn't have known, but I found a bundle of letters in her bureau once, and couldn't help seeing the top one. I only vaguely remember Rex's parents. They died years ago. But Aunt Alice has always been devoted to Rex. So you see, if her two darlings got married, she would die happy.'

'Gemma is very fond of him, but only in a childish way, I'd have said.'

'I don't know,' said Madge slowly, blowing a smoke ring above her head. 'There's a lot about young madam that isn't childish.'

'And Rex?'

Madge shrugged her shoulders.

'Gemma is heiress to a fortune, and he likes her. That's good enough for any man, I'd say.'

Ann said nothing. Whenever one talked to Madge, the conversation got round to money.

'Anyway, don't let on to anybody,' went on Madge. 'It's never talked about in such crude terms. Aunt Alice is much too refined. I believe in calling a spade a spade, myself, so that's the low-down for you. If you want to keep on the right side of Aunt Alice, don't play gooseberry to Rex and Gemma.'

'I was asked to give up some of my time to Gemma.'

'Ah yes, when she's on her own. Aunt Alice would like to know what she's up to. Gemma never says much about her days out, and Aunt Alice wanted a watchdog. That's you. But you'll not be wanted when Rex is available for Gemma. I'm only passing on the tip so that you can avoid being roped in for some ghastly reading party, as you were tonight.'

'Thanks. I'll bear it in mind.'

'You're welcome to come and share my telly any time you like. It helps to while away the time in this dump. Thank goodness you and Rex have joined the outfit. The more the merrier, I say.'

'It must have been very lonely for you before.'

'Oh, I've got to know a few of the village types. Not a word to Aunt Alice, of course.'

'What about the mysterious Uncle Barney who lives in the stable flat? I haven't set eyes on him yet.'

'Oh, he's ga-ga,' said Madge, yawning. 'Keeps to himself and studies his plants. Mad as a hatter. We hardly ever see him. Well, I'm for bed. The love birds are still in the games room, I believe. Best not disturb them. Good-night.'

'Good-night Madge.'

When Ann passed the games room, she could hear voices but no sounds of a game in progress. She wondered whether to knock and say good-night, then decided against it, fearing to intrude, and walked slowly upstairs to her room. Madge's revelations had given her much to think about, and she found none of it very reassuring.

CHAPTER V

DURING the next two weeks, everything ran smoothly enough. Ann found Rex a good person to work for in that he gave clear instructions, dictated well, and made no unreasonable demands, but she was sometimes unnerved by the cool appraising inspection of those dark eyes. Mrs Pendine, too, was affable and appreciative. Ann, following Madge's advice, never allowed herself to join Rex and Gemma if they were together, but she found herself growing very fond of Gemma and enjoyed her company whenever they escaped together. She was a warm-hearted, frank child, devoid of all vanity, even though her mirror gave her good cause for it, and full of a gay vitality that was irresistible. Ann had as little to do with Madge as was possible without giving offence, for there was something about her that was repellent. For all her hearty, robust manner and ready laughter, there was a false note somewhere. Behind her 'I'm easy,' philosophy, there was something that was not easy at all. She and Rex appeared to get on very well, but Rex had the kind of urbane manner which always appeared friendly and, in fact, revealed little of his feelings. It merely oiled the wheels of personal contacts. To Ann, he remained an enigma, and in spite of her curiosity to know what lay behind the mask, she made little progress. Watching him with Gemma, she was still unable to decide whether it was avuncular affection he felt for her or something warmer, whether he contemplated her as his future wife or whether he would have found the idea ludicrous.

On the Monday of her fourth week at Rosevean, Ann woke from one of the nightmares to which she had been subject since the accident. She could never recall the details clearly when she awoke, but always her heart was pounding and she was shaking with fright. conscious of having been pursued. That morning, it left her with a headache and lacerated nerves, the control of which took all her willpower. When, at the end of their session together, Rex asked her if she felt all right, she said, 'Yes, thank you,' and collected up the papers feeling like an over-stretched bow.

'Leave the book, if you feel under the weather. I'd just like the two letters typed if you can manage them.'

'I've said I'm quite all right. Just a headache. It will pass.'

Mrs Pendine fortunately had nothing for her that morning but asked her to spend the afternoon with Gemma.

'She told me that she was taking the trap out. Her manner was so airy and vague that I suspect she was concealing something. I shall tell her at lunch time that you will go with her. You look washed out and the air will do you good, my dear,' said Mrs Pendine, and walked out of the study as though there was no more to be said.

Ann leaned her forehead on her hand. Watchdog. She could not play the spy for her employer or for anybody. When she felt better, she would have to make that clear to Mrs Pendine, but she was unequal to a clash with that iron will just then. Stubbornly, she typed four pages of Rex's book from his manuscript, which was not easy to read. As the technical terms of engineering were as unfamiliar to her as Chinese, she was not able to work up much interest in the subject matter. By the time she had finished, the typewriter keys seemed to be hammering inside her head. She took the finished sheets to him and waited while he signed the letters.

'By the way,' he said, as he screwed up his fountain pen, you skipped a page of Friday's quota. I've just checked them.'

'Impossible.'

He looked up, eyebrows raised at her curt tone, then said,

'Just look into it when you feel better, will you? There's another page that goes between pages forty-five and forty-six.'

'Then you couldn't have given it to me. I've typed every page I've had.'

'It isn't here. I've already looked. Just go back and check what's on your desk.'

'It's clear.'

'Then go back and look on the floor. When you find it, type it. I'd like it before lunch. If you want to be a bad-tempered martyr, so be it.'

She found the missing page under one of the armchairs and remembered that Gemma had sent a pile of papers flying from her desk on Friday afternoon when she sat on the corner and shared Ann's pot of tea. Looking at the page now, she could have wept. She typed it and took it back to Rex with a stony face and an apology which quavered in spite of all her efforts.

'That's all right, but why are you being so obstinate this morning? I can't stand martyrs. I'd much rather you said you felt like chewed string and couldn't work today.'

'I hate admitting defeat, and I'm not ill. Just screwed up.'

'I haven't seen you like this before. You're always so composed. What's caused it? Has Madrina been playing you on a line?'

'No. I had a bad night. Please forget it.'

'Righto. If I hadn't already noticed that my company is unwelcome, I would suggest that you came for a stroll with me round the garden before lunch, but that might perhaps merely add indigestion to your present woes, so I won't.'

She hesitated, trying to find some way of explaining to him why she refused his invitations to join Gemma and him, but could think of nothing that would not cause trouble. He smiled a little mockingly as she remained tongue-tied, and shrugged his shoulders.

'I have a very tough skin, Ann. You need never fear telling me the plain truth. I must see if I can overcome your aversion, since we are all shut up here together and needs must make our association as pleasant as possible.'

She left him then, and went to her room where she took two aspirins and tried to forget the wicked challenge in his dark eyes. As though fate had decided to be her enemy that day, Gemma gave her the slip after lunch. While Ann was waiting with Hilary by the trap, the housekeeper came down the drive with a note for her. It was hastily scribbled on half a sheet of ruled paper.

'Sorry, I've changed my mind. In any case, your headache will get better quicker without my chatter. G.'

And so Sambo was unharnessed and Ann went for a walk instead, for although she had learned to drive the trap, she felt that walking might help her to relax more quickly. She hoped that she would see Gemma, but there was no sign of the girl, and that was going to take some explaining to Mrs Pendine.

The afternoon was grey and cheerless, and although Easter was only a week off, the day seemed autumnal in its mood, and despondency seized her. There were too many undercurrents in this job. She could not cope with the conflicting personalties here, and she did not like the feeling that she was a pawn in Mrs Pendine's hands. Straightforward by nature, nothing in Ann's experience had prepared her for the dark strategies that lurked here at Rosevean, where nothing was plain or straightforward. Was Rex a cynical fortune-hunter or not? Why did Madge go ferreting about in her aunt's bureau, as she had on the previous day? She had tried to cover it up by saying that she had been sent to fetch a letter when Ann had opened the door on her, but Ann knew that Mrs Pendine no longer kept her private papers in the study bureau, but had transferred them to the small desk in her bedroom, giving the bureau up for Ann's use. Gemma was a lovable, delightful girl, but why was she so secretive, disappearing like a wraith? That was probably explained by her grandmother's too powerful personality, for any child would seek to get away from such weight, but Ann felt hurt that she had slipped off that afternoon when the trip together had been seemingly welcomed.

Walking slowly back along the lane, she remembered how happy and excited she had felt on that first morning drive to Rosevean. Everything had seemed so fresh and full of promise. A car hooted suddenly behind her and she jumped at the shock of it and felt her heart pounding. Rex drew up just ahead of her.

'Like a lift back? You look a bit tired.'

'No. No, thank you. I prefer to walk.'

'You mean, you can't stand me. Righto.'

'No, stop Rex. Mr Vernon,' she added hastily, her cheeks flushed.

'Rex will do.'

'Not in Mrs Pendine's hearing.'

'I shouldn't let that hamper you,' he said dryly.

'Could you step out for a moment? I want to explain something to you,' said Ann, awkwardly.

'Good. It's about time, I fancy.'

They strolled along to a gate nearby and Ann leaned on it and looked across the meadow, which was full of cowslips. Rex took out a cigarette and waited for her to speak. She found it very difficult.

'I'm sorry I've behaved so badly today. I've felt dreadfully on edge. Ever since my parents were killed in a car accident last December, I've had recurrent nightmares that leave me in this jittery state for about a day. I haven't had one since I came here, though, and I thought I'd finished with them, until last night. It's a foolish thing, and I dare say last night's was the final performance, because I've not been haunted by it nearly so much since I came to Rosevean. Too many other things to think about.'

'So that's what you were running away from. That's why you came here.'

'Yes. I wanted to get right away from home and change my life completely.'

'I see. Rosevean can't have provided a very comfortable escape route, though.'

She gave him the ghost of a smile.

'It's better than feeling like a mummy.'

'I'm sorry, Ann. Why didn't you tell me before? It's not always a good policy to bottle things up, you know.'

'I couldn't bear to think about it. My mind just turned away from it.'

'And now?'

'This is the first time I've spoken about it to anybody. You see, we were a very tightly knit little family. When I was left alone, there was nobody to turn to. The whole world seemed empty. But I don't want to be morbid about it. I was excited about this job. I really came to life again when I first came down here, and I'm all right now, with all the complications of life at Rosevean to involve me.'

'You're happy here, then?'

'Involved, I said. And until you know what it's like to be numbed to life, you can't understand how much better it is to have feelings of any sort again.'

'About those nightmares. Have you consulted a doctor? Sedatives might help.'

'No. When I left the hospital, I was warned that I might get some delayed reaction from the shock, but I was lucky to be alive and unhurt except for minor scratches, and I'm over the worst now. Being able to talk to you proves it.'

'How did it happen? Tell me,' he said gently, putting his hand over hers on the gate.

'We were going round a bend and met two cars abreast. It was as simple as that. The road was narrow. My father was driving too fast, perhaps, for that twisting road. I don't remember much more. I was at the back. I only remember how slowly the time went before the impact. The rest is blank. I was thrown out of the car.'

'I had the same experience of time standing still once. I was climbing and found myself in the path of an avalanche. It looked like slow motion and I swear I experienced my whole life again in those seconds before it reached me. There was a curious feeling of detachment about it all, too.'

'Yes, I remember that, too.'

'And now,' he said quietly, 'I'll drive you back to Rosevean and you won't mind getting in the car at all. We'll go slowly.'

Her brown eyes met his a little anxiously as he opened the car door for her, but he just smiled and put a hand under her elbow, and she got in. When he stopped the car inside the gates of Rosevean, he said,

'Good girl. It won't ever be as bad again, you know.'

'You've been very kind.'

'I have my softer moods. Are you going to stick this job? You're much too sensitive for it.'

She looked at him and knew that she was going to stick it.

'Yes. I shall try to make a go of it.'

'I admire your spirit, but I think you're going to get mauled. I should have thought you'd taken enough punishment from life.'

'Life is full of paradoxes, my father maintained. I don't think you find happiness by avoiding trouble, or peace of mind by avoiding difficulties. That was what my father believed, anyway, and he was a very wise person.'

'Yes, it's true. How dark this drive is! The trees want thinning to let some light in.'

'I feel that's true of Rosevean as a whole. It needs some light let in. About the avalanche. Were you injured?'

'Not much more than winded. It was only the fringe that caught me and swept me down about fifty feet. It happened years ago. I used to be a keen climber.'

'Not know?'

'Been too busy these past few years and now I'm a bit past the strenuous work. You know, you sound a whole lot friendlier. Can I assume that the defences are down and peace signed?'

'There was never any war. Only a slight wariness.'

'Why?'

She found it difficult to explain her reluctance to yield to the personal magnetism which she had felt from their first encounter.

'Just an instinct for self-preservation,' she said, laughing.

'Oh, I'm a very harmless person, I assure you.'

Ann shook her head and refused to be drawn.

'Anyway, you would be perfectly safe with Gemma there, too,' he went on, his eyes teasing her.

'Perhaps, but Mrs Pendine doesn't want too much fraternizing.'

'Is that why you've been refusing?' he asked, frowning.

'More or less. She wants me to be a companion for Gemma when she has nobody else. I wish I knew where the imp disappeared to this afternoon. We were supposed to go for a ride together.'

'I know. I heard the arrangements. What happened?'

Ann told him and he grinned.

'Young madam has as strong an objection to being organized as Madrina, and she's worked out a very clever strategy in dealing with her grandmother's supervision. Evasive action brought to a high art. I thought you two hit it off pretty well, though.'

'We do. That's why I was disappointed about this afternoon.'

As they approached the house, they saw John Hilary driving out of the wood with a cartload of brushwood.

'Looks as though some thinning has been taking place somewhere, anyway,' observed Rex. 'An estate like this needs half a dozen men, not Hilary and the boy. They're just not obtainable, though. And here comes our truant.'

Gemma had emerged from the wood and waved to them. They waited as she ran up, her eyes shining, her face radiant.

'Hullo. I'm glad you kept Ann company this afternoon, Rex. I've been feeling a bit guilty about leaving her.'

'And so you might. Very impolite of you, my child.'

'You didn't mind, angel, did you?' Gemma put her arm round Ann's waist. 'I've been helping the Hilarys clear some of the undergrowth in the woods. Just had to do something active. Forgive me?'

'Of course, but you may have to answer to your grandmother.'

'Need she know?'

'If you mean, will Ann tell lies for you if she's questioned, the answer is no, Gemma,' said Rex firmly. 'Pay for your indulgences, my child. That's a rule of life.'

'Righto. She may not ask, anyway. It's been a wizard afternoon, hasn't it? Molto bello.'

'Well, the sun may have been shining on you, but I don't think it appeared for us, did it, Ann?'

'It was a much better afternoon than I expected,' said Ann, smiling up at him as they went in.

CHAPTER VI

THE storm broke over Gemma's head while they were drinking sherry in the drawing room before dinner. That Mrs Pendine had deliberately waited until they were all assembled no longer surprised Ann, but she wondered how she had found out so soon, for Ann had not seen her and she doubted whether Rex would have told her. She was soon enlightened.

'You did not keep your promise to go out with Miss Forrester this afternoon, I hear, Gemma.'

'No, I changed my mind, Grandma.'

'With no more than a scribbled note to Miss Forrester, who was waiting at the gates for you.'

'It was sufficient. I didn't think Ann minded,' said Gemma, sending a reproachful look at Ann.

'Miss Forrester has said nothing. I learned this from Madge. Mrs Vincent told her.'

'What business had she to do that? I suppose she read the note, too. Nosey old woman.'

'Rudeness and abuse of others does not make you appear in a more agreeable light, Gemma. Mrs Vincent wanted to explain her absence to Madge, who had gone into the kitchen to consult her about something. I suggest, before we go any further, that you apologize to Miss Forrester.'

Rex studied his glass, Madge crossed her legs and sat back with her sherry as though settling in for the evening. Ann said quickly.

'Gemma has already apologized, Mrs Pendine. I met her when I got back this evening.'

'I see. I'm glad to learn that you have some small sense of one's social obligations, Gemma. Don't ever do such a thing again. If you had other plans, you should have said so at the time.'

'I don't need a nurse-maid,' said Gemma, her face white, her eyes blazing.

Mrs Pendine's face was cold and composed, and her eyes were steady as she studied Gemma's mutinous face.

'It is quite obvious from your behaviour tonight that you do. I'm sorry Rex has to witness such insolence.'

'He wouldn't, if you didn't choose to make such a fuss about nothing. I'd already explained to Ann and Rex. I'm not a child. Why should I be lectured just because I choose to make my own arrangements about how I spend my time? I didn't make the arrangement with Ann. You did.'

'That's enough, Gemma. This exhibition is deplorable. I think we had better wait until you are calmer before we say any more about it. We'll go in to dinner.'

'I don't want any. This atmosphere would put anyone off their food. I'm going out for some fresh air.'

As Mrs Pendine was about to call her back, Rex laid his hand on her arm and said.

'Let her go, Madrina. She needs to cool off.'

'Yes, you're right. Tomorrow, I must have a serious talk with Gemma. I really cannot permit such tantrums. Now, if you will give me your arm, Rex dear. My leg is a little tiresome tonight.'

'If you ask me,' said Madge, downing her drink as Mrs Pendine went out on Rex's arm, 'that girl needs a jolly good hiding.'

At dinner, Mrs Pendine asked Rex if he would play the piano for her that evening.

'Right you are, Madrina. I'll play you something nice and soothing to calm our shattered nerves, and Ann shall sing for you.'

Ann saw Mrs Pendine's eyebrows lift at his use of her Christian name. It was the first time he had used it in her presence. She turned to Ann with a little smile, however, and said,

'Do you sing, Miss Forrester?'

'Not seriously. Only for fun sometimes. My voice has never been trained.'

'Trained or not, it sounded very pleasant when I heard you singing Greensleeves the other day,' said Rex.

'Where were you? I thought I was alone.'

'On the terrace. You sang it better than you played it.'

'I never can do both. It was a favourite song of my mother's. She had a lovely voice. When she was young, she used to sing at concerts.'

'You shall let us hear yours, dear,' said Mrs Pendine graciously. 'I do like to hear music in the home.'

'Gemma has a nice clear soprano,' said Rex. 'I always thought it a pity you didn't have it trained, Madrina.'

'I don't think she would have the diligence for serious training, Rex, and I shouldn't want her to be a professional singer, anyway. There's no need. Gemma will never want for money, and she can enjoy singing just as well with an untrained voice. It will never need to fill a hall. There's nothing wrong with amateurism, my boy.'

In spite of the uneasy recollection of Gemma's white face and hungry state, Ann enjoyed that evening. From the first few bars that Rex played, she recognized a true musician. He drifted easily from a Beethoven sonata to Chopin and Bach. She sang Greensleeves and two Schubert songs out of the album which Gemma used. Rex transposed the key of the second one for her after the first few bars, saying,

'You're a mezzo. You'll not get the range in that key.'

Just before ten, Mrs Pendine thanked them and said to Ann,

'Would you go and tell Madge that I'm ready for her, dear? I feel too tired to stay up longer, much as I've enjoyed this little concert. You will find her glued to the television set in her room, I have no doubt.'

After Ann had left them, Mrs Pendine said,

'Do you think it's wise to call Miss Forrester by her Christian name, dear?'

'Why not?'

'I have always found it fatal to treat employees as personal friends. Sooner or later, they take advantage of it. To maintain discipline, you must keep your footing clear from the start. She works for you, as she does for me.'

'Never fear,' said Rex, half laughing. 'I shall be able to maintain discipline.'

'I still think it's a bad habit. People so easily forget their place.'

'Times have changed, Madrina. You're out of date.'

'They've changed for the worse, and this kind of slackness is a contributory cause. People should be kept in their proper place. That's what grieves me so much about Gemma's behaviour. Choosing to spend the afternoon with the gardener, or fishing with that Dakers' family. It's not fitting for a girl in her position. I shall soon have Hilary telling me what to do, and I already see in young John a very independent attitude. Gemma's behaviour, of course, encourages it.'

'She hasn't many suitable companions to choose from, you know.'

'That's one of the reasons I engaged Miss Forrester, who is a nice, refined young woman. And she has you, Rex. She is deeply attached to you. Always has been.'

47

'She's a warm-hearted poppet. Needs careful handling, you know.'

'I've brought her up, Rex. I know best how to handle her, and believe me, indulgence is not the answer.'

'I don't suggest that it is, but she's growing up, Madrina. If you want to dress her down, do it privately. At eighteen, one's dignity is easily hurt.'

'Yes, perhaps you're right, and I was a little premature with my scolding. I shall talk to her seriously tomorrow about her position, her place in the world. But I want her to be happy. Rex, I have an idea.'

'Go on.'

'About what you said. Her dignity being hurt. There's the annual charity ball at the Grand Hotel on Easter Monday. Would you take Gemma? I bought her a new evening dress last Christmas, a really grown-up affair, and I would like to give her one of the family pieces of jewelry to wear with it, as a gesture of recognition of her status. If I could tell her about this tomorrow, after I have had this talk with her, it might help her to understand, and restore the dignity you say I've affronted.'

'A good idea. I'm game. Not that I'm much of a dancer, but I'll enjoy giving Gemma a night out.'

'You're sure you feel up to it?'

'Quite sure. I'm practically fit again now, you know.'

'You're very dear to me, Rex. Take care of yourself.'

'I've always been able to do that, Madrina.'

'So you have. You're very like your father. Having you here brings back many ghosts. I find I live more in the past than ever now. Ah, there you are, Madge.'

After Mrs Pendine had said good-night and departed, leaning heavily on Madge's arm, Rex went back to the piano and began to play a Brahms waltz quietly, as though preoccupied. Ann leaned on the piano and looked at her reflection in its black, polished surface. Her hair curved smoothly round her forehead and hung in a bell shape from her cheeks as she leaned forward. In the light of the lamp, it was the colour of ripe corn and shone like silk. Something in the classic line of it round that oval face pleased Rex, and he watched her as he played. Her dark eyes were hidden, but he knew already that there were flecks of gold in the brown iris, and he approved the smooth clean line of the eyebrows. Nature had provided some interesting juxtapositions in that face, he thought: dark eyes and brows but fair hair; a beautifully symmetrical framework to uneven features, for the unusually mobile mouth was too wide and the nose a little too short for classical perfection; a high forehead and widely spaced eyes. Altogether, an interesting whole, and a sensitive reflector of feeling, for all her composed manner.

She looked up and flushed a little under his scrutiny.

'Penny for them,' he said.

'I was feeling a little worried about Gemma. I knocked at her door just now, but there was no reply and the room was empty.'

'She'll turn up. Probably waiting until everybody's gone to bed. You shoot off, and have a good night. I shall stay up and have a word with the kid. She'll listen to me.'

'You're very fond of her, aren't you?'

'Yes. Known her all her life. I've always felt sorry for her. A thousand pities she lost her parents when she was so young. Madrina's devoted to her, but they live in different worlds, and I don't think this is a good atmosphere for a youngster. Too intense. Gemma needs riding on a very light rein, then she's most responsive. I think I hear her scuffling about outside now. Buzz off, there's a good girl. I want to see her alone.'

'Good-night, then. And thank you for helping me today.'

'I hope the nightmares won't come back. Good-night, Ann.'

She went, half wishing that she could have stayed, and Rex went to the French windows and opened them.

'Come along in, young woman. How long have you been skulking out there?'

'Ages. Why is everybody so slow in going to bed tonight? I didn't want to see anybody. That doesn't include you, of course.'

'Of course,' echoed Rex gravely.

Gemma took off her coat and seized an apple.

'I'm starving.'

'You shouldn't make defiant gestures of scorning food.'

'I couldn't face dinner with you all, after that,' said Gemma a little wanly, crouching by the embers of the fire and taking a huge bite out of the apple.

'It's difficult for you, I know, Gemma, but you must try to remember that your grandmother belongs to a generation which never answered its elders back, and you were very rude to her tonight, you know.'

Gemma chewed her apple and looked up at him with wide, appealing eyes, but said nothing. He took out a cigarette and sat down on the music stool.

'She's an old lady, Gemma, and to her you are a child. To

old people, we all owe a certain respect, however we differ from their outlook.'

'She shouldn't have talked to me like that in front of everybody. I'm not going to be watched and reported on like someone on probation, either. Whatever I do, Madge or Mrs Vincent or Ann or somebody has to keep Grandma informed. Why? Other people don't have to account for all their movements. It's got worse lately.'

'You have a lot more freedom than most people, my girl. You're not tied down by a job.'

'That's what I thought when I agreed to come home after leaving school. I'd so hate to be shut up in an office or tied down by some dull routine, and I was sick to death of being organized at school. But somehow, freedom doesn't seem to exist here, either.'

'We're none of us free. We all have obligations to somebody or something.'

'Oh, well, I'll make peace with Grandma tomorrow. Don't you lecture me, too, Rex.'

'All right. Just one other thing, though, Gemma. Remember that Ann Forrester is employed by your grandmother. If you try to make her an ally, you'll put her in an impossible position. She's fond of you, but she has a duty to your grandmother. Conflicting loyalties get one in the devil of a mess.'

'Pay for my own indulgences, you mean.'

'Exactly.'

'She's nice, isn't she? Ann.'

'Yes, I think so.'

'I wish Grandma had had a huge family, and then it wouldn't matter so much what I did with my life. I wish my name wasn't Pendine and I wish I belonged to an ordinary family.'

'You have my sympathy, poppet. The concentration on you must be a bit trying, but responsibilities put chains of some sort on all of us sooner or later, you know.'

'Yes, but responsibilities you've chosen to shoulder are different from those you've had forced on you by accident of birth. Look at old Grandfather Pendine up there. He gives me the jitters. That foreboding eye always seems to be following me. Did you ever see such a gloomy lot of forbears as those that darken the walls here?'

'Shockers,' agreed Rex, smiling. 'The men resemble hanging judges and the women bear a look of awful resignation. I've one in the turret I've had to take down. Right opposite my bed. I couldn't bear that look of mute suffering. Great Aunt Lucy Pendine, isn't it?'

'M'm. You know, Grandma's side of the family seems more human. I mean, Gubbie, or I suppose I should call him Great-uncle Barney, is a darling even if he is a bit dippy, and although I don't like Madge much, she's not stiff-necked. I guess Grandma must have been infected by Pendine-itis when she married him,' concluded Gemma, nodding at the portrait with disapproving eyes.

'The world of the Pendines has crumbled to dust, my child, and with it some good things as well as bad ones, and that's why we must have patience with your grandmother, whose world has died but who clings to its ghost for the few years she has left. You have all your life in front of you, Gemma, and it won't always be restricted as it is now, so cheer up and mend your manners to Madrina. A little discipline, my girl, never did anybody any harm.'

She wrinkled her nose at him as she scrambled to her feet.

'Whatever you say, maestro. Grandma wants to have my portrait painted. If she does, I shall look my wickedest and wake the outfit up.'

'You'll be the prettiest thing on these walls, that's a cert. I hope they'll hand you in my turret room instead of luckless Lucy,' said Rex, putting an arm round her slim waist.

'Nice Rex,' said Gemma, rubbing her head against his shoulder. 'I wish . . . Oh, well, never mind. You know, I hate hurting people. Especially people I'm fond of. But sometimes, you can't help it.'

'If you're ever in a spot, you know I'll always do anything I can to help you.'

'I know. But you've told me yourself that you have to pay for what you want.'

He looked down at her thoughtfully, sensing that she wanted to confide in him.

'What are you wanting now that's going to call for payment?'

But her mood suddenly changed and she skipped away from him.

'You'd be surprised. Good-night, angel.'

Rex closed the piano and stood by the fire for a few minutes, finishing his cigarette, while the forbidding face of Charles Pendine looked down on him. Gemma's words had stirred up recollections of that old story he had learned from his father. How Alice Rockford at nineteen years of age had been forced by rapacious parents into marriage with Charles Pendine although she was in love with Philip Vernon, then in his last year at medical school. If she had stood out for the man she loved, her history would have been very different, but she had done what she conceived to be her duty, and had become imbued with all the arrogance that Pendine wealth bestowed and had been moulded by Charles Pendine into the family image. He must have been quite formidable, reflected Rex as he threw his cigarette end into the dying embers of the fire. But the Pendines had thinned out, and now young Gemma was the last of his name, and in her veins the blood of her Italian mother was dominant. It was odd, how things turned out.

CHAPTER VII

'Oh, how beautiful!' exclaimed Gemma as she took the necklace from her grandmother. The sun drew flashing colours from the diamonds as she held the necklace round her throat and looked in the mirror. 'It must have been made for a slender neck; it wouldn't go round a fat one.'

'Your grandfather gave it to me at our engagement party. It had been in the family for several generations.'

Mrs Pendine adjusted the necklace so that the diamond and sapphire pendant was central and stood back to admire it.

'Your white skin is the right background for it, darling. It's yours.'

'Thank you a thousand times. Weren't you thrilled when you first wore it?'

An odd expression crossed Mrs Pendine's face as she recalled that night so long ago. She had felt trapped. Perhaps no moment in all her life had been as bad as when Charles had clasped the necklace round her neck in front of the assembled supper party. His badge of possession. She was labelled Pendine property from then on. How foolish she had been, she thought, dismissing the recollection as she replied,

'It made a great impression on me. I'd better keep it in the safe, Gemma, but you may have it whenever you want it.'

'Grandma, treat me as though I'm really grown up. Let me take care of it. After all, it's no use talking to me about responsibility if you won't give me any.'

Mrs Pendine hesitated, then smiled.

'Very well, my dear, but do look after it. We're not likely to be burgled here at Rosevean, and it's insured, anyway, but remember its value.'

Gemma smiled delightedly and kissed her grandmother's cheek.

'I really will try to remember all you've said. Isn't Rex a dear to take me to the dance? It's ages since I've been to one, and that was only a kids' affair.'

'When you marry, you shall have the rest of the family jewelry. I have no use for it now.'

'Do you believe in marrying young, Grandma?'

'It depends. I would like to see you married to a good man, darling. If he came along now, I wouldn't say it was too soon. Choose someone like Rex, and you'll have my blessing.'

She watched Gemma closely but could detect nothing from her grand-daughter's smiling face but frank mischief as she said,

'I'll see what I can do.'

She was much too attractive to have running around unattached, thought Mrs Pendine. She and Rex must make a match of it. She had set her heart on it, and it would relieve her of so much anxiety on Gemma's behalf. It would be such a suitable union in every way. Gemma needed a man older than herself to guide her and keep her in order, and there was no mistaking the affection they had for each other. So few things in her life had turned out as she wished. Surely God might grant her this last, most dear wish.

* * *

On Easter Saturday the sun shone with such brilliance that Ann decided to go down to the cove and have a swim. Gemma walked half way down the cliff with her, then went off to help the Hilarys, who were still clearing the woods of undergrowth. Down in the cove it was hot and the sand burned her feet as she walked to the edge of the waves to test the temperature. It struck very cold, but she decided to have a quick dip. Climbing back on to the cliff path and using a grassy clearing for her base, she had taken her dress off when a familiar husky voice hailed her from the path above.

'Hi, there. Are you contemplating a sun bathe or a swim?'

'A swim.'

'No go. The tide's turned.'

She waited, buttoning up her dress, until Rex joined her, when she said,

'I'm a good swimmer.'

'Doesn't count. The current's too strong here when the tide's going out. Hasn't anybody told you?'

'Yes, Gemma mentioned it once. I'd forgotten.'

'They could be your last words, my girl, so don't forget again. Where's the child?'

'Helping the Hilarys on the cliff. Didn't you see her?'

'No. Do you mind my company or did you count on having the cove to yourself?'

'Of course I don't mind. I thought you'd settled for an afternoon on the river.'

'I had, but Madrina suggested that I came after you girls when she saw you going off, and when she said it looked as though you meant to swim, I put on speed. I don't fancy myself as a life-saver here unless I'm attached to the shore by a rope.'

'I'm sorry to have caused you the bother.'

'Not at all, Miss Forrester. Allow me,' he said wickedly as he jumped from the path to the beach and held out a helping hand, which Ann ignored as she jumped.

Leaving Rex stretched out on the sand with his head pillowed on her towel and swim-suit, she paddled along the edge of the waves. The sea looked too calm to threaten danger to anybody, but the fringe of sea-weed and shells was about a foot higher than the curling edge of the waves and she knew that the Cornish coast was not without its hazards. She could not understand why she felt prickly when Rex took control of her, as he often did, for there were usually good reasons. It was as though she feared to yield too much to him. And why? She faced the question honestly for the first time and the answer was plain. It was because in her heart she knew that it would be all too easy to yield her whole citadel of reserve to Rex Vernon, and she feared the consequences if she did. There was too much about him that she did not know. He eyed her lazily when she rejoined him.

'Want your towel?'

'No. My feet will dry quickly enough.'

'The sun on your face and the sound of a quiet sea in your ears. That's bliss,' he said.

Ann sat and stared at the sea, hugging her knees, until he pulled her back.

'Relax, girl. Use my shoulder for a pillow as I've got your towel.'

Gradually the warmth of the sun and the murmuring of the sea cloaked her in peace, too, and she stretched like a cat before relaxing against him.

'Comfy?'

'M'm.'

Drowsiness stole over her and she remembered turning and thinking how smooth his white shirt was against her cheek before a beautiful velvety darkness closed over her and she slept. The first thing she was aware of when she awoke was the ticking of a watch close to her ear. The wrist to which it belonged was resting on her shoulder. She moved cautiously and found him looking at her with a quizzical expression. His face stood up well to inspection at such close quarters, she thought, then full consciousness flooded back and she sat up, blinking.

'How long have I been asleep?'

'Don't look so guilty. Only half an hour.'

'Have you been asleep?'

'Just in that pleasant state between sleeping and waking.'

'I hope I don't snore.'

'Quiet as a dormouse,' he assured her.

Ann let the hot sand trickle through her fingers. A herring gull soared round the headland and glided down to the water's edge. Folding its wings neatly and efficiently, it walked along the sand probing for food, its pink feet washed now and again by the smooth swirl of a wave. She was like the gull, Ann thought. She wanted to keep in the safe shallows. On such a lovely, peaceful afternoon, it was hard to think that life here at Rosevean was not as calm and pleasant as this sunny sea. Rex, in the uncanny fashion that he had, echoed her thoughts when he said,

'Life would be simple if it was all like this, wouldn't it?'

'Yes. What cold eyes that gull has!'

'Have you had any more nightmares?'

'No.'

'You're still wary, though, aren't you?'

'Of what?'

'Me. Life in general, perhaps.'

'A little. I'd like to paddle in the shallows for a bit. I'm afraid of getting out of my depth. Do you think that's cowardly?'

'No. It's natural after a bad shock, anyway. I warned you that Rosevean wasn't the place for convalescence, though.'

'It is this afternoon,' she replied, smiling.

'This is the first time you've really let your defences down with me, you know, and you'll shoot them up again at any moment, I feel. And yet, confess. Isn't it a relief to let them down?'

'Yes. But it could be dangerous.'

'I've told you. I'm quite harmless.'

As harmless as dynamite, she thought, looking down at him, but she merely said smoothly,

'The shallows for me. A very ignoble type, I'm afraid.'

'On the contrary. It's because you're sensitive and capable of very deep feeling that you suffer more than most from emotional stress and naturally want to steer clear of it if you can. After recent events, that's an instinctive recoil. The trouble is, you can't change your nature. You have sensitive antennae for feeling, and feel you will, whatever defences you try to put up.'

'Are you a student of psychology, too?'

'Fruits of my long and sordid experience,' he said, grinning. 'But some people interest me. You do. You're such a complete contrast to the other inmates of Rosevean that it adds a nice note of variety. An observant little fawn among the tigers, but not without its own resources.'

'It doesn't look as though I shall have a very long life, then.'

'You need some kind tiger to look after you.'

'You're right. I wish I had some of Madge's toughness.'

'Heaven forbid! You'd lose far more than you gained.'

'What would I lose?'

'You'd lose that vivid appreciation of yours for natural beauty and for music and poetry, for a start. You'd take the stresses and strains more easily, but would it be worth it? You can't just graft on the odd bits of a nature that you'd like. Wouldn't fit.'

'I suppose not.'

'Moreover, you would become that horror of horrors, a managing type, and I should detest you.'

'You don't detest Madge.'

'She has her good points, and she's reliable, but I have to take her in very small doses. She has a larger fund of blue jokes than any man I've ever come across. I think hospital life must have a coarsening effect on the fibres. No, stay as you are and pay the penalties, Ann. Or find a nice kind tiger,' he added wickedly.

'You tie me in knots. Let's stop talking about me. You're looking a lot fitter now. Are you troubled still by that fever?'

'Not much. I shall certainly reckon to get into harness again in the autumn.'

'Start as a consulting engineer?'

'Yes. I shall put out feelers for some offices in London next time I go up.'

'Why do you want to start on your own? That last project you were on must have been fascinating.'

'Yes, it was. But I shall get more variety as a consulting engineer, and I like to be my own boss.'

'The managing type, in fact.'

He laughed as he stood up and held out his hands to her. As she came into his arms, he held her for a moment and ruffled her hair in gentle admonishment.

'Not exactly. Just a dislike of being managed. It's not quite the same thing.'

'The sun has softened me, or I'd argue that one out. Don't count on me always being so meek, though, although you approve of meek women.'

'Not at all. I never said that. I dislike the managing type of woman. Doesn't automatically follow that I approve of the meek ones, and I have never entertained the idea that you were a meek person. The reverse. You've plenty of spirit. That's different from being bossy, and I approve of it. After all,' he added slyly, 'it adds spice to the mixture, doesn't it?'

'I shall never get the better of your tongue, that's obvious,' said Ann, as she shook the sand out of her towel. 'I'm for tea.'

The sun had moved round behind the cliff and it was suddenly cool. As they started off up the path together, Rex took her arm, whistling a tune to himself, as though in good spirits. After a few moments, she recognized it.

'The Choral Symphony. Beethoven's greatest.'

'Yes. I wonder what put that into my head. Ode to joy. Perhaps an unconscious feeling of gratitude in my miserable little soul for sunshine and sea and a quiet little cove.'

'I love it. I go and hear it whenever I can.'

She sang the melody with him until the path climbed too steeply to leave them breath to spare. At the last bend, she stopped and looked down at the cove again before they plunged into the wood behind Rosevean. She could see the blur of their resting place on the sand and the faint tracks their feet had left, no larger than the tracks of birds from that height. A corner of tranquillity. She knew that she would never forget it as it had been that afternoon in the Easter sunshine. . .

　　　　°　　　°　　　°

Gemma carried the last pile of brushwood to the cart and stowed it in.

'There,' she said triumphantly. 'I said we'd get it done by five.'

John Hilary collected up the tools they had been using and looked round to see if anything had been forgotten.

'Thanks for your help, Gemma. You're a jolly good worker, you know. You look such a dainty little thing, but you've gone through almost as much as I have.'

'I'm strong, and I've got plenty of energy, and I love working out of doors.'

'Well, you've surprised me. When you first volunteered to help, I must confess I thought you'd be more ornamental than useful.'

'A spoilt little rich girl. Come on. Admit it. Isn't that what you thought?'

'No. Do you know what I thought?'

Gemma shook her head and looked up at his sunburnt face with wide eyes. His white shirt was open to the waist, his sleeves were rolled up to reveal the smooth brown muscles of his arms. The sun glinted in his fair hair and he seemed to her the finest specimen of manhood she had ever seen.

'What did you think?' she asked.

'That you were the only worth-while thing the Pendines had ever produced.'

'You don't like it here, do you?'

'I'm not a servant. That's how your people treat me, though. I only meant to give my father a helping hand for a few weeks and make him see that this wasn't my life.'

'What are your plans, then?'

'To go to Canada and start a fruit farm of my own. We've an uncle out there, you know. He farms. Arable, though. I've got to save up enough for my fare and a bit to start me off. I'd begin in a small way and hope to expand. My uncle says the prospects are good.'

'Canada. Where does your uncle live?'

'In British Columbia. Uncle Bill was over here for six months just before I started at the agricultural college. Brought loads of photographs and used to talk to me for hours about the life out there. I knew then that it was my kind of life. A man's life. He would have liked me to go back with him. He stayed at the pub here in the village for a few weeks and spent a lot of time with us, but you were at boarding school then and wouldn't have known about the goings-on in the servants' quarters.'

'Don't blame me for that, John.'

'Sorry. It makes me a bit jaundiced sometimes to see the old man behaving like a serf and Mother working so hard. They can't seem to see that this kind of life is an anachronism. My father's a skilled man. He could have got a decent job as a Parks Superintendent or in commercial horticulture at any time. Instead, he's stayed here all these years, ordered about like a dog, being stable lad, gardener, odd job man, for a small wage and a cold, cramped little cottage. I can't make him see how foolish he's been. Now, of course, he's too old to change. But he's kidding himself if he thinks this is good enough for me.'

'You and I are in the same boat, really, John. I'm caught in this feudal prison, too, you know. Grandma expects me to do just as she did when she was a child. I shall escape one day, too, but Grandma is old and Rex says we must be patient with her. He's a dear, you know.'

'Never had much to do with him. Oh, well, I suppose I'd better get back. Coming in the cart?'

Gemma hesitated and he smiled wryly.

'Not done to be seen with the servants?'

'I was going to look for Ann. I left her to go down to the cove on her own.'

'You don't have to make excuses. I understand.'

Gemma stooped to brush some leaves from her slacks to hide the tears that blurred her eyes. When she spoke, her voice trembled.

'You don't understand.'

He looked at her quickly but her face was hidden. When she straightened up, he took her by the shoulders and saw the tears in her blue eyes.

'I can't bear it when you talk to me like that,' she whispered. 'It's so unfair.'

'Do you really mind so much?' he asked, his eyes searching her face.

She nodded and gave a little sniff, and suddenly he held her against him tightly and said,

'Dear little Gemma. It was unkind, and you don't deserve it. There's something in the atmosphere of this place that's

59

poisonous. I'm growing a large sized chip on my shoulder. I was so different at college, away from here. Forgive me?'

He tilted her chin and when he saw the expression on her face, he kissed her. The warmth of her response left him in no doubt, and when he kissed her again, they both knew that they had entered an amazing new private world. Gemma tore herself away when she heard voices.

'Ann and Rex. I can't face anybody now. I shall go to see Gubbie after dinner tonight. Will you come, too? He likes you. Then we can go for a walk afterwards.'

'I'll come, my darling.'

She flashed him a radiant smile and ran off through the woods. John was moving off in the cart when Ann and Rex came in sight.

CHAPTER VIII

THE next morning, Ann was walking along the river bank hoping to see the heron which Gemma told her was sometimes to be found fishing for his dinner, when a flash of brilliant blue wings on the far bank drew her attention. Hurrying forward to keep the kingfisher in sight, she suddenly found herself on the ground, having fallen over what she presumed to be a tree trunk. When she sat up, a little dazed, she found herself beside the prostrate body of a long, thin man with a shock of white hair who was lying face down, holding a magnifying glass in his hand. He was looking at her with mild surprise on his pale, bony face.

'Dear me! Are you hurt, young lady?'

'No, I don't think so,' replied Ann, sitting up and moving her arm gingerly.

'Well, stand up and find out,' he said, and turned his magnifying glass again on a small yellow flower.

Ann did as she was told and found that everything was in order. There seemed to be nothing more to say but,

'Good morning. I'm sorry I disturbed you.'

'Are you Ann Forrester?'

'Yes.'

'I'm Barnabas Rockford, Mrs Pendine's brother. Gemma has told me about you. Quite extraordinary,' he added, peering through his glass. 'I've never seen wood crowfoot here before.'

'It looks like a buttercup,' said Ann, stooping to peer, too.

'Same family. This is not its usual habitat, though. Very interesting. Do you know anything about the flora and fauna of our countryside, young lady?'

'A little. I lived in London before I came here, so I haven't had much opportunity for nature study. I'd like to know more.'

'I'll lend you some books if you're really interested, but only if you give a sacred promise to return them within two weeks of borrowing.'

'Thank you. I'd be grateful.'

'Don't like lending books, mind you. But you should know what grows in your native soil.'

'You're a great botanist, Mr Rockford, aren't you?'

'How do you know?'

'Mr Vernon mentioned it. He said you'd been a plant collector.'

'Quite right. I have one species of a genus named after me. Rockfordiana. Foolish business, really, but if I'm going to have any memorial at all, a plant is better than most. Why didn't you see me when you were walking along? I'm big enough to be seen.'

'I was following a kingfisher.'

'Well, good morning.'

'Good morning,' echoed Ann, a little bewildered. 'May I call to see your books some time?'

'Don't like visitors. I see the child, Gemma. Pretty little bird. Don't mind John Hilary. Knows a lot about plants. But I don't encourage callers. Not from the castle of Mammon.'

'Well, I only work there.'

'You'll get infected. All vultures after the pickings. You can't serve God and Mammon, you know.'

'Well, I'll leave you to your crowfoot, then, Mr Rockford.'

'Wood crowfoot. There are several different species. If you really want to see my books, you may call any evening after eight. I can't guarantee to let you in, though. It all depends on how I'm feeling. I live in the flat over the stables.'

'Yes, I know.'

'Of course. Cranky Barney. That's what they call me. Doesn't bother me. As good a way as any to keep the tribe away.'

He stood up, nodded to her, and walked off briskly, his haversack swinging from one shoulder, magnifying glass at the ready. Ann went on her way, thinking that, cranky or not, Uncle Barney was the most reassuring person she had met at Rosevean. The river flowed silkily beside her, dark beneath the overhanging trees, but her thoughts turned from her surroundings to Rex, as they did so often now. He had taken Gemma out boating that morning. They had not asked her to join them, and as she watched them go off arm in arm, laughing together at some private joke, she had wondered again whether Rex was in love with Gemma or intended to marry her even if there was no more than affection between them. Now they haunted her along the river path and when she saw Madge approaching, she half welcomed her as an antidote to her unprofitable thoughts, but Madge only echoed them.

'Grand weather,' she said, as Ann quickened her step to keep up with her. 'If it didn't make me as sick as a dog, I wouldn't mind being out on the water with Rex and Gemma. It's a confounded nuisance. I've tried all the usual drugs, but my stomach just won't adjust itself to the sea. Are you a good sailor?'

'Yes. I love the sea. In it or on it.'

'Oh well, best leave love's young dream together, I suppose. Not that Rex is exactly a freshman at the game.'

'Isn't he?'

'Sticks out a mile, doesn't it? He's enjoyed life all right. He's got something, and he knows it.'

'Yes. Do you think they'll be announcing an engagement soon?'

'Could be. The old lady wants it, and what she wants, she gets. That's what money can do for you. Give you power over others.'

'Not if the others can't be bought.'

'Everybody has their price. Haven't you learned that yet, Ann?'

'No.'

'You will. Not that Rex will have to make much effort. Gemma's an attractive little thing. No hardship at all."

'How cynical you are, Madge!'

Madge laughed as she trudged along.

'Bless you, I'm not cynical. Just know this old world, that's all. You're in danger of putting Rex on a pedestal and looking all starry-eyed at him, like Gemma, are you?'

'No.'

'Just as well for you. I'm speaking as a pal. Rex likes to

amuse himself, like most men, and it doesn't do to take him seriously. It tickles his vanity and he likes to exercise his skills. That's why he may not be in a hurry to tie himself up with Gemma. Wants a few more diversions before he becomes a husband, because the old lady will see that he behaves himself then, you may be sure.'

'I am in no danger,' said Ann stiffly.

'My dear girl, don't get me wrong. I'm not narrow-minded. I'm easy. A bit of fun and games on the sly is all right by me. Lord knows it's deadly dull down here, and males in short supply. Just thought I'd give you a word of advice. You strike me as being a bit inexperienced where men are concerned.'

'Thanks. I'll bear it in mind.'

'Don't mench. Here's Aunt Alice just back from church. By the way, she was a bit put out because you and Rex apparently lost Gemma yesterday afternoon. Watch your step, girlie.'

The trap passed them on the drive and Mrs Pendine smiled at them graciously. Ann looked at the retreating trap with dismay in her heart. How did she know everything that went on? She must watch all their comings and goings like a cat watching its prey, or else she employed spies to do it for her, and Madge, Ann suspected, performed that office willingly.

She spent the afternoon in her room, listening to some records she had brought with her, but found it difficult to dismiss her disturbing thoughts. She felt herself trapped in this archaic house while gossamer threads were being spun round her. She could not discount Madge's words. All that she had said about Rex could well be true. He was conscious of the charm he exerted, and she knew that he had deliberately set out to overcome her wariness with him and enjoyed seeing her yield her position, step by step. Was it just vanity? A sop to boredom while he was convalescing here? An indulgence of a familiar kind? And did he intend eventually to marry Gemma and the Pendine fortune? That he could bend Gemma to his will, she had no doubt. Round and round went the thoughts against a background of Beethoven and Brahms until in desperation she stopped the music and made herself a pot of tea. This at least had the effect of making her face the issue honestly. None of Madge's assertions that morning would have mattered to Ann if she had not felt herself half way down the slippery slope to Rex Vernon's feet.

* * *

Rex was alone in the drawing-room when Ann went in on Monday evening to fetch her book. He was playing the piano while he waited for Gemma and had graced the occasion with white tie and tails, carnation and all. When Ann came in, he stopped playing and said,

'Hullo there. Haven't seen much of you on this fine bank holiday. What have you been doing with yourself?'

'I borrowed Madge's bicycle and went exploring along the coast.'

'Very nice, too. How far did you get?'

She told him. She had nearly reached the seaside town to which he was taking Gemma that night, but she did not add that she had stood on the cliffs and looked down on it, searching for the Grand Hotel and wishing with all her heart that he was taking her to the ball there. Such thoughts were particularly annoying when she had decided to keep a safe distance between them in future, and she hoped that she was going to show greater strength of mind than that. All the effort in the world, however, had not sufficed to blot out the picture of the two of them waltzing together down there in the hotel ballroom and driving back through the night together. She had pedalled away so furiously afterwards that she had given herself a stitch and was forced to dismount and rest for ten minutes. Altogether, a perfectly idiotic exhibition which she tried to forget, but seeing him there, in front of her, waiting to take Gemma and looking disgustingly attractive, did not make it easy.

Mrs Pendine came in before the conversation went further, closely followed by Gemma, who swept Rex a curtsy.

'Do you like me? Will I do?' she asked.

Ann never forgot the picture that Gemma made that night in the tea-rose pink tulle dress which left her white neck and shoulders bare and billowed away from her tiny waist in soft clouds to the floor. A single satin tea-rose broke the line at the waist, and from it flowed two broad satin ribbons. The diamond and sapphire necklace glittered against her white throat, and two small diamond clips held her black hair back from her face to fall softly free at the nape of her neck. A shy little smile hovered at her lips but her deep blue eyes shone with excitement. In all her life, thought Ann, she would never see a lovelier sight, and their silence was a tribute to beauty. Ann looked quickly at Rex, and saw on his face admiration, and something more, as he went to Gemma.

'A very beautiful signora,' he said, taking her hand. 'I shall be the most envied man at the dance tonight.'

Mrs Pendine looked at them with a little smile. Ann read triumphant assurance in that steady gaze, and felt the strength of the will that lived behind Mrs Pendine's calm, chiselled features. She would get her way, thought Ann. She would always get her way. Stifling the little chill at her heart, she congratulated Gemma with genuine affection, for the girl was as unaffected as she was lovely, and she had brought a radiance into the room that none of them would forget.

'I promised to show Gubbie my ball dress. I'll join you at the car in five minutes, Rex,' said Gemma, slipping into the black velvet coat which he held for her.

'Oh darling, must you?' asked Mrs Pendine. 'You'll catch your dress on the bushes along that path.'

'No, I shan't. I'll lift up my skirt. I promised him.'

'I didn't think he approved of worldly pleasures,' said Rex.

'He approves of me,' said Gemma, dimpling, and had gone in a rustle of silk before they could say more.

'And who is Gubbie?' asked Ann.

'Great-uncle Barney. Haven't you met him?' said Rex.

'Yes. I met him yesterday morning for the first time. I thought he was rather a dear.'

'Eccentric, but harmless,' said Mrs Pendine. 'Look after Gemma and enjoy yourselves, Rex, dear. She does you credit, I think.'

'You've certainly hatched a beauty here at Rosevean, Madrina. Away from this hermitage, she'd have the men round her like bees round a honey pot.'

'A very good reason for sheltering her until the right man takes charge of her.'

Rex picked up his silk scarf and coat from the chair and said goodbye to Ann over his shoulder as he followed Mrs Pendine out of the room. Ann collected her book and went to her room before her employer returned, for she was in no mood for reading Trollope aloud. In the silence of her room, she sat on the couch thinking of the look on Gemma's face; the look of a young woman in love. Ann was sure of it. She sat there for a long time, hoping that she would be generous enough to rejoice and wish them happiness with all sincerity when the time came.

Gemma, hurrying along the path to the stable flat with lifted skirts, ran up the steps to the door with her heart beating quickly. It opened as soon as she knocked, and John Hilary closed it behind them.

'Is Gubbie in there?' she whispered, nodding towards a door on the right of the little hall.

'Yes.'

She slid out of her coat and stood before him, her eyes lifted to his in shy triumph.

'I wanted you to see me.'

He looked at her in silence for a few moments, then said with a despairing note in his voice,

'You're so lovely, Gemma. But it only makes you seem unattainable. You're more in my world when you wear slacks and a shirt.'

'I'm the same underneath. What does all this matter? I just wanted to show you how I looked.'

'Why?' he asked harshly, but Gemma put a finger on his lips and whispered, 'Walk a little way back with me and I'll tell you. I must spend a second with Gubbie.'

John walked back with her as far as the drive, where she stopped him.

'Don't come any further, John, or somebody will see us.'

'And you'll be told off for talking to the gardener.'

'I'm sorry I arranged this,' said Gemma, her voice trembling. 'I really only dressed up for you. All the time I was dressing, I was thinking of you and hoping you'd like me.'

'Like you! Gemma, darling.'

In the deep shadow of a laurel, he took her in his arms, and held her tightly to him as he kissed her. When he released her, he said gently,

'Don't you see, Gemma? Can't you understand how I feel when we have to skulk around as though we're doing something to be ashamed of? When I have to see you go off to a dance with another man, and feel that all I'm entitled to is just a glimpse before you go?'

'I'm sorry. I didn't think. Grandma arranged this dance, you know, as a sort of treat after we'd had a row.'

'What about? Running round with undesirables?'

'I can't stop, John. Rex is waiting for me. Will you meet me down in the cove tomorrow morning? It's easiest for me in the mornings when everybody's busy.'

'All right. I'll be there at ten. There's some wood to be stacked on the hill there. That'll serve as an excuse. But we'll have to settle something, Gemma. I'm not going skulking around indefinitely.'

'I know. But it's so lovely just to be together. Can't we enjoy that for a little longer in secret? I dread the outside world breaking in.'

He tilted her chin and kissed her again, gently this time.

'You're so young, but I'll take care of you if you'll let me, darling. I love you, and I'm not scared of your family, with all their money. It's a free world. At least, outside this place, it is.'

'Give me time to think out a way of making it come right. We've only just discovered each other, John. Let's enjoy our secret world for a little longer.'

'And watch you going out with other men, and having to treat you as a stranger when anybody's about?'

'You don't have to worry about Rex. He's more like an uncle. I've known him all my life and he's a dear. He might help us, if I can convince him that we're truly in love. But don't rush things, John. When things are complicated, you have to take them slowly.'

'Truly in love. How sweet you are, Gemma! All right, darling. I'll be patient. But uncle or not, I bet you'll have him and a lot of others at your feet tonight.'

'I shall be thinking of you all the time. I shan't wear this dress again until you're my partner.'

'Promise?'

'Promise.'

'What a child you are!'

'Don't say that. I'm always hearing it. Tonight is the night of my emancipation, though. The family jewels prove it. I've left childhood behind.'

'Then still stay simple and natural and sweet, as you are, even if you look as seductive as Eve tonight.'

Beneath the velvet coat, his hands moved over her bare shoulders and held her close again for a kiss before she pulled herself away with a despairing little laugh.

'Now I don't want to go at all, but Rex will be livid if I keep him waiting any longer. Good-night, darling John. I love you, and nothing else matters if you love me, too.'

'Do you doubt it?'

'No. Can it only have started the day before yesterday, though? It feels as though it must always have been.'

'That's only because everything that happened before then has suddenly become dim and unimportant.'

'You feel that too?'

'Yes.'

'As though life only really started then. It's wonderful, isn't it?'

'Wonderful,' he agreed, kissing her again, and then she did manage to tear herself away, and went running down the drive, her skirts held high, while he watched her from the laurel bush.

CHAPTER IX

'REX.' Gemma hovered in the doorway of his study uncertainly.

'M'm?'

'Here's another letter for you. It went up with Grandma's post by mistake.'

'Oh, thanks, pet.'

He was sitting at his desk, surrounded with papers, correcting a page of typescript, and he glanced at the envelope she handed him and tossed it aside without opening it.

'I couldn't bear not to open a letter,' observed Gemma.

'It's from the Institute about a paper I've promised them, I expect. It can wait.'

She hesitated, and he looked up at her.

'What's on your mind?'

'You're busy. I don't want to interrupt. I thought you wouldn't have started yet.'

Rex leaned back in his chair and held out his hand.

'Come on. Shoot.'

She sat on a corner of the desk and found it difficult to start. This new experience which had come into her life seemed so miraculous that she could not yet bring herself to talk of it in any but the vaguest terms, even to Rex, but she needed his help.

'Oh, it's nothing particular. I just wanted to thank you again for last night. It was a lovely evening.'

'So it was. You made a great impression. Shouldn't be surprised if some of those young men who partnered you turned up here in search of you. That fair chap looked as keen as a greyhound after a hare. Are you trying to tell me that you made a secret assignation?'

Gemma's cheeks dimpled and she seized the opportunity to lead the conversation in the direction she wanted.

'Would you disapprove?'

'Of course not. A very proper occupation for a pretty young girl. You ought to get around more. You're too cut off here.'

'You mean, I'll never get married if I stay hidden here?'

'Oh, I wasn't thinking of marriage. A bit early for that, pet. But I do think you ought to meet more people, learn a bit about the world. Fall in love half a dozen times, if you like.'

'That sounds a very risky programme.'

'Oh, there's no risk in calf love, and it all helps to educate you.'

'How do you know it would be calf love? It might be a grand passion,' she declared dramatically.

Rex chuckled as he took out his cigarette case.

'You're about ten years too young for that, pet. No. You'll fall for a handsome young man with beautiful blue eyes and think he's marvellous for a time, until he begins to bore you.'

'How do you know? Is that how it took you when you were young?'

'So long ago that it's a job to remember, but I do have some dim recollection of a procession of insipid young things, more ornamental than intelligent. At eighteen, my child, take my word for it, you don't know a thing about the opposite sex.'

'You wouldn't approve, then, if I got engaged now?'

'I certainly would not. Far too young to know your own mind. Getting impatient, are you?'

'I just wondered what you'd think. Grandma would favour me getting married young, she said.'

'Did she? That was her own fate. You don't have to be married off to the man of your parents' choice now, Gemma. You take your time and make sure you know what you're doing before you take that step. There's a great big world to be explored outside Rosevean, you know. This limited life won't last for ever, and when you emerge, I'll take you around and show you the ropes, if you need any guidance.'

He had picked up the page of typescript again and was running his eye over it. Gemma stood up and said lightly, but with a desperate little quiver in her voice,

'No good relying on your support if I want to marry that fair young man who danced the last waltz with me, then?'

'To have fun with, yes. To marry, decidedly no. You're far too young to embark on anything like that. You're getting ahead of yourself a bit with that young man, aren't you?' he asked, giving her a playful smack.

'Wanton Gemma, that's me.'

'Well, run off and tempt some other male, my dear. I can see that wearing that delightful dress and the family jewels last night has put ideas into your head. La Traviata herself.'

He was teasing her, and she knew, with a sinking heart, that

69

he would not help her. If he knew about John, he would even perhaps try to stop it because he thought her too young to be the judge of her own happiness. It was the first time he had failed her, and it marked a turning point in their relationship. To him, she was a child. But she had grown up. As she went to the door, he said,

'Tell Ann I want her, Gemma, will you?'

He thought about Gemma for a few moments after she had left him, then dismissed it all as growing pains. The dance and the attentions of several young men last night had stirred up these feelings. He was making the last alteration to the script when Ann came in.

'Sorry, but I've had second thoughts about this page and have made an awful mess of it. Think you can read the amendments?'

Ann looked at it and said,

'Yes. I'm getting used to your writing now. Any post?'

'A couple of letters. Oh, and I'd better open this and see what it says.'

After he had dealt with his correspondence, he said casually,

'I saw a concert advertised in the hotel last night. Next Saturday at the Pavilion Hall there. Beethoven seventh and the Empero Concerto. Will you come with me?'

Her hesitation was fleeting.

'Thank you. I'd like to.'

'Good. That's brave of you.'

'And Gemma?'

'Three's an awkward number, don't you think?'

'That is for you to say.'

'Well, I do say it. Gemma prefers lighter weight music.'

'And has had her treat,' said Ann, a gleam of mischief in her eyes which did not escape him.

'That's better. You've been as formal as a toast master with me lately, in spite of my efforts to be sociable.'

'I shall look forward to the concert.'

'You know, you do make me work hard. I tunnel away like a beaver to get those defences of yours down, and having managed it, I sit back for a breather and find they're up again when I approach to reap the fruits of my hard labour.'

'And what fruits are you expecting?'

'Why, the exploration of a personality that interests me.'

'But perhaps I don't want to be peeled and quartered and cored like an apple.'

'And eaten?' he asked with a wicked grin.

'And have a bite taken out of me as a sample.'

70

'Ah, now we're getting somewhere. You think I'm an apple-sampler, taking a bite and throwing the rest over my shoulder. Is that it?'

'This conversation is getting out of hand. I must go back to my work.'

He put out a detaining arm.

'No, you don't. I'm getting tired of these coy retreats. Let's have the cards on the table. Has anybody been warning you off or is this your own idea?'

'A little bit of both, perhaps. One thing I will say, though. Mrs Pendine does not approve of our association on any but a business footing.'

'Oh, humbug! It doesn't do to take any notice of Madrina's old-fashioned foibles.'

'But she is my employer.'

'She won't sack you because she wants to keep me here for the summer, and she knows I won't stay unless I can work. I need you for that. She hasn't an earthly chance of getting anyone else, and in any case, I shall opt for you. Has that disposed of that?'

'Yes,' said Ann, but he saw the doubt on her face.

'Good heavens, girl, here we are, all shut up together in this place for the summer, with few visitors. If we can't be friendly in our leisure hours, it's a pretty dim prospect. Leave Madrina to me. She's a good soul, but one has to take a firm stand with her on some issues.'

'She's not an easy person to be firm with. The opportunity, somehow, doesn't seem to arise.'

'I can cope. Now we're just left with those unfounded suspicions of yours.'

'They must wait until another time,' said Ann and fled.

As she hurried back to her office, she reflected that he was like a slippery eel to handle. At breakfast, she had half feared to hear the announcement of his engagement to Gemma, but both parties had been singularly uncommunicative. When Ann had asked if they had enjoyed the dance, Gemma had given a fervent but brief affirmative and Rex hadn't commented at all, being immersed in the paper. If this was a couple on the brink of an engagement, the atmosphere was surprisingly cool. Madge had winked at Ann, whose spirits rose nevertheless at all lack of evidence to bear out Madge's contention.

In the sanctuary of her room, she had to admit that the prospect of the concert was a delightful one. What a weakling she was, she thought, half humorously. Whatever he might say, her

71

defences were about as strong as paper where he was concerned. It was no comfort, either, to feel pretty sure that he was well aware of the fact.

. . .

'It didn't just start on Saturday,' said John, smoothing the hair from Gemma's face. 'It started the first day I got back here. Remember? We met you and Miss Forrester. I think I knew then. I was quite certain after you'd spent a couple of afternoons helping us.'

Gemma, lying on the slope of woodland above the cove, looked up at him with soft eyes. It was a grey morning and the wind was chilly, but they were not aware of it.

'I think I knew that first afternoon I helped. You were a bit stiff with me until I tripped over the tree root with that pile of brushwood in my arms. When you lifted me up, I knew. You looked so concerned, as though I was terribly fragile,' said Gemma, smiling at the recollection.

'And now I know you're as tough as wire, but you still look as fragile as fine glass, and I find you completely and utterly adorable. Will you marry me, Gemma?'

'Yes, John, I will. I can't think of a life without you now. But we'll have to go carefully. It's not going to be easy, you know.'

'You're telling me!'

'I tried to sound Rex out this morning, but he thinks I'm far too young to know my own mind about getting married, so I didn't tell him. I'd hoped he would help us.'

'Well, it's not a crime to want to get married. If only that grandmother of yours wasn't such a terrible snob and so concerned with the family name and fortune.'

'She's good-hearted underneath, you know. I'll think of some way of getting round her.'

'Well, I'm all for coming out with it, and be blowed.'

'No, John, we've got to be tactful. If Grandma gets her back up, she's hopeless. She'd separate us somehow. I'm not of age yet. She'd send me away to a finishing school in Switzerland or stop it somehow.'

'Well, what are we to do? Run off?'

'Oh, I couldn't do that. It would break her heart. I'm all she has. No, it'll have to be gradual. I do wish Rex had been more encouraging. He's so good with her. He can make her see reason. It's just that he thinks I'm still a child.'

'Or wants to keep you for himself.'

Gemma's peal of laughter brought a reluctant smile to his face.

'Oh, John, how silly! Fancy being jealous of Rex. He's old enough to be my father. Or nearly. He was quite relieved last night when so many young men freed him from the duty of dancing with me. He doesn't like dancing and he was able to spend most of the evening in the bar talking to the man who organizes these annual balls. Rex knows him. He was a climber once, and so was Rex, and they had a grand old natter about the peaks they'd climbed.'

'I can't help thinking that any man who sees you must fall in love with you. I feel it's a miracle that you love me, but as you do, I can't wait to stake my claim. I want the world to know.'

'So do I. It's terribly hard to hide something so big, but wait a little, John. After all, we can meet easily enough and not have to worry about other people. I'll sound out Gubbie. He would approve, I know, but I'm afraid he hasn't any influence. Anyway, let's enjoy our happiness in secret just for a few weeks.'

'Whether we make it known or not, we're engaged, aren't we?'

'Yes, John.'

'I shall buy you a ring at the first opportunity.'

'And I'll wear it next to my heart until we announce it,' said Gemma solemnly, then smiled as she added, 'Where is my heart?'

'Here,' said John firmly.

'Well, that might be a little awkward. I'll wear it on my long silver chain and it won't be far off, anyway.'

'If only your name wasn't Pendine," murmured John as his lips moved over her cheek, and then her arm tightened round him and drew him close, and they forgot the hostile world.

Gemma met Rex as she returned to the house for lunch. He was doing something to his car, but straightened up and closed the bonnet when he saw her.

'Hullo, mia Gemma. You look very blooming, for all your late night frivolity. A date with the fair young man, I presume?'

'Correct.'

He put his arm round her shoulders as they walked up the drive together.

'And what have you been up to this morning, really?'

'Went down to the cove. Saw Jim Dakers.'

'And how was he? Paying more attention to you than to his lobster pots?'

Gemma smiled and did not think it necessary to tell him that she had only seen Jim chugging out to sea in his boat from the shelter of the woods.

'He's not very forthcoming,' she said demurely.

'Too bad. So it's sweet eighteen and never been kissed, is it?"

'You've said it.'

'Then accept a modest salutation from one who has always been your most devoted admirer,' said Rex. Stooping and bestowing a light-hearted kiss on her forehead.

Gemma laughed, but felt a small chill inside her. It was the first time she had ever misled Rex. Trying to console herself with the thought that she had not actually lied to him, it still troubled her honesty that she should have given him a fake impression. Life, she thought, as well as being most wonderful, was also very complicated.

To Ann, standing by the dining-room window and witnessing that kiss, it was not at that moment at all complicated. The maestro was merely sampling another apple, she thought drily, and turned away to find Mrs Pendine behind her.

'How happy those children look!' she said. 'While it is in my mind, Miss Forrester, I wonder if you could put a little more time into the library cataloguing. We're not getting on very fast, are we?'

'No, I'm afraid not. Mr Vernon is keeping me pretty busy with his book just now.'

'And other things, perhaps, too. You must not allow yourself to be diverted too much, my dear.'

'My working hours are strictly observed, Mrs Pendine.'

'I'm sure they are, but Rex is a diverting rascal. I expect he wastes more of your time than he should in talking. I'm not blaming you, my dear, but perhaps a little firmer stand about the time taken up with matters not strictly business might give you more time to give to the library. I hesitate to ask you to do overtime, but I do want the library catalogue completed this summer. At this rate, it won't be finished this year.'

'What won't be finished this year?' asked Rex, coming into the room with Gemma.

'The re-arrangement and cataloguing of the library. Miss Forrester isn't making such good progress as I'd expected.'

'That's a big job for one, Madrina. I'll give Ann a hand with it.'

'I'm afraid that won't reassure Mrs Pendine,' said Ann lightly. 'She thinks you waste my time.'

'Unwittingly, of course, dear boy. But Miss Forrester has

quite a lot to do here, you know, and when you keep her talking over tea and coffee, as you sometimes do for a considerable time, it means that she can give very little time to the library.'

'Then I shall help her with the library,' said Rex blandly, but the gaze which he turned on Mrs Pendine was steady.

'I wouldn't dream of it, Rex,' said Mrs Pendine. 'You're working too hard on your own account as it is. This is a convalescent period for you, remember.'

'I'm practically fit, and a peaceful few hours in the library now and again will be most soothing. You've got a magnificent library there, Madrina. It will be a pleasure to help sort it out. We mustn't work Ann too hard, or she might leave us, and then it would be London for me, you know. I had a letter from my old secretary last week asking me to let her know when I would need her. Poor girl's got stuck with a job she hates in the firm now.'

'I bet you're a jolly nice person to work for, Rex,' said Gemma. 'Isn't he, Ann?'

'Very. I can well understand his secretary not letting him go.'

'I'm too old to blush. Don't worry, Madrina,' he added, patting Mrs Pendine's shoulder. 'We'll sort that library out in no time.'

And Mrs Pendine, with the ground neatly cut from beneath her feet, was too well controlled to show any feeling at all as she said,

'That's very kind of you, dear boy. What's happened to lunch?'

'Excuse me. I must clean up. I've been tinkering with the car,' said Rex, and his eyes met Ann's for a moment as he passed her, and she fancied she saw him wink.

Machiavelli, she thought, unable completely to stifle the smile hovering at her lips. If she was to be the battlefield over which Mrs Pendine and Rex fought, her prospects were far from comfortable. Not that any aspect of Rosevean had been comfortable from the start. It was a jungle she walked in, and even kind tigers were dangerous.

CHAPTER X

AFTER the concert, they walked along the sea front. The night was calm, with a sky pricked with stars and a crescent moon like a silver sickle among them. The tide was high, but the wash of the waves was gentle. Ann, pleasantly conscious of the firm hold of Rex's arm in hers, hummed the last movement of the Emperor concerto. She had thoroughly enjoyed the evening from the moment they drove out of the gateway of Rosevean. They had dined at a nearby hotel before the concert, and Rex had been on his best behaviour, neither teasing nor challenging. The music had been well performed and Rex's knowledgeable appreciation of it had added to her own enjoyment. She refused coffee afterwards, but welcomed the walk before they drove back to Rosevean.

'You sound happy,' observed Rex.

'I am. Away from Rosevean, the atmosphere seems so much clearer, somehow.'

'Don't let it affect you too much. Just hold your own course steady.'

It was rather like asking her to keep a steady course over Niagara, she thought.

'Don't you find it oppressive, Rex? The sense of being watched and manipulated, and the feudal atmosphere of Rosevean itself. It's so beautiful, and so mournful, somehow.'

'I know. Out of its time. In the old days, I suppose it was bustling with servants, full of the family and their friends. The Pendines were a big family, and they entertained a lot. Parties were met at Truro with a procession of carriages, I believe. That was at the turn of the century. When Madrina talks about it, you realize just how much change has been packed into one life's span.'

'No wonder she find it a little difficult to adjust herself to the modern age. She married young, I take it, Rex.'

'Nineteen. He was much older. They had a town house as well as Rosevean, but they gave the London place up at the beginning of the last war. It was a terrible blow to the old man

76

when their only son was killed, with Gemma's mother. He never really got over it and died soon afterwards.'

'What about the other Pendines? You say they were a big family, but Mrs Pendine always speaks as though Gemma is the last of the Pendines.'

'She is. They've had a tragic history, one way and another. Two world wars took a big toll. There are some distant relatives-in-law, so to speak, who turn up hopefully every summer to remind Madrina of their existence, but they're batting on a bad wicket. Pendine money goes to Pendine blood, and that means Gemma.'

'What about Mrs Pendine's own family?'

'There's only her brother, and Madge, who was her sister's only child. She'll look after them, of course, but in a pretty modest way, I guess. She rather despises her own family, the Rockfords, you know. She helped her sister, who had a hard struggle after her husband died, but was never really fond of her. Thought she was a weak fool. And as for Barnabas, he's written off as a crank.'

'Not a very happy family history. When did you come on the scene, Rex?'

'Spent part of my summer holidays here every year from about the age of six. Madrina was very fond of my father and he of her. They had a violent row over her marriage, but a few years later, when my father married, they ran across each other again and the two families struck up some sort of friendship. Anyway, Madrina was my godmother, and has taken her duties very seriously. I'm sorry for her.'

'She seems a hard person to be sorry for.'

'I know. But she would have been different, perhaps, if she'd not been forced into a loveless marriage for money. That, at least, was my father's contention, but then he was doubtless prejudiced. I only know that her life has been far from happy.'

'And having sacrificed herself to duty, she now puts it on a pedestal and thinks nothing else counts.'

'She has to, to make it all seem worth while.'

'It's frightening, how one wrong step can have such enormous consequences.'

'We pay for our sins all right, if that's what you mean. This kind of thing is right outside your experience, I imagine. Your background was a happy, peaceful one, I'd say.'

'Yes, it was. I'm a little out of my depth at Rosevean. I've been glad to escape from it this evening.'

'You've been really relaxed, haven't you? Not once have you looked at me as though horns sprout from my head.'

'It's the music,' she said lightly.

'I shall know in future how to get those defences down, without pushing. With music.'

'You're very good at getting defences down, with or without music.'

'I don't think they're necessary between you and me. Will you keep them down from now on, Ann?'

She looked up at him and felt the pressure of his arm tighten.

'They were never really very firm, were they?' she said a little ruefully.

'No. Just time-wasting.'

'You win,' said Ann helplessly. 'Just peel me gently, will you?'

He chuckled as they turned round.

"That depends on you,' he said.

*   *   *

During the weeks that followed, it seemed to Ann that a halcyon lull came over Rosevean, although she remained conscious that her capitulation to Rex and her enjoyment of their friendship was spiced with danger. Mrs Pendine passed no further comments on her association with Rex, Madge's blunt strictures were diverted to some distant relatives who turned up at Whitsun to pay their respects, and Gemma was at her happiest, doing all she could to please her grandmother. When June came in, it seemed to cast a benign warmth even over the cold stone walls of Rosevean, and Ann was beginning to think that some of her earlier fears were the result of an over-active imagination, a sensitivity still raw from the loss of her parents. She knew afterwards that it was the light cast by being in love with Rex which induced this mood of optimism and misled her.

As she walked through the woods one Saturday afternoon in June, however, the mood of confidence still held and she was looking forward to Rex's return from London that afternoon. He had been away only three days, but she had missed him sorely. When a grey squirrel suddenly darted across the path ahead, she moved silently after it and watched it sitting on the ground beneath a tree, a nut held between its paws, but a slight movement on her part sent it flying up the trunk of the oak tree, from whence it leapt to a neighbouring ash tree and then away out of sight. Picking her way back to the path, a flash of yellow among the trees off on her right caught her eye. It was Gemma and John Hilary, locked in a close embrace. She heard John murmur something, and hastily returned to her footpath, thinking herself unseen. Gemma and John. The peace that had reigned over the past weeks was suddenly split right open. So that was why Gemma was so elusive, disappearing for hours. Ann, dismayed by the knowledge that such a love affair was doomed, drew a little comfort for herself in the discovery that Gemma's heart was not involved with Rex. But it was a disastrous choice for Gemma to make, for Mrs Pendine would never permit it and Gemma was still under her control.

She had gone only a short way when a rustle of feet brought Gemma beside her.

"Ann. John said he thought it was you. You saw us?'

'Yes, Gemma. It was quite accidental. I was following a squirrel.'

'Oh, I know. You're not a spy. Thank goodness it wasn't Madge. I was afraid it might be, though Madge would have made more noise, I expect. Please, please, Ann, you mustn't say anything about it just yet. Not to anybody.'

'Is it serious, Gemma?'

'We're going to be married one day, and John wants to announce our engagement now, but I must work Grandma round to it gradually.'

Looking at her intent little face, Ann had not the heart to say that never in her lifetime would Mrs Pendine consent to the marriage of her grand-daughter to the gardener's son.

'You're quite sure this isn't a flash in the pan, dear?'

'Quite, quite sure. We love each other now and for ever. I would have liked to have told you about it, Ann, you're so kind and understanding, but Rex said I mustn't involve you in any troubles with Grandma. It's awfully lonely when you haven't anyone to confide in, though.'

'Not Rex?'

'I tried to tell him, but he made it so clear that he thought me a child that I realized he wouldn't help, and might even stop it if he could. He said I wasn't old enough to know my own mind and that I ought to have lots of love affairs before settling for marriage.'

'Did he, indeed?'

'Oh, nothing serious, of course. Just to educate me,' said Gemma, her eyes twinkling.

'Enjoyable diversions. I get it.'

'You see, he wouldn't realize that this is something deep,' said Gemma with a simplicity which touched Ann's heart and made her say gently,

'Other people's hands can be very rough on something precious.'

'That's it, exactly. I'm afraid of letting it be known, although John doesn't like this secrecy. I've thought and thought about telling Rex, but he's an ally of Grandma's in a way, and I think he'd feel it his duty to tell her, don't you?'

'I think he might. But it will have to be known some time, dear.'

'I know. But I'll find some way of softening Grandma up. Try to get her to know John as a person first. She's so rigid, that's the trouble. You won't think it your duty to give me away, will you, Ann? I know it's awkward for you, and I didn't ever mean to involve you, but the wrong way of breaking it to Grandma would be disastrous.'

'I'll say nothing for the time being, Gemma, but there's something I do feel it my duty to do. Get to know John better.'

'You'll find that I'm in good hands. He's such a fine person, really. Honest and not a bit afraid of my family, and he hates this position. I have to work hard to persuade him to be patient.'

'You realize the risk you run of being discovered, Gemma? Madge is always around and your grandmother has a remarkable way of finding out what's going on.'

'I know. I'm careful. This morning, it overwhelmed us. Gubbie is our sanctuary.'

'Does he know?'

'He never knows what's going on under his nose, but he likes John and he has a soft spot for me, so we're always welcome about the place, as long as we don't bother him too much, and we don't,' said Gemma, dimpling.

'You're very happy, in spite of the difficulties, aren't you? I've thought for some time that there must be a special reason for it, but I didn't suspect John.'

'Yes, I'm wonderfully happy. I can't think how I endured that empty life before. You won't give a hint, will you, not even to Rex? I hate leaving him out, and I don't like deceiving anybody, but I just want to do it in my own time.'

'All right, dear. I promise. But let me know when you come to any decision, and I'll see if I can help in any way. That is, if my investigation of your John proves satisfactory,' added Ann as she took Gemma's arm.

'Bless you. I knew you would understand.'

They came out of the woods together to see Mrs Pendine stepping out of the carriage. Ann understood now why Gemma so often appeared at the last moment of one's outing and thus gave the impression that they had been out together. The young woman showed a good deal of tactical skill, thought Ann, as Mrs Pendine waited, smiling, at the door.

She could not help feeling worried about the whole affair, though. Gemma had convinced her that she was wholly committed, that this was no light-hearted flirtation, and Ann could see nothing but heartbreak in store for her. For all her ardent, high-spirited nature, she was fond of her grandmother and would in the end have to tell her. She could be trusted not to do anything underhand or desperate to get her way, but Mrs Pendine's ruthless will would crush Gemma's dreams. Ann could not see the old lady compromising on this issue, and she wielded sufficient authority over the girl to defeat her in the end.

This way and that, her thoughts turned about this alarming situation. She would have liked to have confided in Rex, but Gemma's observations about him had been valid, and in spite of her friendship with him, Ann still could not quite dismiss Madge's assertion that Rex was biding his time with Gemma. Diversions for all before the serious business of getting married. There was only one constructive thing she could do, and that was to make sure that John Hilary was worthy of Gemma and could be entrusted with her, for she was very young and inexperienced.

Rex looked tired when he arrived back, and Mrs Pendine swept him off to have tea with her in her room. Madge watched them go with a thoughtful expression.

'Wonder what commissions Rex executed at her solicitors. Did he say anything about it to you, Ann?'

'No. Just said that he had some papers of Mrs Pendine's to leave with Mr Cardew.'

'I shouldn't be surprised if she's making a few changes in her will. That hypocritical Lawson lot certainly went out of their way to curry favour at Whitsun.'

'I don't think Mrs Pendine was taken in. It struck me that she was getting a certain amount of cold amusement out of them.'

'The old lady's no fool,' said Madge, smiling. 'It would be a smart Alec who could take her in. Just as well. With all that money, she's a target for the vultures.'

'Well, I'll take my tea into the library and catch up on some work there.'

'On a Saturday afternoon? You're getting keen, aren't you?'

'I nearly finished the poetry section yesterday. I'd like to finish it off.'

She perched on top of the ladder dipping into a poetry anthology when Rex came in.

'Hullo, my dear. Madge told me I'd find you here. Everything all right?'

Everything all right. Could that ever be said of life at Rosevean, she wondered, but she smiled and reassured him, adding,

'You look fagged out, Rex. Was London too gay for you?'

'Not exactly. Had a lot to do. Commissions for Madrina as well as office hunting for myself.'

'But you're not going yet, are you?' asked Ann, a sudden cold clutch of fear at her heart.

'Not until September, but offices aren't easy to find and I want to have everything organized by the time I leave here. You look a refreshing sight perched up there. Miss me?'

'Very much.'

'Good. Me, too. What are you reading?'

He held out his hand and she gave him the book open at the page she had been reading, saying,

'The Shakespeare sonnet. I've always loved it. I'm afraid I'm the wrong person to sort out a library. I can't help dipping.'

' "Let me not to the marriage of true minds admit impediments." A favourite quotation for idealists,' said Rex, handing the book back to her.

'I don't think it's idealistic. I think it's true. Don't you?'

'Love is a dangerous subject to generalize on. I need more experience,' he said lightly.

'You're hedging, but let it go.'

'We'll go into it more thoroughly another time. Would you like to come out for the day with me tomorrow? Take a picnic lunch and find a quiet spot? I need some fresh air and quietness after London.'

'I'd love to.'

'Good. Now I'm going to have a bath. I feel as stiff as a poker after that drive down. Be seeing you.'

Ann looked down at the book in her hand. She was a little disappointed in his observation about Shakespeare's description of true love, but not altogether surprised. "It is the star to every wandering bark". She thought of herself and Gemma. It was a star that was leading them both into trouble, she felt, and with the dangerous rock of Rosevean looming over them, their wandering barks seemed very frail.

CHAPTER XI

'MISS FORRESTER.'

Ann stopped as John Hilary caught her up in the drive. She had just stowed the picnic basket in the car.

'Good morning, John.'

'Could you spare me five minutes?'

'Of course. Let's take the path through the woods.'

'Gemma told me that you'd promised to keep quiet about us, Miss Forrester, but I wanted you to know that it's no wish of mine to hide it as though we're ashamed of it.'

'I'm sure it's not, John, but it is a difficult situation, and I think you must both go carefully. I gather that this is equally serious for you both.'

'I'm not giving Gemma up for anybody. I can earn a decent living and look after her away from this place. I'm qualified, and Gemma is no spoilt darling. She's a grand girl.'

'She's only eighteen, John. Mrs Pendine could stop it, you know.'

'If I got to, I'll wait until she's twenty-one, but I hope to heaven we don't have to wait that long. I intend to get some land of my own and go in for fruit farming in Canada, you know. There's a decent living to be got out of it and Gemma's as keen as I am on the idea.'

'I'm sure you'll do well, John, but Mrs Pendine's approval won't be easy to win, and Gemma is well aware that she is the centre of the old lady's life.'

'I know. If only Mrs Pendine was a different sort of woman! She's so out of date. She'll think I'm after the Pendine money, of course. I wouldn't touch a penny of it. She's used it to buy people as though they're serfs. Look at my parents.'

'They're happy enough here, aren't they?'

'Is a dog happy in a kennel? It's security and regular meals. But they're both scared of her, and too old to lose their servility now. I guess. It's her arrogance I hate.'

'I know. I've suffered from it, too. But she's old and one must make allowances, or else leave.'

'I shouldn't be here now if it weren't for Gemma, believe me. Now old Mr Rockford, he's quite a different cup of tea. Nice old boy. Hard to believe he's her brother. Money's given her power, and power has corrupted her, I suppose. Anyway, I wanted to thank you for standing by Gemma, and to let you know that I'm not playing with her. She means everything in the world to me, and I'm fighting for her.'

His face was serious and determined, and she knew that he spoke the truth. She laid a hand on his arm, and said gently,

'I think you've a hard task in front of you, but I wish you all the luck in the world. I think you're right for Gemma. She needs a strong arm.'

He smiled and immediately the years dropped from him and he looked a boy as he said,

'A little devil sometimes, isn't she? But as lovable as they come. Hullo, here's Vernon. I sometimes think he's the one marked down by Mrs Pendine for her son-in-law. He needn't think I'm going cap in hand to him or anybody here, for that matter.'

Rex saluted them casually as he came up, saying,

'Good morning, John. All set, Ann?'

John nodded and strode off as Ann said,

'All set. I'm so glad it's warm. We can be really lazy.'

'You two looked as though you were discussing grave matters of state.'

'Just talking about Rosevean. He's a nice young man.'

'I shall have to keep my eye on you, I can see. That's a pretty frock. I like you in white.'

'I'll just fetch my cardigan, Rex, and then I'm at your disposal.'

'Right. I'll be waiting in the car, deciding how to dispose of you.'

The cherry red cardigan trimmed with white looked well over her dress, and her eyes shone back at her as she looked in the mirror. Everybody must know how she felt if she went about looking like this, she decided. As she ran downstairs, she tried to pin a less ecstatic expression on her face.

Although she was still not fully at ease in the car if Rex drove fast, her confidence had returned and she stepped in beside him now without a qualm.

'Gemma wants me to drop her off at Dr Lloyd's. She's going boating with them today, I gather,' said Rex.

Gemma came running down the drive, and Ann was struck again by the graceful movements of the girl. Dressed in a tangerine-coloured shirt over bottle-green slacks, she could yet look as delicate as a fawn. Fond as Gemma was of slacks, she could never look anything but completely feminine. She flashed them a smile and slid into the back seat.

'Thanks for waiting. Got held up at the last minute by Grandma. She doesn't approve of slacks on Sunday, but what else can you wear in a boat?'

'I don't think she really approves of boating on a Sunday. It's a good thing it's the Lloyds and not the Dakers you're going with. The Lloyds add a little note of respectability.'

'Grandma's a bit shocked that they go boating on Sunday morning instead of going to church, but I explained that you can feel just as reverent in a boat as in a church. Anyway, I've promised faithfully to go to church with her next Sunday.'

'Well done,' said Rex, as he eased the car forward and turned through the gates.

Ann wondered just how long Gemma was committed to spending with the Lloyds, and rather suspected that the impression had been given that she was spending the day with them when she was, in fact, only spending the morning with them, and it needed little imagination to guess who was sharing the rest of the day with her. When she left them at the doctor's house, Ann turned round and waved to her as Rex moved off, and for a moment she thought how lonely the girl looked standing outside the doctor's house, looking after them. She was so gay and so plucky, thought Ann. She never visualized defeat in what seemed to Ann to be a hopeless campaign. She hoped with all her heart that things might go well for her.

They drove for about half an hour, when a cliff covered with thrift suggested a pleasant resting place. They carried the picnic basket some way down the slope of the cliff. Below them lay a sandy bay, and on each side of them a rocky headland. The thrift made huge hummocky cushions, and Rex sank down with a contented sigh.

'This is bliss,' he observed. 'I could almost fall for the solitary life and cast off London's grime and noise for ever. Almost, but not quite. Perhaps when I'm sixty.'

Ann adjusted her back more comfortably to her cushion of thrift, and said,

'We should have come here a few weeks ago. The flowers are past their best now. It must have looked a lovely sight.'

'M'm. I'd forgotten this spot. Haven't been here for years. How do you make your hair hang together so smoothly? If I ruffle it, will it go back?'

'It's well-behaved.'

'Spun by a silk-worm,' he observed, laying a hand on it. 'Most inviting after the mop heads that seem the rage in London now. Hair like crows' nests starting to disintegrate.'

'What did they feel like?' asked Ann, teasing him.

'I didn't sample any. The only young woman I met was my former secretary, and she's not so young and certainly not the sort to play games with.'

'She's very constant, anyway.'

'M'm. I've booked her from September onwards. She's a splendid organizer and I'll need her to get started.'

'Don't talk about going away yet, Rex.'

'Why not? It will mean your release from Rosevean, too, won't it?'

'I don't know. I can't look ahead, somehow. Yes, I suppose it will. There won't be much for me to do after you go, and I expect Mrs Pendine will find me redundant.'

'Oh, well, time enough to think about that when my book's finished.'

They lapsed into silence, lulled by the sunshine and the murmur of the sea below. Ann found it difficult to visualize the future. It was as though Rosevean cast an obscuring fog round it. Without Rex, she knew that she would find it intolerable, and yet she wanted to see how Gemma fared, and would not like to desert her if she needed her. The sunshine glittering back from the glassy surface of the sea seemed to have a hypnotic influence, for her thoughts dwindled away and a calm vacuum took over. . . .

When she awoke, Rex was unpacking the picnic basket. After lunch they climbed down to the bay and had a swim. When they returned to their base on the cliffs, Ann had to spend some time rubbing her hair dry. Rex watched her with a thoughtful air.

'Here. Let me,' he said after a few minutes, taking the towel from her.

When he had finished, he framed her face with his hands and kissed her gently before handing back the towel.

'Nice Ann. The more I peel, the more I like. I'm going to enjoy the rest of this summer, aren't you?'

'Yes,' she said simply and hoped that her face did not betray as much as she feared.

'Not wary any more?'

She shook her head. She had gone far beyond that. He smiled and took her hand.

'Don't worry at things. Time is our friend.' He kissed her

hand, then said, 'Now show me how you restore that hair of yours to its usual smooth perfection.'

The sunny hours they spent on the cliff together that day dispelled all Ann's doubts about Rex. She decided that Madge's insinuations sprang from her own money-ridden outlook on life. She was obsessed with her aunt's wealth and thought that everybody else was after it, too. Nothing in Rex's behaviour had ever indicated this, and Ann was sure now that his affection for Gemma owed nothing to the fact that she was Mrs Pendine's heiress, and was entirely platonic. That she herself was deeply in love with him, she now admitted, and the warmth of his attitude to her that day held a tenderness which she had never seen in him before and which made her heart sing with happiness and dismiss the cowardly pictures of frail barks threatened by rocks. Love, she thought, was a wonderful source of courage and optimism. Everything would come right for her and Gemma. Time was their friend.

.   .   .

Mrs Pendine was walking slowly towards the stable flat with a few eggs for her brother. Madge had gone out and forgotten them, and the fine evening had tempted her to make the short walk herself, although she had to rely heavily on her stick, and paused once or twice on the way. She considered it her duty to see Barnabas now and then, although he was a very unsatisfactory person to visit, making it all too plain that he was not glad to see visitors.

She sat down for a short rest on a wooden seat in front of the laurel hedge. The hedge needed trimming, she thought. It was nearly seven feet high and jutting too far out into the path. She must tell Hilary in the morning. Then she heard Gemma's voice floating over the hedge.

'Let's stay here for half an hour, John. I'm not expected back yet.'

'Suits me. I'm not the one who's afraid of being spotted.'

'Darling, don't let's start on that now. Gubbie's safely tucked up in his garden and nobody else is likely to come this way. Love me?'

'Madly. I hate the hours we're not together.'

'I know, darling. So do I. When you're my husband, I hope you'll never want to spend evenings with your cronies. I hope you'll always want to spend every spare minute with me.'

'Your husband. That sounds good. Say it again.'

'My dear husband. Sounds too stodgy for you, John, some-how,' said Gemma, giggling.

'Doesn't to me. I love you so much, Gemma.'

'Show me,' whispered Gemma.

Mrs Pendine sat there, under the laurel hedge, as though frozen, her face deathly pale, her hand clenched on her stick so that her knuckles showed white, until the endearments and rustlings ended in a scuffle and Gemma laughed.

'I'll race you back through the woods to your cottage. Then we must say good-bye.'

'Wait a sec. . . . Gemma, come back.'

But Gemma's footsteps continued to retreat, and then his followed. It was a long time before Mrs Pendine moved. When she did, she walked straight back to the house, left the eggs in the kitchen, and went to her room. Madge, summoned to her room by her bell just before supper, found her in bed.

'Hullo, Aunt Alice. Not feeling too good?'

'A little tired, dear. Just bring me a milk drink. I shan't want anything to eat. Have you taken the eggs to my brother?'

'Yes. Just got back, as a matter of fact. I think you'd better have a couple of your tablets. You do look poorly.'

'It's nothing. I went out for a short walk and the sun was a little warm. I shall be glad of a quiet evening.' She leaned forward so that Madge could arrange the pillows behind her back, and picked up a book from her bedside table. 'Thank you, dear. That will be all.'

When Madge had gone, Mrs Pendine put her book down and gave herself up to the nightmare situation that she had discovered. The one thing she had decided was that she was going to handle this alone; that nobody else was going to be told anything about it. Now that the first shock was over, she must think out the best method of scotching this disgraceful affair without alienating Gemma's affection. Angry as she was at Gemma's deception and amazed that this affair could have been going on under her nose for so long without her discovering it, for their words and behaviour had revealed the extent of their familiarity, she knew how dangerous it could be to try to crush Gemma. That way, she would make an enemy of her and perhaps drive her to heaven knows what desperate folly, for her power over Gemma was not absolute. The girl was as spirited as her mother had been, and needed clever handling. Deliberately, coolly, she set about planning her course of action. Much was at stake. There must be no false move.

•   •   •

88

As Rex and Ann walked up the drive together, Gemma came out of the woods and joined them.

'Hullo, folks. Hasn't it been a grand day?' she observed.

'Marvellous,' agreed Ann.

'Good boating?' asked Rex, putting an arm round her shoulder.

'Super. Where did you go?'

They told her, and Rex put his other arm round Ann as they came to the porch.

'You two girls sound as happy as larks,' said Rex, 'which is as it should be on a summer day.'

In the sombre hall, Ann looked at Gemma's smiling face and then up at Rex's, his dark tan all the more marked beside the delicate magnolia complexion of Gemma, which defied all wind and sun and remained petal smooth and pale.

'A day to remember,' said Ann softly.

Gemma bounded off upstairs, but Rex stood behind Ann and looked over her head at their reflection in the hall-stand mirror.

'A day to remember,' he echoed, and putting his hands on her shoulders, stooped and kissed her cheek.

CHAPTER XII

A FORTNIGHT later, Rex had to go up to London again and Mrs Pendine suggested that Ann and Gemma should go with him.

'I feel Gemma should see something of London, and this is a splendid opportunity for Ann to show her. It will make a nice change for both of them, and I'm sure you won't mind, Rex dear.'

'Not at all. Plenty of room in the car. It will make my trip more agreeable, having the girls there in the evenings. What do you say, Ann?' asked Rex.

'I'd love it. Thank you, Mrs Pendine, for the kind thought. We could do some shopping and perhaps go to the ballet, Gemma.'

Gemma's hesitation was barely perceptible as she said,

'M'm. It would be fun. I can do with some more clothes.'

'I thought you weren't interested in them. I never seem to see you in anything but slacks,' said Rex.

'I need some more undies,' said Gemma airily.

'Well, Ann will show you round during the day and Rex can look after you when he's free,' said Mrs Pendine.

'Mind you look after yourself while we're away, Madrina. You've been overdoing things a bit, I think,' said Rex.

'Just a little tired, dear. The hot weather doesn't suit me. How long will you be staying in London, Rex?'

'I had intended to go up on Friday and come back on Monday. If the girls are coming, though, I think we might extend the trip by a day or two.'

And so it was arranged. Ann, happy to think that she would not be separated from Rex, planned a programme for herself and Gemma which would fill the days, and looked forward to the trip with eager anticipation.

For Gemma, it was not so simple. Apart from her own reluctance to be separated from John, the latter greeted the news with marked displeasure.

It will be less than a week, John, and I couldn't very well refuse.'

'Oh, I expect you'll enjoy yourself, but how long are we going on like this, Gemma? Are you serious, or just playing about with me?'

'John, how can you talk like this?' Gemma's voice quivered and she sat up and looked straight ahead with blurred eyes. It was a chilly day, and they were sitting in a hollow of the cliffs with a grey sea before them which almost matched the grey sky above.

'Sorry, darling. I think we're both a bit edgy today. But don't you see, Gemma? We've got to make a stand some time. We can't go on like this indefinitely.'

'You're so impatient, John. We've only known each other for a few months after all.'

'Have you doubts, then?'

'Don't look so fierce. Of course I haven't. I'm only afraid of being parted from you. I've got to find some way of getting round Grandma.'

'But you keep saying that, and we're no nearer to it.'

Gemma pulled at a piece of bracken. The situation was getting beyond her. Both of them were frayed by the constant need for vigilance, by the snatched meetings, by the pretences they were driven to when other people were around.

'I don't know what to do,' said Gemma helplessly. 'If I tell

Grandma, I think she might send me away to a finishing school in Switzerland.'

'Good grief! Anyone would think we lived in the dark ages. If you don't think she'll agree, there's no other course but to elope.'

'I couldn't do that, John. It would break her heart.'

'Has she got one? I haven't noticed it. Did you hear her order me to clean out the toolshed this morning? As though I was the char. Nice for me, with you and Rex Vernon standing by. I don't know how I stopped myself walking out there and then.'

'I know. She was in a frigid mood yesterday, but I expect her leg was hurting her. She has a lot of pain from it.'

'Well, it boils down to this, Gemma. You'll have to choose between your grandmother and me if she won't listen to reason, and I want you to tackle her when you get back from London. I'll be beside you, and I'm not afraid of anything that her ladyship can say.'

'Can't we just have this summer together, without anyone knowing? I'll be nineteen then, and it won't sound so young to Grandma.'

John took her face between his hands and searched it.

'You're not playing with me, Gemma, are you? No, darling, of course you're not. Forget I asked. But you mustn't be frightened of standing up for our happiness. I'll be with you.'

'All right. I'll do my best,' said Gemma, burying her face on his chest.

He could feel her trembling against him, and he smoothed her black hair with his hand as he said gently,

'I love you. I'll work for you, Gemma. You won't ever regret it, I swear. I'll make up for all the trouble you'll have with your grandmother. I'm sorry I'm not a more eligible suitor,' he concluded a little dryly.

'You're the best in the world. Perhaps I'm frightened for nothing. Perhaps Grandma will agree without any trouble.'

'Perhaps,' said John, and then turned her face to his and kissed her.

The knowledge of what lay before her when she returned to Rosevean kept Gemma a little subdued in London, but on the whole the expedition was a happy one. Ann took Gemma on a sight-seeing tour of London, and they paid a visit to the ballet on their own and to a theatre with Rex. On their last evening, Rex took them to a concert at the Festival Hall, and afterwards they walked back to their hotel on a fine, mild night, with the lights along the river to delight their eyes and

show them London at her loveliest. Gemma seemed tired and
went to bed as soon as they arrived back, but Ann and Rex
sat on in the lounge together over a drink.

'Has this been a satisfactory trip for you, Rex?'

'Very. I've arranged to take those offices in the city I told
you about, from the beginning of October.'

'And where will you live?'

'Sufficient unto the day. Start off in a hotel, I expect, until
I can find a house or a flat that suits me. There's a chance
that some friends of mine may have a flat to let for the winter.
That would give me a breathing space.'

Again it chilled her to hear him discussing his future, a
future that did not seem to have anything to do with her, and
something of this must have shown in her face, for he smiled
and said,

'We'll have to think that one out later. You shall advise
me.'

'I think you're the sort of person who needs very little
advice, but I'll be glad to help.'

'Gemma's seemed unusually quiet, don't you think?'

'Yes.'

'Anything wrong?'

'Not as far as I know. It's been pretty strenuous. Maybe
she's tired.'

.'Never known Gemma tired before. She always seems to
have boundless energy. You've thrived on the programme
anyway.'

'I've enjoyed it immensely. Being away from Rosevean is a
relief, too. It's not a peaceful house.'

'But you're a peaceful person. You would create peace in a
home. I'm glad you've found your balance again. After that
accident, I mean.'

'Yes. I've come together again. You helped me there.'

'It was only a question of time, I guess.'

She wondered if he knew just how he had helped her, for it
was not so much his kindness, although that had helped, a
the fact that he had invaded her life so deeply that the loss
of her parents now left only a dim ache where before it had
been a void too agonizing to think of. Into that void, Rex Ver
non had stepped, and there was room for little else. She wished
that they had not to return to Rosevean the next day. She felt
safer with him away from that house.

When she went up to her room, she was surprised to see
Gemma sitting on her bed. She was wearing a red silk dressing
gown over her pyjamas, and looked a little lost as she sat there

her elbows propped on her knees, her hair a black cloud round her shoulders. She looked up with a wan smile as Ann came in.

'Hullo. You've been a long time.'

'Gossiping. What is it, pet? You look tired out.'

'I feel it. I simply had to talk to someone. Do you mind?'

'Of course not.'

Ann sat down in the fireside chair as Gemma said,

'I promised John I'd tell Grandma about him when we get back, and I'm scared stiff. Do you think there's any chance of her agreeing to our engagement?'

'I think it's very doubtful, dear. After all, you are only eighteen.'

'I know. And John's the gardener's son. Oh, it's all so silly. What does it matter? John's young and strong and clever, and he's trained to do a good job. Who could object to him, except Grandma? She's old-fashioned.'

Ann stooped and switched on the electric fire. She felt helpless to advise the girl, for the predicament seemed to her fraught with danger whatever Gemma and John decided to do. She made the best suggestion she could.

'You know, I think Rex is the one to tell first. He understands your grandmother, and she will listen to him. And he's very fond of you.'

'I know. But when I sounded him out, he didn't seem at all promising. And John doesn't like him very much.'

'Why not?'

Gemma hesitated, then said.

'Well, it's awfully silly, but I think he's jealous of him. He thinks Rex is Grandma's idea of a perfect match for me. I laugh at him. It's so absurd. Rex is like a favourite uncle. He's a darling, but it's quite different from John and me. I did think of trying to get Gubbie's support, but I don't think he carries any weight with Grandma, do you?'

'The reverse. I think she would automatically take the opposite view of her brother.'

'That only leaves you, Ann. Could you do anything, do you think?'

'I would if I could, Gemma, but I am only an employee of your grandmother. She would soon make that fact known if I attempted to interfere in personal matters which she would think were no concern of mine. I'll be glad to stand up for John, because I think he's a fine young man, but I don't think my opinion would be sought or listened to.'

'I wish John would wait a little longer. I'm so afraid of what will happen. I suppose it's cowardly of me. John's beginning to think I'm not serious.'

'Shall you and John and I have a little conference when we get back before you do anything? And are you sure it wouldn't help to have Rex in?'

Again Gemma hesitated. There were dark circles under her eyes and all her usual resilience had left her. Not serious, indeed, thought Ann.

'You suggest it to John when we have our conference, Ann. If he agrees, then so do I. Rex is very kind and understanding as a rule. He's always been good to me,' said Gemma.

'Yes. Cheer up. Four of us may be able to find a way of influencing your grandmother.'

'Grandma did say she was in favour of marrying young,' said Gemma, pathetically grasping at any straw.

'Did she? Well, we may be making her into too much of a bogey. Perhaps if John goes away and gets a good job and proves that he can look after you, she will agree. But you mustn't expect her to welcome an engagement at this stage, Gemma. You'll have to wait, I'm sure.'

Gemma fingered the little ring which she could feel through the thin silk of her pyjamas.

'John hates waiting, and so do I. I shouldn't like him to go far away. That would be awful.'

'We'll see what we can hatch up between us. Don't worry too much, dear. Get some sleep. If you're both true to each other, the world can't come between you.'

'How nice you are, Ann! I do feel a bit more cheerful now. It's such a pity, all this, because Grandma really wants me to be happy, you know.'

'I know. So do we all.'

'Don't say anything to Rex until we've talked to John, will you?'

'I won't,' said Ann. 'Now to bed, young woman. John will think you've been having a giddy time in London if he sees saucers under your eyes, and blame Rex.'

In bed, sleep eluded Ann for a long time. In spite of her attempts to comfort Gemma, she felt deeply troubled by the thought of Mrs Pendine's reaction to the situation. When at last she fell asleep, she dreamed of Rex and Gemma. They were in trouble and she could not reach them. Running after them, she fell over the brambles which divided them, and Rex came back to pick her up, but when she looked up, it was John Hilary, and Rex and Gemma had gone.

CHAPTER XIII

Mrs Pendine sat behind the study desk and eyed the two men in front of her. Hilary shifted his feet uneasily and stared at the paperweight. His son looked at her steadily, his lips tight, his face as grim as hers. She kept them standing there for a moment or two before she spoke.

'I shall make what I have to say as brief as possible, Hilary. First of all, may I ask if you are aware that your son has been trying to seduce my grand-daughter? I want no denial from you,' she said, holding up her hand as John broke into a protest. 'Did you know, Hilary?'

'No, Mrs Pendine. I can't believe it. I've seen them together sometimes, but all friendly like and nothing to object to. Is this true, John?'

'I am not interested in any pretences your son may make, Hilary. Do you think I would make such an accusation if it weren't true?'

'It isn't true,' broke in John angrily. 'I love your grand-daughter, Mrs Pendine, and I want to marry her. Gemma feels the same, and nothing you can say will make any difference to that.'

'That you would like to marry the Pendine fortune is readily understandable. Gemma is a child. No doubt you have been able to make some impression on her. Such an infatuation will soon fade away. I have other plans for her. Plans which Gemma is not unwilling to fall in with, believe me.'

'And what may they be?'

'I am not discussing them with you, and please do not speak to me in that aggressive manner. You have behaved contemptibly with a girl scarcely out of the schoolroom for your own mercenary ends. Marry my granddaughter, indeed! The idea is laughable. When she is old enough to know her own mind, I have little doubt that she will marry Mr Vernon, to whom she has been devoted for years. What I will not tolerate is to have one of my staff sneaking about making love to a child too young to realize her foolishness. You will leave at once, John Hilary, and don't expect any good references from me.'

'I wanted Gemma to make this known before, Mrs Pendine. It was none of my plan to keep it hidden.'

'Indeed? Then you are a very ingenuous young man if you thought it would be tolerated for one moment. You are dismissed, but before you go, there is one thing I have to say. Unless you give me your word that you will never communicate with Gemma again, I shall dismiss your parents at once. Your conduct doesn't suggest to me that your word would be reliable, but if you broke it, and I should know, your parents would be turned out of here immediately.'

'After all these years' service, Mrs Pendine?' said Hilary, half stupefied.

'I'm sorry, Hilary. I believe you when you say you knew nothing of this, but such a scandalous state of affairs must be stopped. You will have to pay the price if your son will not give his word.'

'So you use my parents to blackmail me into leaving Gemma alone, do you?'

'John,' interjected his father, plainly at a loss to know how to deal with the situation.

'I don't choose to discuss the matter any further with you, John. If you refuse to give your word, I shall not hesitate to seek the protection of the court for my grand-daughter. She is not of age, and I must protect her until she is. You would not be allowed to marry.'

'She would hate you for that.'

'She would live to thank me. Naturally, I do not wish to make Gema unhappy or antagonize her. She will soon forget you and be happy again with Mr Vernon if you leave her in peace. I am sure, Hilary, that you see the sense of that.'

'Of course, Mrs Pendine. Be sensible, John. It's not fitting. No good can come of it. Looking above yourself like that. There are plenty of other girls.'

'Exactly,' said Mrs Pendine. 'However, I don't intend to spend time arguing. You know what is involved. Think carefully before turning your parents out of their home and their job, my boy. And robbing them of a comfortable pension for their old age, as I have naturally provided for them in my will. It rests with you, and don't think you can promise, and then get in touch with Gemma on the sly. I shall know. From now on, Gemma will be carefully guarded until Rex Vernon can take care of her. The choice is yours. Let me know by twelve o'clock, and whatever you decide, you will leave

Rosevean for good this afternoon. Whether your parents go with you is up to you. Come back here at twelve both of you, and tell me what you have decided.'

'I'm really sorry about this,' faltered Hilary. 'I wouldn't have had it happen for the world, Mrs Pendine.'

'Come on, Dad,' said John savagely, and almost pushed his father out of the door, slamming it behind them.

Mrs Pendine leaned back and closed her eyes. It had taken more out of her than she had expected. That presumptuous, brazen young man. No sign of guilt. She could have whipped him as he stood there. The intensity of her feelings frightened her. She must calm down. Such turbulence was dangerous. She fancied that she had won that battle, but it had exhausted her.

Madge, creeping away from the window, beneath which she had been crouching most of the time, went round to the terrace and sank down on the garden seat.

'Well, I'll be blowed,' she said softly.

For the past week or two, she had sensed that something was on Mrs Pendine's mind. She had not looked after her all these years without developing a sixth sense where her aunt was concerned. When she had sent for the Hilarys that morning and had told Madge that she had estate matters to discuss with them and was on no account to be disturbed, Madge's instinct told her that something was up. The study window was half screened on one side by a holly bush. It had been a simple matter to open the window a little wider at the top and to be in position before the Hilarys arrived. She had not suspected anything like this, though. The sly little puss. Having fun and games with young John Hilary, and nobody any the wiser until now. She wondered how Mrs Pendine had found out. Her precious little Gemma. If it weren't for her, Madge would inherit the Pendine money, for she was the next of kin, ignoring Uncle Barney, who was not in the running at all. She stood to inherit a bit, anyway. Her aunt had made that clear. But if Gemma cut loose and made a disastrous marriage, Madge stood to inherit the lot. She pulled out a packet of cigarettes from her pocket and lit one. This needed thinking out.

John Hilary faced his parents with a desperate, unhappy face.

'It's like this, my boy,' said his father. 'You know your mother and I put your happiness first, but this girl won't bring you happiness. It doesn't do to marry out of your class. She's used to a soft life. As nice a girl as you'd meet, but she's no more than a child, as Mrs Pendine says.'

'She loves me.'

'Young people fall in love easily, I'm fifty-eight. Your mother's fifty-five. We're too old to start a new life, John. This is our home as well as our job. Our future, too. Are we to lose it all for the sake of a love affair with a young girl who won't be allowed to marry you?'

'They can't stop her once she's of age.'

'That's more than two years ahead. A lot can happen in that time. Meanwhile, you'll ruin her home life.'

'You could get a job somewhere else, Dad. There's no difficulty these days.'

'And a home?' asked his mother, her lips trembling. 'John, dear, you know how much you mean to us, and we wouldn't stand in your way for the world, but you've only known Miss Gemma for a few months. You're young, with all your life in front of you. This affair can never bring you happiness. Miss Gemma will never defy her grandmother. Must we sacrifice everything for a dream which will never come true?'

John looked at them helplessly. It was true. They were too old to face such an upheaval in their lives. Had they been more independent, if they had known more of the world, they would have felt differently, but they had lived most of their adult lives at Rosevean. They were afraid to leave its familiar walls. Mrs Pendine held all the cards. Money. It all boiled down to money, for that meant power. And Gemma? Was she strong enough to fight her family? He remembered how she had trembled against him like a frightened bird at the thought of telling her grandmother. If he plunged his parents into fear and uncertainty, how firm would Gemma be? It was because she had such a lovable nature that she would find it difficult to defy her grandmother, backed up by Vernon. It would tear her to pieces. She was utterly ruthless, the old lady. Hard as granite. She would stop at nothing.

As he turned aside and stared out of the window, accepting defeat, the recollection of Gemma's eager little face went through him like a sword. Perhaps she would soon forget. Perhaps Vernon would see to that. But he would never forget her. He turned back to his parents.

'All right,' he said quietly. 'I'll get out. I'll see you up at the house at twelve, Dad.'

As he went out of the house, his mother started to cry, and Frank Hilary put an arm round her shoulders.

'There, there, my dear. Don't fret. He'll get over it soon

enough. Be finding another young woman within the year, I guess. Mustn't take these young people's love affairs too seriously, you know. Let's hope he'll find a decent woman like I found, who'll be a good wife to him. Miss Gemma's not of our world.'

When John informed Mrs Pendine curtly that he would leave that afternoon, she said,

'I'm glad that you have some sense of responsibility to your parents. There is one more thing I have to say to both of you. Nothing that has passed between us here this morning must go any further. Is that clearly understood, Hilary?'

'Of course, Mrs Pendine.'

'Nobody else knows about this disgraceful affair but me. I shall say nothing of it to anybody, not even to Gemma, who will not know that I found out about it. This seems to me the wisest course. You will see that nothing leaks out from you or your wife, Hilary?'

'Yes, Mrs Pendine.'

'Gemma will be told that John has found a job elsewhere, and left of his own free will.'

'I must leave a note for her, Mrs Pendine,' said John quietly.

'I want her to forget this affair, not brood over it. It will be better to leave without any goodbyes.'

'How can you be so brutal? What will Gemma think?'

'That you were enjoying a flirtation, as you doubtless were. It is kinder to make the break clean and complete than to have harrowing, sentimental goodbyes. In a few weeks, Gemma will have put it behind her. There must be no communication between you of any sort again. I have warned you what will happen if you don't keep to my terms.'

'It's no good doing things by halves, John,' said his father.

'Very well. You've used your power to ride over our feelings like a steamroller, Mrs Pendine. I hope you'll get what you deserve,' said John bitterly.

'I leave it to you, Hilary, to see that your son's whereabouts remain unknown here. I don't wish to hear any more of him at Rosevean. He no longer exists as far as we are concerned. Now, please go.'

As the two men walked down the drive together, Frank Hilary looked up at the grim face of the boy who seemed to have become a stranger, and said,

'I'm sorry, John. Don't take it too hard. It may all be for the best. You weren't happy here, anyway.'

'Happy! Living like a serf. Where's your pride, Dad? How can you stick it?'

'Pride? Never had much time for it, John. I do my work well, and I suppose I take pride in that. But I've never wanted to set myself up as being more than I am. Nothing to be ashamed of in that. I've nothing to grumble at. You young people are so dissatisfied. It's all this education, maybe. We thought we were doing the best for you when we sent you to college, but it's taken you from us, John, I'm afraid. We're no longer good enough for you.'

'That's not true, Dad. It's because you're too good for this job here that I get so mad.'

'You can't change your nature, my boy. It suits me here. You're ambitious, like your uncle. What will you do?'

'Go to Canada. Join Uncle Bill, until I can start on my own. I'm not staying here in this snob-ridden country.'

'Fruit-farming, you mean?'

'Yes.'

'I thought you would. It's what you've wanted ever since Bill came over. Well, it's a good country for a young man, I guess. Don't think too badly of us because we're not young any more, John. You'll do well, I'm sure. It'll be a blow to us to lose you.'

'In these days of aeroplanes, I shan't disappear for ever. May even persuade you to make the trip some time. The world's changed since you were a boy, Dad.'

'Where will you go for the time being?'

'Oh, find some digs in London while I make arrangements. You don't have to worry about me.'

No, thought Frank Hilary. The young had their own ideas, knew what they wanted. It was no use thinking you could guide their lives. This affair with Gemma Pendine was unfortunate, but it had probably only hastened what was inevitable, for John had set his heart on fruit-farming in Canada a long time ago. He sighed. You had children, you made sacrifices to give them what you hadn't had, and then you lost them. That was life. . . .

CHAPTER XIV

IT was beginning to rain as Rex drove through the gates of Rosevean, and said,

'We'll defy all regulations and drive up to the house. Don't see the sense of getting wet or asking Hilary to lug the suit-cases up the drive.'

'Where else but at Rosevean would such conditions be imposed?' said Ann, chilled by the fact that they had arrived back.

'Eccentricities can't be pandered to beyond a certain point,' declared Rex, bringing the car round to the front of the house. Madge opened the door to them, grinning.

'Couldn't believe my ears. A car on the sacred precincts! The old lady's in a bad mood already. This will cap it, Rex.'

'Too bad. All right, Ann. I'll bring your case. You carry the small one, Gemma.'

Mrs Pendine came down the stairs while they were sorting themselves out in the hall. She leaned heavily on the handrail of the staircase and was very pale. Her skin looked almost transparent, thought Ann, but her voice was as firm and resonant as ever.

'Hullo, Gemma dear. Did you have a good journey, Rex?'

'Not too bad. You look very elegant, Madrina. Don't say you're going to a party.'

'The Lloyds and the vicar and his family are coming to dinner tonight, dear. I've made it eight o'clock, to give you time for a bath and a short rest. And did you enjoy yourselves?'

'Yes, thank you, Grandma,' said Gemma.

'I shall look forward to hearing all about it later. Now be off with you and get ready for dinner.'

'Rushing us a bit, Madrina, aren't you?' observed Rex blandly. 'Driving all day, and a dinner party to greet us.'

'I know, dear boy. If you feel tired, we'll excuse you. Gemma can't be tired, though, so change into something pretty, dear. Would you mind having dinner in your own room this evening, Miss Forrester? Family friends, you understand.'

Ann flushed at the arrogant dismissal, but said quietly,

'Of course not, Mrs Pendine. I shall be glad of a quiet evening.'

'There's tea for you in the drawing-room, Rex. I hope you'll feel ready to join us after a rest, but please yourself, dear boy.'

'You look in need of the rest, my dear,' said Rex, picking up his case.

'I'm all right. Glad to see you and Gemma back. Leave the cases, dear. Mrs Vincent or Hilary will see to them. It was naughty of you to bring the car up here, Rex.'

'I know, Madrina. Too wet to walk, though. I'll get you inside a car one day, if it's the last thing I do.'

'Never. Despoilers of our country. Polluters of the air. But I'll overlook it this time. I wouldn't do as much for anybody else.'

Rex bowed ironically.

'I will remove the obnoxious machine directly when it stops raining. In the circumstances, Madrina, it would be kind to your visitors to rig up some sort of canopy over the drive. It's quite a long walk in the rain.'

'People managed quite well before cars,' replied Mrs Pendine dryly. 'There are such things as umbrellas and mackintoshes, and our legs were made to walk with.'

Rex grinned and put an arm round her shoulders.

'So they were. But you can't stop the march of time, my dear. Now, where's that tea?'

He went into the drawing-room with Mrs Pendine, and Ann picked up her suitcase. Gemma delved into her hold-all, withdrew a small parcel and seized an old mackintosh from the hall cupboard. As she slipped out through the front door, she flashed a smile at Ann. Her destination was not hard to guess, and rain would make no difference to Gemma. As Ann turned to go upstairs, she caught Madge looking after Gemma with a curious expression on her face. It did not seem an auspicious return to Rosevean.

Mrs Hilary opened the door to Gemma.

'Good evening, Mrs Hilary. Is John in? I've brought the book he asked me to buy for him while I was in London.'

'John's left, Miss Gemma,' said Mrs Hilary through tight lips. She considered that this girl had caused them all quite enough trouble. She blamed her. Running after the boy like that. Took after that Italian mother of hers, no doubt. John trying to seduce her? The other way about, more likely.

102

'Left?' Gemma smiled a little uncertainly. 'I don't understand.'

'Had the chance of a better job and took it. Mrs Pendine released him. He went last Friday afternoon.'

'But I only saw him on Thursday and he didn't say anything about it.'

'He had a cable from his uncle in Canada.'

'But where is he now?'

'Couldn't say, Miss Gemma. He said he'd let us know when he arrived in Canada.'

'I can't believe it. He must have given you some address.'

'Why? He'll be sailing any day. If you want my opinion, Miss Gemma,' said Mrs Hilary with the cruelty of a jealous mother, 'I think he was glad to get away from here. Got sort of complicated. Now, if you'll excuse me, I must see to our supper.'

'Didn't he leave any message? He must have done,' cried Gemma, bewildered by Mrs Hilary's attitude.

'Why should he? I've just been explaining to Miss Gemma that John's left for Canada,' said Mrs Hilary to her husband who had loomed up behind her, paper in hand.

'That's right. He'd always set his heart on it. Only wanted Uncle Bill to say the word. He'd saved up enough for his fare, and I guess it's a good thing for the boy. Did you have an enjoyable trip to London, Miss Gemma?'

'Yes, thanks. There wasn't any . . . trouble before he went?'

'Trouble? Why should there be? All a bit rushed, of course. But John was always a boy to make up his mind quickly. Not let a good chance slip. It was his ambition to go to Canada.'

'Yes, I know. I don't understand why it was all so sudden, though.'

'Well, young men are a bit impetuous, you know, Miss Gemma. Now, you mustn't stand about there in the rain any longer. You'll get soaked.'

Gemma looked at them helplessly, and then as the door started to close on her, she turned away and walked blindly out of the front gates and down the lane. It couldn't be true. And why was Mrs Hilary so hostile? Had John decided that she would never tell her grandmother and was not serious about marrying him? She remembered how he had searched her face when he had asked her. But he couldn't have gone without leaving any message. Bewildered and stunned, she arrived back at Rosevean soaked through, and managed to reach her bedroom unseen. She looked at the sodden parcel still in her hand. It was a book on fruit-farming which she had seen in the window of a bookshop and had bought as a small surprise for him. The thin wrapping had disintegrated in the rain and the cover was ruined. Rain had even trickled down the flyleaf on which she had written, "To my darling John, with love from Gemma", and smudged the words. She threw the book on to the window still and sank down on the floor by her bed, burying her face in the eiderdown to smother her sobs. She paid no attention to the dinner gong, and when Mrs Vincent knocked at her door, she told her that she had a blinding headache and would not be down that evening.

'I expect she's over-tired,' said Mrs Pendine when she received the message. 'I think you gave her too good a time in London, Rex.'

'No. We were very moderate. She seemed quiet and not her usual self all the time we were there, though,' said Rex, looking at his glass of burgundy as though seeking interest there, for he was finding the dinner party appallingly dull and was tired after the day's driving.

'Growing pains. I think she needs a change of air.'

'Why not ask her if she'd like to come with us to North Wales tomorrow week?' said Doctor Lloyd. 'She'd be a welcome companion for Grace, wouldn't she, my dear?'

'Yes, it would be lovely,' said Grace, who was a pleasant looking girl, a year older than Gemma, who had known the Pendines for as long as she could remember, but who had never overcome her fear of Mrs Pendine, before whom she was seldom other than tongue-tied.

'That's a very kind thought,' said Mrs Pendine. 'I'll certainly ask Gemma, and I'm sure she'll be delighted with the idea. How long will you be away?'

'Two weeks. All I can manage, I'm afraid. No country lovelier for walking than Snowdonia, tell her.'

Mrs Pendine thanked him again with a gracious smile, thinking that it would be just the thing to take Gemma's mind off that wretched boy. The vicar then embarked on a discussion of how to raise funds for heating the church hall, and the dinner pursued its formal course.

When Gemma knocked at Ann's door before breakfast the next morning and came in with an ashen face, Ann's smile turned to a look of dismay.

'My dear girl, what *is* the matter?'

'John's gone.'

'Gone? What do you mean? Here, sit on the sofa and tell me.'

Gemma told her in a voice flat with exhaustion.

'It's impossible,' said Ann.

'I've been thinking about it all night. There are only two explanations that make any sort of sense. Either he thought it was all hopeless and I'd never tell Grandma, so he left. I know he only stayed because of me. He hated it here. Or else his uncle cabled him, as Mrs Hilary said, and he'll be writing to me later. After all, he couldn't very well leave a message. There was nobody he could trust,' ended Gemma pathetically.

Or else he had become more deeply involved than he intended, and had decided to get out while the going was good, thought Ann, and then remembered the determination on his face when he had talked of marrying Gemma. She could not believe that he had been playing with the girl's affections.

'You don't think somebody found out and told your grandmother?'

'Mrs Hilary said there had been no trouble. John wanted to seize the opportunity and Grandma released him. I shall ask her about it this morning.'

'Will you tell her how you feel about John?'

'No. There's no point until I hear from him. I must hear from him. I'm sure he would never leave me without a word. He loves me.'

'I know he does, dear. You'll hear from him, I'm sure. After all, he knew that you wouldn't be back until last night. There may be a letter for you this morning.'

'Yes. It's wrong of me to doubt him. He knows what he's doing, I'm sure. Only . . .' Gemma hesitated.

'Go on, dear.'

'Mrs Hilary seemed so hostile last night. As though she blamed me for John going. She sort of hinted that he wanted to get away from me.'

'It's all very puzzling, but there may be a letter explaining everything, or your grandmother may be able to throw some light on it.'

'Yes. There's the postman coming up the drive. I'll go. Don't say anything about it to anybody yet, will you, Ann?'

'No, dear. Try and run some colour into your cheeks. You look ghastly.'

But Gemma had gone. When she returned, it was obvious from her face that there had been no letter for her.

'There will be,' she said with a gallant attempt at confidence. 'I'm sure there will be.'

When Mrs Pendine came into Ann's office with some letters that morning, Gemma was waiting for her.

'Can you spare a few minutes before you start with Ann, Grandma?' she asked.

Ann looked at the two of them as they faced each other, the tall handsome old lady, impeccably dressed in her favourite lavender colour with white lace at her throat, the classic regularity of her features sharpened by age and as unrevealing as those of a statue, and her grand-daughter, pale and tense, but outwardly composed. Ann admired the girl's courage as she stood there, opposing her immaturity to all the years of experience behind her grandmother's authority.

'If it's important, dear. You know I like to keep to my routine.'

'It will only take five minutes.'

'Very well. We'll go into the drawing-room.'

Gemma was not the only one to feel a new hostility chilling the air around her, thought Ann, as the door closed behind them. She would have liked to hear the conversation. Gemma would doubtless tell her about it, and Ann hoped desperately that something reassuring would be forthcoming, but the whole situation seemed to her ominous, to say the least.

'Now Gemma, dear, what is it? You look very poorly. Does your head still ache?' asked Mrs Pendine.

'It's not too good.'

'The long car journey has upset you. Far better travel by train.'

'Grandma, Mrs Hilary told me that John has left.'

'Yes, dear.'

'Why?'

'Because he wanted to. He wasn't satisfied with his job here, and I must say I was not impressed with his work. Wasted far too much time, in my opinion. However, I would have kept him on for his father's sake, but he had the chance of a better job. I didn't try to stop him.'

'But it was very sudden, wasn't it?'

'Young people are like that these days. Restless. They think the world owes them an easy living. He'd grown too big for his boots, that lad. He'll learn, however. Now what was it you wanted to talk to me about, dear?'

Gemma looked at her helplessly.

'That was all. I wanted to see John to give him a book I brought back for him. On fruit-farming.'

'That was kind of you, my dear, but not very wise. It might have put ideas into his head. You're far too trusting, Gemma. You mustn't encourage people to step out of their place. It's not kind to them, although you might mean it kindly. By the

106

way, dear, Doctor Lloyd has invited you to join them on their holiday in North Wales at the end of next week. They are going for two weeks. I said I thought you'd be delighted at the idea. A change of air will do you the world of good, especially after London, which really doesn't seem to have suited you at all, and I'm not surprised. Foul air. Not fit for human beings to breathe. I've no doubt that it is all the petrol fumes which have given you this upset.'

'I'm all right, and I don't want to go away with the Lloyds, Grandma.'

'I'd like you to think about it, dear. The country in the Snowdon district is lovely and I'm sure it would brace you. Now I must give Miss Forrester the letters. Quite a lot of correspondence has accumulated while you've all been away. Why don't you ask Rex to go walking with you this afternoon? It will do you both good, and you have been neglecting Rex a little, you know, darling.'

'Have I?'

'Yes. I think he was a little hurt that you didn't enjoy the visit to London more. You know how devoted he is to you. Try to give him a little more of your time. I know you're fond of him.'

'Yes,' said Gemma, and went across to the window.

Mrs Pendine watched her for a moment, then went out. Rex could catch her on the rebound with very little trouble, she thought. He was just the kind, older friend Gemma would turn to for comfort. She must have a talk with Rex as soon as possible. Good might yet come out of this deplorable episode. Meanwhile, she intended to take a very firm line with Miss Forrester. If anybody knew about John Hilary's goings-on with Gemma, it would be that young woman. She and Gemma were very thick. As she had been appointed to keep an eye on Gemma, it was lax, to say the least of it, if she hadn't known what was going on, and if she had, her duty to her employer should have made her reveal it. Moreover, Miss Forrester was getting much too familiar with Rex. She would have to be curbed. The situation was delicate, but not as black as it might have been. Although on first discovering Gemma's secret, she had been angered by Gemma's deception, she was glad that the child had not burst out with it when she found that young Hilary had gone. Better far to ignore the affair now. It would die a quick death that way. A little careful manipulating of Gemma, Rex and the Forrester girl, and all would be well.

CHAPTER XV

Mrs Pendine took the opportunity of speaking to Rex when they were sitting on the terrace alone together before dinner that evening. The weather had changed, and the evening was fine and warm.

'I'm a little worried about Gemma, Rex. She seems very peaky. I wonder if you could spare a little more time for her just now. You always cheer her up, and I think she's been rather disappointed that your work has kept you so tied up.'

'Bless the girl, I always like to have her around, but she's been rather elusive this summer.'

'Well, she's a sensitive girl. Perhaps she felt she wasn't wanted. She was counting so much on having you here this summer, and Miss Forrester has rather monopolized what little free time you have, dear.'

'It shall be attended to, Madrina,' said Rex, taking out his cigarette case. 'Wouldn't hurt the child for anything.'

'I know you wouldn't. And, of course, she thinks the world of you. Always has.'

For the next few days, Rex was as good as his word, and devoted most of his spare time to Gemma, and it seemed to Ann as though the girl did lose some of her unhappiness under his influence, although she haunted the postman persistently. Ann was kept too busy by Mrs Pendine to be able to spend much time alone with Gemma, and when, on the following Tuesday evening, she was about to go with Rex and Gemma for a drive, Mrs Pendine called her back.

'I wanted to have a little talk with you this evening, Miss Forrester. Would you mind letting Rex and Gemma go off on their own?'

'Of course not, Mrs Pendine. I'll just tell them.'

'There's no need. I have already told them.'

There did not seem much point in asking her if she minded, then, thought Ann, feeling her heart contract at the sight of Mrs Pendine's cold face. She had known something was brewing and she wished she felt less vulnerable. Rex was right. She was not tough. She did need a kind tiger to protect her from the unkind type that inhabited Rosevean. It was not that she lacked spirit, but cruelty sickened her and violence of any kind shocked her sensibilities. She felt both behind Mrs Pendine's icy façade.

They went to the study, where Mrs Pendine took the chair behind the desk. Ann's mind went back to that first interview in this room. It seemed a long time ago.

'I won't keep you very long, Miss Forrester. Just sit down there and listen to what I have to say. Your work here has in most respects been perfectly satisfactory, but I'm afraid that you have misunderstood your position here. You are an employee, and not a member of the family.'

'I have never forgotten that, Mrs Pendine.'

'No? Then your familiar behaviour with Mr Vernon is very hard to explain. Is that the way typists behave with their superiors these days? Am I out of date?'

'But I am not on duty in my spare time, Mrs Pendine. I must have some kind of companionship when I'm not working.'

'There are social clubs in the village which you could join. You have your own room here, to which you can invite any outside friends. If you wish for leave to go up to London at any time to see your friends there, you have only to ask.'

'Part of my work was to be a companion to Gemma.'

'A part you have played singularly badly, if I may say so. During the day, you never seem to know where she is, and in your spare time, you are too busy monopolizing Mr Vernon to want to bother with Gemma. It has reached the stage of becoming an embarrassment to me and to him.'

'Has he said so?'

'He realizes that he has been neglecting Gemma. He has promised to give more time to her. I do not want you pushing yourself in and edging Gemma out. In brief, you are Mr Vernon's typist, and if you cannot remember that, I am afraid I shall have to ask you to leave.'

Ann's cheeks were scarlet, and anger almost pushed her into resigning there and then, but before she could speak, Mrs Pendine's tone changed to a more tolerant note and she went on.

'Now please don't think I am blaming you and nobody else. Rex is partly to blame, I have no doubt. He is an engaging rascal and may well have encouraged you by his casual manner. You see, I am very old-fashioned, Miss Forrester. Happy-go-lucky modern ways are not mine. What would pass as quite normal behaviour in a London office strikes me as objectionable. Rex is no more averse to flirting with a typist than most other young men, I expect, and if he has encouraged you to behave in a manner I have to condemn, I am sorry, and it is not kind of him. I shall speak to him. Perhaps you haven't realized, either, that there is an understanding between him and Gemma. Nothing definite has been said, but I have every hope of Rex and Gemma marrying one day.'

'I have never heard any suggestion of it from them.'

'Probably not. After all, it is not your business, is it? And in any case, Gemma is too young to know her own mind, and Rex realizes that. Now, my dear, I hope I haven't been too hard on you. Put it down to my age if you think I have. But when I employ people, they have to fall in with my ways. So, a little more formality with Mr Vernon, please, and I suggest that you look outside Rosevean for your leisure. Madge can put you in touch with the village community association, and of course the church has all kinds of social activities, some of which I am sure would prove worth while. I'll ask the vicar to get in touch with you.'

'That won't be necessary, thank you, Mrs Pendine. Reading and music more than fill my leisure time, and those I can enjoy in my own room,' said Ann cuttingly, anger now swamping her fear.

'Very well. Now that we've had this little talk, I'm sure we understand each other better. That will be all, my dear.'

Back in her room, Ann stood by the window and tried to calm her outraged feelings. Things could not go on like this. She would ask Rex outright where he stood on this battlefield. Meanwhile, the house seemed intolerable, and she made the return of a book she had borrowed the excuse for walking across to the stable flat and having a talk with Gubbie, who in his eccentric way was always reassuring. She found him studying a horticultural journal, but he seemed pleased to see her, and offered to make her a cup of coffee.

The room was in the usual muddle, littered with books and papers. Ann picked her way across the floor round the raincoat on which a cat was asleep, over a pile of horticultural journals, picking up a tray of tea-things as she went. There was no room for it on his work bench, which held a microscope, dissecting knives, slides, a jam jar of wild flowers, and a drawing of a flower section, so she took it to the adjoining kitchen, where she proceeded to clear it.

'Why must women always start clearing up?' demanded Gubbie. 'One clearance at the end of the day is quite enough. You're as bad as that Hilary woman. She will come in every

Wednesday and clean up. Nearly drives me mad. I go out, of course, and can't find a thing when I get back.'

'Dirt must be removed sometimes, Gubbie.'

'Too much fussing about inessentials. That's women. Find that book interesting?'

'Very. Now I have a longing to go to China and see all those wonderful flowers.'

'A lot of our best garden plants came from there. Here, stop fussing with those cups and carry the coffee pot for me. I'll bring this.'

This was the top of a biscuit tin on which he had set the cups and a jug of hot milk.

'I've emptied the tea-tray now. Wouldn't it be safer to use that?' asked Ann.

'Safer? My hands are steady enough. If you're going to argue about my hospitality, young woman, it's withdrawn. Come on now.'

Ann removed an old sweater and a magnifying glass from the arm chair opposite him, and acccepted her coffee with a smile as she observed,

'You're quite right. We do fuss about unimportant things. But can you find anything here? I always get so cross if I can't find things.'

'Always know where everything is, except after Mrs Hilary's tidied up. You're looking a bit harassed, girl. Relax. House of Mammon getting you down?'

'Yes. I've just been lectured for forgetting my place. It's rankling and I feel as though I'm sitting on thorns. I thought you might restore my sense of proportion.'

'False values are infectious, like measles. Live with them, and they invade your own healthy ones. Little Gemma now. Even she's getting infected. That natural gaiety of hers, quite gone when I saw her yesterday.'

'It's not a happy house, Rosevean.'

'Couldn't be, ruled by such principles as my sister's. Poor soul. She's not happy herself, you know. You'd think when people find life permanently out of tune, they'd examine their philosophy and try to alter it. But there. We can't change our natures much, I guess. The penalties are apt to get heavier with the years, though.'

'They fall on others, too.'

'Circumstances never shape men, my dear. Only reveal them. I forget who said that. Lamennais, I think. But it holds a lot of truth. You, I would say, have a gift for happiness. It won't flourish at Rosevean, though. Polluted air. You'll wilt,

111

like evergreens in industrial towns. Soon recover in clean air, though. If I were you, I'd seek a better habitat.'

'Will you stay here always, Gubbie?'

'Until I've exhausted the flora and fauna. Don't know how long that'll take me. It suits me at present, but then I'm free of Rosevean here. Don't allow it to impinge on my life. You can detach yourself easily enough when you're my age. Not so easy for young folk, though. Where's young John Hilary got to? Haven't seen him for some time. Nice lad.'

'He's left. Didn't Gemma tell you?'

'No. Only saw her for a few minutes. Where's he gone?'

'Canada, we believe, but nobody seems to know much about it.'

'He was too good for this job. Plenty of scope for a young man with his qualifications. Wonder he didn't come and say good-bye, though. Probably did, when I was out. I'm not indoors much.'

'Did he strike you as a reliable character? The sort of person who means what he says?'

'Certainly. Have you any doubts, then?'

'Not really. I just wanted your confirmation. There's something odd about the way he left without a word to Gemma or me. We were all so friendly.'

'Expect he had a row with my sister, and went off in a temper. Understandable.' He was running his finger along one of the bookshelves which lined the wall. 'Here. This will interest you, I think. Expedition to the Himalayas. I went with that party, plant hunting, and was responsible for the photography.'

Ann took the book and thanked him. She had half wondered whether to seek his advice that evening, but she knew that, good and understanding as he was, he was not the man to confide in. His interest was not primarily in human beings but in nature, and he had no wish to be involved in family troubles. She envied him his self-sufficiency.

It was dark when she arrived back at Rosevean, and she met Rex and Gemma arm in arm in the drive. At the front door, Gemma remembered a message she had to give Mrs Hilary, and left them.

'I want to have a talk with you, Rex. Alone, where we can't be interrupted,' said Ann.

'Suits me. In my work-room, then.'

In the turret suite, they were safe from all eyes and ears. Rex perched himself on the desk, took out his cigarettes, and said,

'Shoot.'

'I've been told off for being too familiar with you, Rex.'

'Dear me. Are you?'

'I'm serious. The interview I had with Mrs Pendine this evening wasn't at all pleasant, I assure you. She accused me of running after you and keeping you from Gemma.'

'Well, so you have,' he said, grinning, and Ann wished she had a missile handy. Her nerves were raw still, and his attitude infuriated her.

'I am to find companions from the village community association and remember that, at Rosevean, I am an employee only. I was hard put to it not to resign on the spot.'

'Why didn't you?' asked Rex with a twinkle.

'I don't know,' she said fiercely.

'You do, you know. Come on. I want an answer to my question. Why didn't you?'

She looked at him as he sat there, assured, mocking, waiting for her to pander to his vanity, knowing why she stayed, but leaving her still in doubt about his feelings for her. Was he amusing himself? Was it a friendship that he would soon forget when he left Rosevean? Or was it more? She could not say which was true.

'Before I answer that, I would like to know what you think about Mrs Pendine's accusation that I am coming between you and Gemma, or trying to.'

'She's worried about the kid, and wants me to cheer her up. Seems to think Gemma's pipped because I've been neglecting her, but I doubt that. Anyway, something's pipped the child and I'll get it out of her, I expect. She's always confided in me, and I'm expecting to have a confession any day now. I have been neglecting her. Your charms, my dear.'

'Mrs Pendine indicated that there was an understanding between you and Gemma.'

'Understanding? Well, of course there is. I've known the kid ever since she was born. Feel a sort of guardian to her, and I know Madrina has appointed me Gemma's trustee until she's twenty-five, if anything happens to the old lady before then.'

'I gathered that it was a special understanding. That you and Gemma would be married one day.'

'Did Madrina say that?'

'She did not use those exact words, but she implied it.'

'You misunderstood her, my dear.'

'I don't think so. Madge told me once that it was Mrs Pendine's wish that you should marry Gemma.'

113

He frowned and his voice had a sardonic edge to it as he said,

'How you ladies do gossip! Comes of being shut up here together, I suppose. I suggest that you stop listening to it. I'm very fond of Gemma and intend to look after her until she's old enough to look after herself. With all that money, she'll need looking after. She has a lot of confidence in me and can help her. Are you jealous of that?'

'How can you ask that? I'm as fond of Gemma as you. What am I supposed to do, though, when Mrs Pendine forbid me to come between you? Treat you as a stranger?'

'Ignore Madrina's lecture and carry on as we are. I'll have a word with her about it. She gets these moods. You're making a fuss about nothing, my dear, if it's Gemma who is in your hair. As for Madrina, I warned you about her right at the start. Unless you can take her dictatorship calmly and still go your way, you're sunk. She won't dismiss you. I'll see to that.'

'But it's so humiliating.'

'She's an old lady. Think of it as humouring her.'

'Whose side are you on, Rex? You peel me with ruthless thoroughness but reveal so little of yourself.'

'Among a bevy of women, it's my only defence.'

'I hate you when you won't be serious about serious things.'

'Come here, Ann.' He held out his hand, but she ignored it and stood her ground, flushing as his eyes raked her. 'Come on,' he repeated gently.

'I won't.'

'How childish! Why not?'

'Because I'm not letting you use your animal magnetism to avoid the issues I've raised.'

He chuckled as he came across to her and took her in his arms.

'You're losing your sense of humour in this place, my dear, and I don't wonder at it. There are no issues. Just a lot of silly talk by women who have nothing better to do than plot and weave fantastic tales. Now tell me why you didn't resign.'

'I've learned one thing about you this evening, anyway. You are disgustingly pleased with the attraction you think you wield over women. What vanity!'

'Alas, the weakness of all men. But, then, you do rather encourage us, don't you?'

'I find you quite insufferable this evening, Rex. Good-night, Mr Vernon. That is what I must call you now.'

'I must summon up my animal magnetism,' he said, and twisted her round as she turned away. In his arms, she looked

114

up at his dark face and tried to remain impassive, but it was no use, and as he stooped to kiss her, she yielded to him. When he released her, he said softly,

'Perhaps that was the nicest way of answering my question. Good-night, dear. And don't worry.'

As she left him, she reflected that all her questions had remained unanswered. She had found it a very unsatisfactory talk, despite the warmth of that good-night. He was as slippery as an eel when he chose.

It was a warm night, and she decided to walk a little way in the garden before going to bed. Her mind was too troubled for sleep. As she came to the seat on the river bank, she heard a sound of sobbing, and found Gemma crouched at one end, crying her heart out on the back of the seat.

"Gemma, darling,' said Ann, putting an arm round the girl's heaving shoulders, 'don't break your heart over him.'

'I can't help it. Every morning, I've thought there was sure to be a letter, and not a word has come from him.' She gulped and went on in a quivering voice. 'When I went to ask Mrs Hilary if they'd heard anything, she was horrible to me. Said I ought to have more pride, running after someone who doesn't want me. Ann, can it be true? That he really did go to get away from me?'

'Gemma, dear, I am sure he loved you. But it looks as though he thought it was hopeless, and went off to save the trouble he felt was inevitable. That's the only explanation I've been able to arrive at.'

'But without a word. Not even a goodbye. It's my fault, I suppose. I should have been braver. He knew I was afraid of Grandma. But we're engaged. I've got his ring here.'

As she took it out of the top of her blouse, she began to cry again, softly and hopelessly, and Ann could find no words to comfort her. John Hilary. Rex. They were all the same. Took what they wanted and left tears behind. When Gemma was calmer, she took her arm and walked her slowly back to the house.

'We shall hear something some time, dear. Meanwhile, try not to lose heart. I'll have a go at Hilary myself tomorrow. See if I can get an address from him on some pretext or other.'

Madge was in the hall. She had apparently just come in, and looked rosy-cheeked and appallingly robust. Gemma averted her tear-stained face and called out a quick good-night as she ran up the stairs. Madge chatted to Ann for a few minutes about the village darts match she had been attending

115

that evening, and then Ann, too, followed Gemma upstairs and went to her room. As she sank down on the sofa, she found herself wishing that she could fly from Rosevean and take Gemma with her, leaving Rex behind with John Hilary's ghost. Selfish, arrogant males, she thought angrily, but she knew that it would be as difficult for her to fly away from the web of Rex's attraction as for any small fly caught in the gossamer threads of a spider's weaving.

CHAPTER XVI

EVERYBODY had gone to bed and the house was quiet when Madge knocked gently on Gemma's door and slid in. Gemma, who had been lying face down on the bed, still fully clothed, turned her aching eyes to Madge, surprised to see her.

'It's no good, kid. I can't see you made wretched like this. I think it's a damned shame.'

Gemma sat up slowly and pushed her tumbled hair back from her face. Madge sat down on the fireside chair and rubbed her chin reflectively as she went on,

'I know all about you and John Hilary, and I'll be blowed if I can stand by any longer and let them do this to you.'

'I don't understand,' said Gemma.

'I'll explain, but I'll have to make one condition. If Aunt Alice ever knew I'd told you, I'd be kicked out without a penny. Will you give me your sacred promise never to tell anybody what I tell you now about John Hilary?'

'I promise. You know something about John? Where he is?'

'Steady. When I say you must tell nobody, I mean nobody. Not Rex or Ann or a single soul. Give me your word on this.'

She handed Gemma the Bible which her grandmother had given her as soon as she could read, and Gemma, wide-eyed and trembling, took it and promised. Then Madge leaned back in the chair and told her about the interview which she had overheard in the study that morning when John was dismissed. Gemma at first was unable to believe it.

'But she's said nothing to me. Never hinted that she knew about us.'

'Why should she? Better get rid of John and let it die a natural death without any rows.'

'But to make him go without a word, and let me believe that he didn't care a straw for me. How cruel!'

'It was effective, from her point of view.'

'And to make John choose between me and seeing his parents thrown out, homeless. Oh, I can't believe Grandma could be so wicked.'

'She doubtless told herself that it was all for your good,' said Madge dryly.

'Grandma, of all people. To deceive me like that! I always thought she was so upright and honourable. It's . . . horrible.' And Gemma, faced with her first big betrayal, was shocked into silence.

"Well, there it is. The rest is up to you. Not for me to advise, but I know what I'd do. Nobody would rob me of the man who loved me, and that boy's dead nuts on you, kid. I could tell that.'

'I know. I couldn't believe he would leave me without a word. Oh, Madge, what can I do? He's probably in Canada now.'

'No, he's not. He's in digs in London, waiting for the O.K. from his uncle. I prised that much out of Hilary when we played darts tonight. And I've got his address. Saw a parcel waiting to be posted in Hilary's cottage when I went in there this afternoon. Here it is.'

Madge passed Gemma a piece of paper with the address scribbled on it and Gemma gazed at it as though a star had been put in her hands.

'If I went to Grandma and told her that I was going to marry John, what would she do, Madge?'

'Get a court order to prevent it. She'll stick at nothing, Gemma. She told John that. But she couldn't do anything, once you were married. Now, I'm not saying any more. Don't believe in meddling. But I thought you ought to know the true facts.'

'How kind of you, Madge, to tell me, and risk so much! You can be sure I'd never let out who told me, not even under torture. You don't know what you've done for me. It's like coming back from the dead. Only, it's been a terrible shock to know that Grandma could do such a wicked thing.'

'She's old and in some ways a bit unbalanced, kid. Can't let her spoil your life, though. Wish I'd had your chance. I'll give you one tip for your own good. Whatever you do, don't give a hint to a soul. These walls have ears, and I do believe Aunt Alice has a built-in radar set. She seems to know everything. Keep your own counsel, and good luck to you.'

'Thank you, Madge. I'll never forget what you've done. I'll have to think it out now. You're so clever at managing things. Have you any more tips?'

'Well, if I were you, I'd change my mind about going away with the Lloyds, or seem to. That would give you two weeks to work in. I know you'd rather defy everybody and come out into the open, but you'll be sunk if you do, my dear. The opposition is too strong. You'll have to use guile, as your grandmother did. Now that's all from me. So long, kid. Take your chance while you can. I'll just make sure that the coast's clear.'

Madge opened the door cautiously, nodded to Gemma and went out, closing the door softly behind her. Gemma, taking the ring from its hiding place, held it in her hand and then slid it on her third finger while she tried to calm the tumult of her heart and make plans.

The next morning, Ann received a note from John Hilary. As soon as she saw who it was from, she pushed it into her pocket and opened a circular, not wanting to attract any questions at the breakfast table. In her room, she drew out the single sheet of notepaper. There was no address and it merely said,

'Please tell Gemma that I love her and shall never forget her, although our hopes couldn't be fulfilled. Don't mention this message to anybody, or let Gemma talk about it. I trust you to see to this. Nothing can be done. This is goodbye. I wanted Gemma to know, that's all. J.H.'

Ann, running downstairs to find Gemma, was told that she had just gone out.

'Anything important?' asked Madge, who had just fetched Mrs Pendine's breakfast tray down and was about to take it through to the kitchen.

'No. Nothing important. I'd like a stroll before starting work. I may see her in the garden.'

Ann found her on the way to the stable flat, and had to sit on the very same seat on which Mrs Pendine had been concealed in order to get her breath back.

'Here,' she gasped. 'It came this morning.'

Gemma read the note. It was all she needed. She knew now what she was going to do. Her eyes were shining as she carefully tucked the letter away in the pocket of her blouse.

118

'Somehow, I knew a message would come to me this morning. Here's Rex. I'll be off. Thank you, Ann. See you later. I've a date with Gubbie.'

'Why all this rushing about?' asked Rex lazily as he strolled up. 'First you go streaking off like a jet plane, and now Gemma's bolted as though she's stung.'

'Are you waiting for me to start work, Mr Vernon? It's just on half-past nine. I'm so sorry. I thought if I hurried, I'd be back on time, but I see that I shan't.'

Her brown eyes looked at him guilelessly and her face portrayed polite regret.

'Too nice a morning to start work on the dot. How about a stroll along the river first?' asked Rex dryly.

'My hours of work are nine-thirty to five-thirty, Mr Vernon. You must not tempt me from my duty. I shall be in my office, filing, if you will let me know when you want me.'

'Ann, don't be an idiot.'

She gave him a smile as bland as any he had foisted on her.

'Mr Vernon, you do make things difficult for me. You must ask Mrs Pendine to release me for such treats. Good morning, Hilary,' she added, as the man approached with a wheelbarrow laden with tools.

'Good morning, Miss Forrester. A lovely morning it is, too. I wonder, Mr Vernon, if you'd be so kind as to look at the motor mower, you being so good at engines. I'm reluctant to tell Mrs Pendine that it's gone wrong again, her being so prejudiced against motor mowers on account of the noise. It was John who persuaded her to buy it in the first place, against her better judgment, she said. So if you could look at it. . . .'

Ann took the opportunity to skip past Hilary and leave them to it, conscious of a very ominous look from Rex as she did so. Two could play at that game, my boy, she thought, and returned in a triumphant mood to her gloomy office. The day had started off well, she considered.

Gemma found her great-uncle washing up his breakfast things in an absent-minded manner.

'Bless my soul, this is an early call. What do you want, young lady?'

'Give me the tea cloth. I'll dry. I want to ask a favour.'

He looked at her suspiciously.

'It's a bad time to ask, but go on.'

'At least, it's not really a favour. If Grandma dismissed the Hilarys, could you find them another job? You know so many people in the horticultural world.'

'Yes, of course I could. Only this week I was asked if I knew of a couple for a National Trust country house. Why, Gemma? Is more trouble brewing up there?'

'Yes. They're out of favour and I know John was worried about it before he went.'

'He skipped off quickly, didn't he?'

'He had a chance to go to Canada. You know that precious fruit-farming scheme of his. This plate's dirty. You haven't washed the egg off.'

'All right. Don't fuss. Egg's wholesome enough. Now don't go embroiling me in any of the battles up yonder, but you can tell Hilary to come to me if he ever wants a job. Decent enough couple, though the woman gets on my nerves when she comes to clean up here.'

'That's all I wanted to know, Gubbie. Thank you. You're a darling.'

'No, I'm not, and you know it.'

'I expect you're one of those people who need to break into the day gently. Rex is the same. A regular monk at breakfast. I'm always at my best early in the morning.'

'You're certainly looking better today than when I last saw you. No need to fuss over the coffee pot, child. Like to do some field study with me this morning?'

'I'd love to, but I've got a lot to do this morning. I know you really prefer to be on your own, anyway. No need to mention the Hilary business to anybody. It may not come to anything.'

'When did I ever go about blabbing?'

Gemma gave him a hug and left him. Her little face was serious and determined as she went about her business that day. Her grandmother's deception had hardened her sense of purpose as nothing else could. She kept her own counsel but when she met Madge returning from the village, she told her about the note from John.

'What did I say? He's got it badly, kid. All the best. But I know nothing, remember,' said Madge, patting the girl's shoulder.

Gemma ran off towards the village, and Madge went on her way. That letter from John to Ann would come in useful, she thought. If a scapegoat were needed, Ann was handy. She hoped to heaven there would be no hitches. So much was at stake. . . .

'And how long are you going to keep up this silly act?' asked Rex, leaning against the bookshelves and looking up at Ann perched on top of the library steps.

'What act? I am merely doing as my employer requires. If you can persuade her to relax the rules, I shall be glad.'

'She's not here now.'

'But I am not wiling to amuse you behind her back and lay myself open to insulting charges. I believe Gemma is waiting for you on the terrace. Aren't you going swimming?'

'Yes. She's a lot more cheerful today. I have a hunch she'll unburden her soul to me.'

'And you'll be able to comfort her with sage counsel, and feel wonderfully noble.'

"Miaow."

Ann ignored him and went on jotting down titles and authors for the catalogue. He had put her in an impossible position with Mrs Pendine, and until he came out into the open and made a stand for her, she intended to follow her employer's instructions. If he refused to do so, she would know that he was merely using her for amusement to make life at Rosevean more tolerable until he returned to London. She descended the steps with as much dignity as she could muster, for it was a difficult feat to accomplish gracefully, and moved the ladder along a section. Rex stubbed out his cigarette and moved to her swiftly.

'Don't be an idiot, Ann. I'm determined to get to the bottom of this trouble of Gemma's.'

'You think I'm jealous of the attention you give her?'

'No,' he said a little doubtfully, 'but I don't think you welcome it.'

'A distinction without a difference. Listen, Rex. We are both fond of Gemma. She's a lovable girl, and I know the friendship means a lot to both of you. The time you spend with her has nothing to do with my attitude now. Mrs Pendine made insulting accusations which I need you to refute. Until you have done so, and she has come to me and admitted that I have a right to your friendship, I must accept her view of the situation.'

'And that is?'

'That you are amusing yourself by flirting with me to pass the time, that I am far too familiar with you and run after you shamelessly, and that although such conduct may be common between typists and bosses in London, she cannot countenance it at Rosevean. She is too old-fashioned. Perhaps I am, too.'

'You take it all too seriously, my dear. It only calls for a little diplomacy.'

'I prefer more straightforward methods. Excuse me, Mr Vernon,' said Ann, as Mrs Pendine came in.

'Oh, there you are, Rex. Gemma's kicking her heels on the terrace.'

'I have already told Mr Vernon,' said Ann coolly. 'I wish he would remember that I have work to do. Perhaps you could remind him, Mrs Pendine.'

'Yes, it's too bad, Rex, when you hold Miss Forrester up. Work gets behind, and she has to take the blame. You look a bit off colour today, dear boy. Get out in the sun with Gemma. It will do you good.'

'It's not sun I need, Madrina. It's work. I'm getting soft. You will only need to bear with me a few more weeks, though. That's not to say that I don't appreciate the rest and the amusements which Rosevean has provided this summer,' he said with his husky drawl and a stabbing smile for Ann.

He waited while Mrs Pendine preceded him through the door, then turned to Ann and said reproachfully, 'Temper,' before he closed the door. She supposed he was right. The previous evening's interview with Mrs Pendine had left her with a slow-burning anger which she could not put out. It was her pride that was the fuel, she knew, but underneath, there was the pain of doubt about Rex. She had no claims on him. He had never been specific about his feeling for her. There was mutual attraction, an affectionate friendship there. Or perhaps she had misinterpreted that. Perhaps he had exerted himself to gain her confidence in the expectation of getting some pleasing payment afterwards. But she loved him too deeply to make a diversion of it. In her hope that he might love her, too, was she trying to force his hand unreasonably? Whatever the truth was, she could no longer remain in this ambiguous position. He must take a stand. The time for diplomacy was past.

As she climbed the steps again, she felt glad that Gemma had heard from John. Just to know that a man returned your love was great comfort, even if you were parted.

That evening at dinner, she learned that Gemma had decided to go with the Lloyds to North Wales. Mrs Pendine was pleased, and attributed the decision to Rex's influence, for she had asked him to try to persuade Gemma to go.

'A pity you can't go, too, Rex dear.'

'Far too busy just now, Madrina. I shall have to go to London again next week.'

'Won't you hate living in a London flat, Rex? I should,' said Gemma.

'It will be convenient while I'm getting my business organized. I'm only taking it over from my friends for six months, anyway. They want it back again in the spring. By then, I shall know better where I stand.'

'You'll build up a very successful practice, dear boy. No doubt about it,' said Mrs Pendine, peeling an apple with meticulous care.

'We shall miss you, Rex,' observed Madge.

'He'll be coming down quite often, I'm sure,' said Mrs Pendine. 'Gemma will be broken-hearted if you don't.'

'You must come to London sometimes and let me take you on a real spree, Gemma. I feel I didn't do the occasion justice last time. Too much business to attend to,' said Rex.

'Some people get all the fun. What about me, Rex?' asked Madge, cutting herself a hefty slice of cheese.

'I'll take on the lot of you, with pleasure,' said Rex, grinning.

'I'll keep you to that,' replied Madge.

'You shall console me, dear heart, while Gemma is whipped up by the young men of my circle,' said Rex.

'I expect you know a lot of people in London, Rex. It would be nice to introduce Gemma to them. I feel she meets far too few suitable people here,' said Mrs. Pendine.

'Would your friends be suitable, Rex?' asked Madge, smiling.

'I know Rex too well to fear that he wouldn't take every care of his Gemma,' said Mrs Pendine.

They spoke of her as though she were a doll, thought Gemma, watching her grandmother pour the coffee from the silver coffee pot. She still found it hard to believe that her grandmother could have behaved with such underhand cruelty. It had shaken the whole foundation of the world she had lived in hitherto. Sitting there, between the ruins of the old life and the promise of the new, she felt lonely and a little frightened, but quite determined. She wished she could have told Ann, whose eyes were always so kind and understanding, and she wished she hadn't to shut Rex out, but he, she knew, would not be on her side. To him, she was still a child in need of protection. Soon, she prayed, John would be the one to protect her.

'Have you told the Lloyds that you are joining them, Gemma?' asked her grandmother as she passed the coffee cups round.

'I'll go round tomorrow morning.'

'Did you say that the Lawsons were coming for a week in September, Aunt Alice, or was it longer?' asked Madge.

'They suggested a week or two. I shall confirm it as one week. Cousin Edith tells me. . . .' She broke off as Ann, who had been silent for most of the meal, rose to her feet.

'If you will excuse me, Mrs Pendine, I'll take my coffee to my room. I know you prefer to discuss family matters privately.'

Mrs Pendine inclined her head as Ann left the table. So she was being mettlesome, was she? So much the better. She wouldn't last much longer, she felt sure, and with Rex nearing the end of his stay, her departure would not matter. There were more ways than one of dismissing people.

Of all the people round the dining table that evening, it was Mrs Pendine who was the least troubled.

CHAPTER XVII

THERE was only one moment when Gemma's courage failed her, and that was when a suspicious-looking landlady told her to wait in the hall while she saw if Mr Hilary was in, and disappeared up a dark staircase. With her two suitcases beside her, Gemma stood there feeling like an orphan of the storm, and for one terrible moment, she wondered whether John would truly welcome her. She fingered the ring on her finger nervously while she waited for what seemed an eternity. Then she heard voices on the landing above, saw John at the top of the stairs, then never knew how he reached her, but suddenly she was in his arms.

'Gemma, darling!'

Oblivious of the landlady's backward stares as she retired down the passage, they remained locked together for several moments, until John said,

'Come up to my room. The cases can stay here.'

In his room, the strain of the past week and the joy of feeling his love round her like a warm cloak were too much for her, and she dissolved into tears. When she was coherent again, she said simply,

'I found out what happened, John, and I came to you. Was I right?'

'You were right, sweetheart. You don't know what these past weeks have been like. Now stop trembling, and tell me all about it.'

Sitting on his lap in a shabby leather armchair, she told him.

'You don't have to worry about your parents, John,' she concluded. 'I had Gubbie's promise that he would find your father another job and a home if they were dismissed.'

'Bless you, what a resourceful young woman you've proved to be! I never thought you would do it.'

'I don't think I would have if Grandma hadn't behaved so cruelly. It broke something.'

'I'll make it up to you, Gemma, I promise you. Nothing will stop me now that you've shown your faith in me. Now, we must make plans. Marriage licence, that's the first thing. My passage is booked for Thursday week. I'll have to do some arithmetic about a passage for you. Hope to heaven nobody finds out before the Lloyds get back.'

'They won't,' said Gemma calmly. 'Nobody knows. And to help you meet the expenses, I've brought my necklace. It should raise quite a bit. It's valuable. And it is mine. Grandma gave it to me.'

'I'll manage without, if I can, darling. If not, it shall be a loan. I've a thing about Pendine money.'

'But I'm a Pendine,' said Gemma gently.

He smiled down at her and smoothed her black hair from her face. Dark smudges beneath her eyes stood out sharply from her delicate complexion.

'A treasure of a Pendine,' he said. 'But Mrs John Hilary is going to sound a lot better to me.'

They sat there in the shabby room with its drab, grubby curtains and dusty artificial flowers on a bamboo table, seeing nothing but a shining vista before them as they talked of the fruit farm and the home they would make in Canada. As dusk fell and the lamp post outside the house cast a pallid light over the room, John came back to the present, and said,

'I'll fix up a bedroom for you with Mrs Gordon, who's not a bad sort when you know her. She's got one vacant on the floor above. Then I'll take you out to dinner. You feel as thin as a rake. We'll celebrate.'

'I am hungry,' admitted Gemma. 'Don't seem to have eaten much lately, somehow.'

'You've had a ghastly time. I know what it must have cost

you to do this, Gemma. I'll never forget it, and I swear you'll never regret it. I'll work my fingers to the bone for you.'

Gemma touched his cheek softly, and said,

'As long as we're together, nothing else matters.'

． ． ．

With Gemma away, Ann found Rosevean heavy and menacing, and she escaped from it whenever she could, avoiding Rex outside of working hours. His attitude was irritating in the extreme, for he seemed to be playing a waiting game, treating her with a lazy, amused kind of tolerance, as though sure of her surrender in the end. Before he left for a few days in London, he came into her office to say goodbye.

'If you'll type the last chapter while I'm away, Ann, we can get the complete typescript off to the publishers as soon as I'm back. That will be a good job done.'

'Yes. I hope the book will be successful.'

'Oh, these text books have a fairly limited sale, I imagine, but I've enjoyed getting it out of my system, and it should be useful. It's helped to keep my brain from rusting here at Rosevean.'

'Yes. Well, I hope you get everything fixed up satisfactorily in London,' said Ann politely as she took the cover off her typewriter.

'You know, I never guessed that you possessed such steely fighting qualities behind that quiet, gentle exterior. You've given Madrina a bit of a shock too, I'd say.'

'There comes a time for taking a stand,' said Ann coolly, wishing he would remove himself from the corner of her desk.

'It's been quite amusing, watching you take Madrina at her word.'

'I'm glad you find it entertaining.'

'How long are you going to keep it up?' he asked gently.

'As long as I want to keep the job, I shall accept the conditions Mrs Pendine laid down. You are not willing to get those conditions changed, it seems. Nobody here seems willing to challenge Mrs Pendine. I wonder why? Can it be her money?'

His eyes narrowed at that but he spoke calmly enough.

'That is a very objectionable suggestion.'

'Is it? I've had so many objectionable suggestions aimed at me recently that I'm getting callous myself, perhaps. I'm sorry.'

'I've known Mrs Pendine all my life. She's been very good to me always. Particularly when I was a kid. Now that she's old and, I admit it, difficult, I'm prepared to humour her. Moreover, I'm a guest here, and although I didn't particularly want to spend the summer at Rosevean, it has got me fit again and provided a most useful stopgap while I planned a new career. Everything has been done here to make me comfortable. It is not for me to abuse hospitality by telling my godmother to change her ways. I warned you that she was difficult and that, at Rosevean, she was dictator. If you want a job at Rosevean, and I use it as a convalescent home, we have to accept that fact. The alternative is up to us. To get out.'

'I am accepting the fact. I am doing exactly as I'm told.'

'Good grief, you really are maddening, Ann. Madrina's whims can be humoured but need not govern every waking hour. You're making a mountain out of a mole-hill on this question of our friendship. Madrina likes to flick the whip sometimes. It annoys all of us at times, but we humour her and don't let it affect our way of life in the slightest. How else would Madge keep going here? Or Gemma? To keep me at arm's length when we're alone is ridiculous. Now come off that high horse and stop being childish.'

'Goodbye, Rex. I hope you have a good journey.'

'All right. Play it your way. When you've had enough of it, perhaps you'll let me know. Goodbye, my dear.'

As the door closed behind him, she wanted to say, 'Be careful on the roads', for always in her heart now lay a fear of road accidents, although he had helped her reduce it to rational proportions. Now, as she sat down at her typewriter, she said to herself, 'Be careful, Rex darling,' and rested her head between her hands, knowing that, whatever he felt for her, she loved him and nothing could change that.

The weather was sultry and thundery while Rex was away, and Ann took the opportunity to work hard in the library, where at last the end of her task was in sight. She had enjoyed the work, for the Pendine library was a fine one, and it seemed a pity to her that it was so seldom used. Shut in with the books, she felt apart from the troubled relationships that made life at Rosevean so difficult, and which seemed to her during those humid July days to be worsening. Mrs Pendine treated her with cold arrogance, while Ann held her ground with quiet dignity, but antagonism lay between them like a gleaming sword. The sands of her time at Rosevean were running out, she felt, for her faith in Rex's championship was now slight. He had been glad of her companionship during these fallow months, but she was beginning to accept with an aching heart that it meant less to him than his deep affection for Gemma and less than his consideration for his godmother.

No news came from Gemma, and as the last days of her holiday approached, Mrs Pendine commented on the fact at dinner one night.

'I should have thought Gemma might have sent us a card. You haven't heard, Miss Forrester, I suppose?'

'No, Mrs Pendine.'

'How slack these young people are! In my young days, a card was despatched announcing our safe arrival as a matter of course, and it was followed by a letter after a few days.'

'A good thing she's with the Lloyds and you don't have to worry,' said Madge.

'Yes. The mountain air will do the child a world of good. I hope that at least we'll have a card telling us what time to expect her home on Saturday.'

'Do you know what time Rex is getting back tomorrow?' asked Madge.

'About tea-time. I had a note this morning.'

'Well, I must get cracking, if you'll excuse me, Aunt Alice,' said Madge. 'I'm due at the Church Hall in quarter of an hour. Promised to help set the tables up for the whist drive. Suppose you wouldn't care to come along with me and help carry the basket of fruit we're raffling, Ann? I've a load of clobber to take, and it's hardly worth troubling Hilary to get out the trap.'

'Of course I'll give you a hand,' said Ann.

'A pity you're not going to the whist drive,' observed Mrs Pendine.

'I don't play whist,' replied Ann politely.

'You should learn. You might make some suitable friends at the village social meetings.'

'Come on, Ann,' said Madge briskly. 'We haven't much time.'

Walking back through the village afterwards, Ann quickened her steps, for the leaden sky and close atmosphere seemed to threaten a storm. The cottage gardens were gay with sunflowers and hollyhocks, phlox and nasturtiums, all looking as though they were painted there, so still was the air. July was almost at an end and there was little birdsong. The trees on each side of the drive at Rosevean were heavy and dark with leaf, motionless, shutting out the light. The elms behind Rosevean seemed to brood over the house with dark menace, and there was no sign of life anywhere. In spite of the bad light, the windows were all dark, and Ann felt reluctant to go in. She skirted the turret, with its acrid smell from the ivy which covered the round base and swarmed upwards with ever encroaching fingers, and walked to the seat by the river. She saw lightning flicker in the distant sky, but heard no thunder. The water looked glassy and still, although the slow passage of a dead leaf indicated a flow. The dark bulk of the turret was reflected in the water. It seemed to Ann on that close, lowering evening, that Rosevean was a dead house, that life could not survive there, as plants could not survive lack of light. She visualized it slowly engulfed by the ivy and the trees, deserted and decaying, the only life that of the birds who nested round its walls and the dragonflies and midges who hovered over the sluggish, silent river. Perhaps the village children might venture here to play, but the gaunt house would probably frighten all but the toughest spirits. In spite of the closeness of the evening, she shivered as she sat there.

At last she summoned up enough resolution to return to the house. As she walked back beneath the trees, a bat darted to within inches of her and instinctively she put up her hand. She often saw them at this time of evening, swooping among the elms. Her thoughts turned to Gemma. It would be good to have her about the place again. How possessive Rex was over the girl! She wondered how long it would take Gemma to forget John. She was young and resilient. And how long would it be before she herself was able to forget Rex? She was not so young and far less resilient. She could not envisage a time when the thought of him did not mean heart-ache. It was a prospect which she could hardly bear to contemplate, and, yet, during his absence, that prospect had come closer. She blamed herself for thinking that he took her seriously, for seeing more than casual friendship in it. Because she had resisted him initially, she had presented a challenge to him. A pleasant diversion during a dull period of convalescence. She had nothing to complain of. His friendship had been welcome, and if she had built dreams which he did not share, that was not his fault. But there was still an element of doubt that left her with a slender thread of hope. At times, she had been sure that she saw in his eyes a tenderness which promised more than friendship. Whatever the truth might be, however, she felt in her bones that they were moving to a climax, that the truth must be revealed soon now. Perhaps it was only the oppressiveness of the night which made her feel so despondent. An owl hooted nearby as she went in, seeming to add mournful confirmation of her mood.

Rex telephoned the next morning to say that he had been detained and would not get back to Rosevean until late that night, so that Ann did not see him until the following day, when the letter arrived from Gemma.

CHAPTER XVIII

THE stormy weather of the past two days had passed, and the sun was shining into the dining-room when Ann went in to breakfast and found Rex standing by the window, hands clasped behind his back, looking preoccupied.

'Hullo, Rex. Did you have a good journey down last night?'

He spun round at her voice and came across to her, putting his hands on her shoulders.

'Hullo, my dear. It's good to see you. No, I had a foul journey. Never knew so many holiday-makers travelled by night. Ran through storms all the way from Somerset, to add to my joys. I shall go by train in future.'

'Good morning, Rex," said Madge. 'Nice to have you back.'

They sat down to breakfast as usual, and the first intimation that anything was wrong came when a scared-looking Mrs Vincent threw open the dining-room door and stook back to reveal Mrs Pendine standing there with a terrible expression on her face. Ann could not tell whether it was anger, pain or hysteria behind it. She wore a pink housecoat dragged round her, and her hair was dishevelled. Madge was the first to move and reached Mrs Pendine as she swayed. Then Rex joined her and they helped her to a chair. She seemed then to take a grip on herself.

'Rex, Gemma has eloped with John Hilary. She never went away with the Lloyds. They were married last Monday and sailed for Canada yesterday.'

'What? No, it can't be true,' said Rex, and took the letter which Mrs Pendine held out to him with a trembling hand.

'Young Hilary!' he exclaimed incredulously.

'Well, I'll be blowed,' said Madge, keeping her hand on Mrs Pendine's wrist.

'But it's just crazy,' declared Rex, who clearly could not credit it, even after reading Gemma's note. 'Did you ever suspect that there was anything between them, Madrina?'

'Look out, Rex. Catch her,' said Madge, as Mrs Pendine slumped forward in the chair.

' 'Phone for the doctor, Ann,' said Rex, and Ann flew to the telephone while Madge and Rex between them got Mrs Pendine back to bed.

During the next confused hour, Ann had only a waiting rôle to play. Her own bewilderment gave way to admiration for Gemma's courage in staking everything on John Hilary's love, and the conclusion that, regrettable as the manner of her going might be, the future for Gemma with John was hopeful. Gemma might be young and inexperienced but John was an honest, hard-working young man who knew where he was going and would look after Gemma with real devotion. Any doubts about Gemma's behaviour vanished when Madge brought her a note.

'From Gemma. There were two enclosed with her letter to Aunt Alice. One for Rex and one for you. Lord, what a bombshell!'

'How is Mrs Pendine?'

'The doctor's given her a sedative and she's drowsy now. Think she'll be all right, although her ticker isn't up to shocks like this. I must rush off to the village to get this prescription made up.'

Ann opened the note and read,

This must be short, as I am so rushed, but I wanted to tell you that John and I are wonderfully happy and looking forward to our new life with the greatest joy, although I am sad when I think of the unhappiness I have caused Grandma. But she gave me no choice.

She found out about us, and dismissed John, threatening to evict his parents if he so much as wrote me a line. And all the time, she never said a word to me, just left me to suppose that John had walked out on me. I can't tell you how I found out, but when I did, I knew what I had to do, and I knew I mustn't involve any of you. Thank you, though, for all your kindness, Ann, and do please write to me. I shall feel a little lonely in a new country at first, even though John is with me, and I would like to hear from you. I will send you our address as soon as we are settled. Meanwhile, we shall be staying with John's uncle, address above.

I am sorry I had to leave Rex out of this. I think he will

131

be hurt, but I have written to him explaining as best I can, and I hope he will write to me, too. I don't think I can expect Grandma to forgive me, but I have forgiven her for what she tried to do.

John sends his kind regards.

With love from,
Gemma.

P.S. Please explain to Gubbie. He has promised to help John's parents if they are dismissed.

Walking to the stable flat, Ann pondered on the web of deceit that had taken Gemma from Mrs Pendine. The thought that it had all been going on behind their backs, that Gemma's grief had been ignored, that Mrs Pendine had manipulated them like pawns on a chess-board, confirmed Ann in her belief that nothing good came from Rosevean. She wondered how Gemma had found out. Had her pumping of the Hilarys at last broken down their front?

Gubbie's reaction was refreshingly matter of fact.

'Gemma was bound to break free sooner or later. Good thing for the child. Nothing wrong with young Hilary. He'll make her a good husband. Poor Alice! She's brought it on herself.'

'Will you be able to help the Hilarys if they're dismissed?'

'Of course. So that was what the young madam was up to when she asked me. Yes, I'll find them a berth. Alice will dismiss them, I'll be bound. Won't be able to bear the sight of them, knowing that Gemma is now their daughter-in-law. That terrible pride of hers is as corrosive as acid. I'll have a word with Hilary today.'

'Can I send Gemma your love when I write?'

'Of course. Bless my soul, I'll write myself. Send them a little wedding present. Here, let me make a note of that address.' He scribbled it down and went on, 'Well, well. Poor Alice's sins have certainly rebounded on her own head. She's had her life, though. Gemma has it all in front of her. Pretty little bird. I shall miss her.'

'So shall I,' said Ann slowly.

When she arrived back at Rosevean, she found Rex pouring himself a stiff whisky in the drawing-room.

'Oh, there you are. I wondered where you'd got to.'

'I've been to the stable flat to tell Gubbie.'

'Want a drink?'

'No, thanks. Do you want to do any work?'

132

'Can't give my mind to it yet. It just beats me. Gemma, to be so deceitful. Never let on by as much as a word. Of course, it was young Hilary's doing. He knew he'd be sent packing if it came out.'

'As he was,' said Ann quietly. 'Did Gemma tell you about it in her note?'

'Yes. Madrina was right, of course. Trouble was, she found out too late. I wish she'd told me, though. I'm sure I could have made Gemma see sense.'

'Is it such a calamity? John Hilary is a decent young man and they were in love.'

'Are you mad? Of course it's a calamity from Gemma's point of view. She's only a child. What does she know of the world or of love? An infatuation for a good-looking gardener, who played his cards well. I can't believe such a tragedy could have taken place here under my nose, when Gemma and I have always been such close friends. When I think of that fellow taking advantage of her innocence, I could. . . .'

Words failed him and he put down his empty glass angrily and began to pace up and down. Ann's heart, which had seemed to grow heavier with every word he spoke, now felt leaden as she realized that this was the rock on which they would split. After a few moments, he went on,

'She took the necklace. He saw to that. They can live on that for a time, I suppose. The cunning way it was all planned beats me. Madrina could have stopped it by making Gemma a ward of court if only she'd known before they were married. Now it's too late, and Gemma's got heaven knows what sort of a life in front of her.'

'It may not be so bad as you suppose. I liked John Hilary. I think he'll make good over there.'

'Do you realize what life can be for the wife of a labourer? Gemma has never had to do a stroke of work in her life. She's been cared for and waited on and given everything she wanted. Do you seriously think she'll be happy as a working man's wife? That child. It's like making a shetland pony pull a coal cart. Look at Hilary's wife. Still charring here. The boy will probably do no better than his father. I suppose he's counting on the Pendine money coming to them eventually.'

'You see it only from a materialistic angle.'

'For heaven's sake, Ann, be your age. Spare us the romantic dreams with which John Hilary doubtless hypnotized Gemma. You're not a child. You know something of the world.'

'And something about human hearts, too, Rex. I think Gemma will find happiness with John. They loved each other.'

He stopped short in his prowling then, and came up to her. Now for it, she thought, with a hollow feeling inside her.

'Did you know that Gemma was in love with him?' he asked quietly.

'Yes.'

'Then why, in heaven's name, didn't you tell me?'

'Gemma asked me to keep it secret until she herself felt able to tell her grandmother. She had some idea of breaking it gently.'

'And you've known all the time, and said nothing?'

'I gave Gemma my word. She wanted to tell you, but when she sounded you out, you made it clear that you wouldn't give her any support.'

'Support! I should think not. That chap would have been sent packing straight away, and I'd have made Gemma see sense.'

'I think you over-estimate your influence.'

'And you seem completely unaware of the irresponsibility of your behaviour. You should have seen the danger and warned Mrs Pendine. It was your duty, even if our friendship meant so little to you that you couldn't confide in me.'

'I wanted to, Rex. When we were in London, I persuaded Gemma to call a conference. You and I were to talk it over with both of them, and she was going to suggest it to John directly when we got back. When we got back, John had vanished. It was Mrs Pendine's fault that Gemma took the law into her own hands and bolted. She was shown that reason would not help her a jot.'

'Did you never suspect that she might elope?'

'No. She was too conscious of her duty to her grandmother until Mrs Pendine deceived her. Then, I guess, Gemma decided that her grandmother had forfeited her right to it. That must have been quite a shock. Gemma is very honest herself.'

'Honest, to keep it all dark for so long? When did it start?'

Ann told him all she knew. His face was grim. It was a tremendous blow to his vanity, she knew, that Gemma should not have turned to him for help and advice, and his concern for the girl, mistaken though Ann believed it to be, was genuine, and sprang from a very real affection. When he turned on her so brutally, however, she wondered again whether he had intended to marry Gemma eventually, whether it was more than his pride and affection that were baulked.

'I consider you've behaved with criminal irresponsibility, Ann. Gemma, up to a point, was in your care. You were asked to keep an eye on her, act as a restraining influence. She is only eighteen. You are many years her senior. You should have foreseen this possibility, but even if you didn't, such an unsuitable attachment should have been made known. As an heiress, you must have realized that she was a particularly vulnerable prey for any fortune hunter. I'm amazed at the way you've behaved.'

'I made it my business, when I found out how serious Gemma was, to get to know John Hilary better. I am not a snob, as you and Mrs Pendine appear to be. I found much in John to admire, and I was absolutely convinced of the sincerity of his feelings for Gemma. He loved her, and he believed enough in his future as a fruit farmer to be confident of being able to provide for her. She was interested in his work, and I am quite sure that they will be very happy together. Although I was surprised that Gemma had the courage to elope, I cannot think that it was the wrong thing to do in the circumstances. You seem to think of Gemma as a puppet, without feelings. She loves John, and he loves her. Is that so hard to believe?'

Before he could reply, Madge came in with some coffee.

'Here we are, folk. I bet you can do with it. Aunt Alice has confounded the doctor by sitting up and taking notice when by all the rules she should be sleeping. She wants us all to assemble in the study at three o'clock this afternoon, including the staff, when she will preside at the meeting.'

'Ought she to get up?' asked Rex.

'You try to stop her. Have a biscuit, Ann.'

Ann refused and took her coffee to the study, where she had some typing to do. Sickened and shaken by Rex's attitude, she was glad to occupy her fingers even if her mind refused to concentrate on the work in hand. Rex did not send for her, and at lunch, he said very little. Without Madge, the meal would have been painfully silent. Mrs Pendine had lunch in her room, but she was in the study, behind the desk, punctually at three o'clock. Ann drew Hilary aside just before she went in.

'Hilary, have you seen Mr Rockford?'

'Yes, Miss Forrester, I have.'

'Good,' she whispered, and saw Rex look at her with a frown as he and Madge came up.

Mrs Pendine, although as white as a sheet, looked in complete command of herself again as she sat there, immaculate and erect. She disposed of them as though they were troops in an army, keeping the Hilarys standing before her, motioning Rex to a chair beside her, and consigning Ann and Madge to more distant chairs. Mrs Vincent hovered just inside the door.

'You all know why we are assembled,' she began. 'My

135

grand-daughter has eloped with the gardener's son. That fact will be known by everyone in the village by now, I expect First, I will make my attitude clear. By doing this, my grand-daughter has disgraced the family and cut herself off from it Henceforth, she has ceased to exist, as far as I am concerned After this meeting, I do not wish her name to be mentioned in my presence again. Is that clear?'

Only Mrs Vincent replied with a murmured assent.

'When I first suspected this disgraceful affair, I dismissed your son, Hilary, and made certain conditions for continuing to employ you and your wife. These conditions have been broken, therefore you are both dismissed. I will pay you a month's money, and I wish you to be off the premises within the next twenty-four hours.'

'We never broke the conditions, Mrs. Pendine,' said Hilary 'I can prove it by the letter John wrote to us. We never told Miss Gemma where he was or anything about it. Mrs Hilary had to be rude to her when she pestered her so, but we never broke the bargain.'

'That is unfortunate for you, Hilary. The fact remains that my grand-daughter found out what she was not intended to find out. For that, I am afraid you will have to pay the penalty It is impossible for me to countenance your presence here any longer. You can go now. I don't wish to see either of you again.'

Hilary opened his mouth, then closed it again and took his wife's arm. They went out in silence.

'You may go now, Mrs Vincent,' said Mrs Pendine.

Me next, thought Ann, as the door closed behind Mrs Vincent, but it was to Rex that Mrs Pendine next addressed herself.

'I want you, dear, to write a letter to Mr Cardew asking him to come down here as soon as he can conveniently arrange it I wish to change my will and I am not able to travel to London myself.'

'Don't you think you'd better think about it a bit, Madrina, before doing anything drastic?'

'I have thought, dear boy. I would like the letter to catch the afternoon post. Will you see to that?'

'Very well. Don't be too bitter about this affair, Madrina.'

'It is the end of all my hopes. I have nothing left to live for now, but let us not be melodramatic.'

Madge poured her a glass of water and said,

'Don't you think you've talked enough about it for the present, Aunt Alice? I'd feel happier if you'd try to rest again.'

136

'You're a good girl, Madge. I shan't forget your loyalty when I'm changing my will. There's one thing more I must clear up before I leave this dreadful affair, though. I'm inclined to believe the Hilarys when they say they did not tell Gemma about John's dismissal or give her any address. They had too much at stake. I shouldn't have been surprised if the boy had broken his word, but I took the precaution of giving instructions to Mrs Vincent to look at the post each morning and bring me any letters addressed to Gemma. Not one came. What I would like to know is, how did Gemma find out where John Hilary was?'

'Search me,' said Madge. 'You could have knocked me down with a feather when you told us this morning. I still can't think how it went on without my getting a clue.'

'Well, you and Gemma never really hit it off, Madge. You were not the person she would have confided in. Rex?'

'Not an idea of it. Like Madge, I find it hard to believe that it all happened while I was here, and Gemma never gave me so much as a hint. Do you think Gubbie might have acted as a go-between? Gemma was very fond of him and it's the sort of crazy enterprise he might lend himself to.'

'I thought of that, and spoke to him just before this meeting. He said he knew nothing about it until Miss Forrester told him this morning, although he intimated that he thoroughly approved; that was doubtless to spite me. He's crazy enough to have done it, but he never tells lies. What about you, Miss Forrester? Gemma liked you and may well have confided in you. Did you know anything of this affair?'

'I knew that she and John Hilary were in love with each other, but I knew nothing about the elopement. When we returned from London and found that John had gone, I assumed that was the end of Gemma's hopes.'

'So you knew about it all the time, and doubtless encouraged it. When I thought Gemma was with you, I suppose she was meeting John and you were their cover. I might have known. You had a very good motive for wanting Gemma out of the way.'

Rex got up and walked across to the window, staring out of it with his back to them. Madge said,

'What motive, Aunt Alice?'

'Jealousy, of course. The strongest motive of all. She knew how fond Rex was of Gemma, and to rid herself of a rival, she encouraged this child to make a disastrous runaway match. To further her own ends, she has helped to ruin Gemma's life.

137

You gave her John's address, of course. He wrote to you. I hadn't foreseen that.'

'I did not give Gemma any address. I didn't know where John was.'

'Do you dare to stand there and tell me that John didn't get in touch with Gemma through you?'

'He wrote a note, with no address given, saying goodbye, and telling her that he would always love her. That was all. I gave it to Gemma, thinking it would ease her unhappiness a little.'

'And the next thing we know is that Gemma joined him. Can you really be stupid enough to expect us to believe that you did not pass on the address with that note? In any case, by your own admission, you have behaved with the most callous treachery to me and to my grand-daughter, because you were in love with Rex. I wish to heaven I'd never employed you here. All I can ask now is that you never let me set eyes on you again. You have played the biggest part in ruining Gemma's life. I hope your conscience won't ever let you forget that, although I doubt if you have much of a conscience at all.'

Ann's voice was composed and her eyes met Mrs Pendine's steadily as she spoke.

'Before I go, I must say what nobody else here is willing to say. It was you who drove Gemma to take this step, Mrs Pendine, by breaking her faith in you. She would never have done it if she hadn't found out that you had lied and schemed to part her from John without any explanation. She was to assume that he had walked out on her. How she found out, I don't know, and I did not know John's address, nor was it on that note I gave to Gemma. I was as much surprised as any of you when I learned what had happened this morning. But Gemma's note made it clear that the decisive factor was your conduct, Mrs Pendine. I don't share your opinion that this is a tragedy for Gemma, nor does Mr Rockford. We both know that John Hilary is a decent young man with good prospects in Canada, and that he has taken Gemma to his uncle's home for the time being. I think she will be far happier as John's wife there than she ever was here. This house is diseased. Mr Rockford calls it the house of Mammon, and he's right. Money is the only God here. I shall be thankful to be free of its poisonous atmosphere.'

'Get that girl out of here, Rex,' cried Mrs Pendine, her eyes glassy with anger.

'I'm going. I don't need your henchmen to help me," said Ann, and walked out, her step unhurried and her head high.

'Wicked creature!' said Mrs Pendine.

'Now, don't get excited, Aunt Alice,' said Madge. 'There's nothing we can do. Good riddance to her.'

'I should have foreseen it. I knew she was after Rex.'

'Forget it. The harm's done,' said Madge.

'To accuse me! But you're right. I mustn't allow myself to get worked up. I have business matters to attend to.'

'About the Hilarys, Madrina. You can't send them packing without giving them time to find somewhere to go,' said Rex from the window.

'They have doubtless saved a good deal of money while they've been here. Their living has been cheap enough. They can stay in rooms somewhere. I'll not have them here to remind me. That's final. If any letters should come to me from Canada, Madge, I wish you to destroy them without mentioning them to me. And please remember, both of you, that the subject and the persons concerned have now ceased to exist for me. They are blotted out. Never mention them in my presence from now on.'

'Perhaps you'll feel differently after a little while,' said Rex.

'Never, dear boy,' said Mrs Pendine with a terrible little smile which chilled even Madge's insensitive heart.

CHAPTER XIX

ANN went straight from the study to the stable flat and was lucky enough to find Gubbie in. She told him what had happened and asked him if she might use his telephone to book a sleeper on the night train and hire a car from Truro to fetch her.

'I didn't want to use the telephone there. I just had to get away from the place. You represent an oasis of sanity.'

'Carry on, my dear.'

Ann was able to take advantage of a cancelled sleeper, and arranged for a car to call for her at nine o'clock that evening. By the time she had finished, Gubbie had made a pot of tea.

'Must say you're taking this very calmly, young woman, although you look as though you've been dipped in whitewash.'

'In a way, it's a relief to have it over. Tension has been building up for weeks now, and I felt disaster in the air. Now that it's all over, I feel quite calm in an unhappy sort of way.'

'Why unhappy? You'll not be sorry to be away from here now that Gemma's gone.'

'No. I could have wished my employment to end less brutally, though. However, that is what Rosevean is like. What have you fixed with Hilary, Gubbie?'

'They're staying with friends in the village for a week or so, while I get in touch with this National Trust job I told Gemma about. My recommendation will get them the job, I'm pretty sure. If it should be filled, and I doubt it, I know enough people in the horticultural world to be able to place them pretty quickly. I shall write to Gemma and John and reassure them about that. Now where did I put that address?'

'In a little red notebook your took from your pocket.'

'So I did. I expect they'll stay with John's uncle for some time. Nice fellow. Met him when he came over here. He thought a lot of John.'

'Well, I mustn't linger, because packing always takes me an age, and I thought I'd write a letter to Gemma, too. If I send it by air, it will be waiting for her when she gets there. I know she'll be feeling a little lost, wondering what's happened here, and someone ought to write and wish them the happiness they deserve. She's a warm-hearted girl, and she'll be worrying about the reaction here. They'll have my good wishes, anyway.'

'She's not the only warm-hearted girl, either. I hope this hasn't damaged you too much, my dear.'

She smiled and shook her head, not trusting to words, and he put his arm round her shoulder as he walked to the door with her. Sometimes she thought Gubbie knew more than he pretended.

Back at Rosevean, she went quickly to her room. As she passed the half-open door of the drawing-room, she heard Rex's voice, and Madge answering him. They were no doubt discussing her treachery, she thought bitterly. All her life, she would remember Rex standing by the window with his back to them, silent, while Mrs Pendine painted the ugly picture of a jealous schemer. She had no reason to suppose that he was refuting it to Madge. . . .

'The sickening part is,' said Rex angrily, 'that all we can do is bleat about it. We're absolutely helpless. Gemma is John Hilary's wife, and that's the end of it. It was planned with diabolical skill, and broken to us only when we could do nothing about it.'

'Not like Gemma to be so clever. I'm afraid Aunt Alice was right, Rex. Gemma let herself be influenced by Ann Forrester,' said Madge.

'But Ann could have known nothing of what happened here while we were in London. It was between Madrina and the Hilary family, and nobody else.'

'Until John wrote to Gemma through Ann. Why did he use Ann as a post office if he didn't know she was an ally and would assist any plan he made?'

'Oh, she was an ally all right, but I can't believe she would have pushed Gemma as far as this.'

'I wonder what was in Gemma's note to her. It would be interesting to know. What did the kid write to you?'

'Here it is. You can read it.'

Madge opened the folded sheet.

Dear Rex,

I am afraid you will be shocked to hear that I have married John Hilary and shall be on the way to British Columbia by the time you receive this.

We have loved each other ever since he came back to Rosevean, but I knew Grandma would oppose an engagement, and you would have, too, because you think of me as a child. I was hoping to find a way to gain Grandma's consent, but I was afraid to tell her until I had some chance of success. But she found out about us, and while we were in London, she dismissed John, threatening to evict his parents if he ever got in touch with me. She said nothing to me, but I found out what she had done, and then I decided that this was the only way.

I haven't time to write much, but please forgive me for being so secretive, Rex. If only I had felt you would help us, I would have gone to you before anyone for advice, but you would have been against it, I know.

We are wonderfully happy, so don't be angry with me for long. I hate hurting you when you have always been so good and kind to me. I hope you will write soon and say you forgive me. The address at the top of this letter is where we shall be staying until we find a home of our own.

In haste. Your loving

Gemma.

'Well, that's clear enough,' said Madge dryly.

'Yes. I'd have given everything I possessed for this not to

have happened. I must be a complete dolt not to have suspected it. I reckon I know Gemma better than any of you.'

'No good blaming yourself, Rex. We were all as blind as bats, except Ann Forrester.'

'She could have stopped it so easily,' said Rex desperately.

'My dear man, no woman in love is going to lift a finger to stop the exit of a rival. I think Aunt Alice hit the nail on the head there. It's your fatal charm that was at the bottom of it.'

Rex, with an expression of distaste, shook his head and said grimly,

'I'm going for a walk. Need some fresh air. So long.'

Madge leaned back in her chair and pulled out her cigarettes. She had already extracted Gemma's note from Ann's handbag, left in the dining-room, and she drew it from her pocket now, lit one corner of it with her lighter, and dropped it in the ash-tray, watching it curl to ash. Gemma made it a little too clear that Ann had not played any part in revealing Mrs Pendine's measures against John. No harm in being on the safe side. She finished her cigarette, then took the ash-tray out to the kitchen and emptied its contents into the boiler. When she returned, she met Ann emerging from the dining-room with her handbag.

'Hullo. I thought you were out,' said Madge.

'I went to see Mr Rockford. Now I'm packing. I'd forgotten where I'd left this.'

'Not surprising, with all this flap,' said Madge, not unsympathetically.

Ann returned to her room and opened the bag to take out Gemma's note, to which she was about to reply. When she could not find it, she thought she must have left it at the stable flat with Gubbie that morning. She decided to write the letter and slip along to the flat to address it, for she could not remember the exact address. When she and Gubbie searched for the note, however, it was nowhere to be found. Looking round at the muddle, Ann did not find it surprising that one small sheet of notepaper should have disappeared, and she contented herself with copying the address from his notebook.

She was finishing her packing that evening when a knock at the door heralded Rex. He came in without invitation and said curtly,

'Well, you've helped to make a fine mess of everything, I must say, Ann. The Hilarys sacked, Gemma disinherited, because that's what Madrina intends unless I can dissuade her before Cardew gets here, and the old lady's life to all intents and purposes finished.'

'If all you've come to do is abuse me, Rex, please go. I've stood enough abuse from Mrs Pendine. Nothing that has happened has been caused by me. Nothing. Mrs Pendine has brought about her own loss. As you remained silent this afternoon when she attacked me, it is obvious that you agree with her.'

'How can you say that this appalling business wasn't helped on by you? At the very least, you acted as a go-between for the two of them. In fact, I believe you played a big part in engineering the elopement.'

'So you think I'm lying when I deny it, do you?'

'What were you and Gemma so busily discussing that morning I came after you? I saw you hand her a note, and then she saw me and ran off like a stag. You were singularly bland, I remember. The incident came back to me this afternoon. That note was from John, wasn't it?'

'Yes. The one I told Mrs Pendine about.'

'The one that gave no address and said goodbye. And two days later, Gemma eloped. How stupid do you think we are, Ann? The most sickening part of the whole business for me has been your deception all the way along the line. You deserved everything Madrina said to you this afternoon.'

Ann fastened the case and straightened up to face him. It took all her self-control to keep her anger in check.

"Then shall we leave it at that? I've no more to say to you, since you think I'm a liar.'

'What did Gemma say in her note to you? Tell me that. Did she give you the news as though it was a surprise?'

'Yes.'

'Then show it to me.'

'I've mislaid it.'

He smiled, then, without humour.

'Too bad.' As he turned to go, he added, 'I'll drive you to the station tomorrow, if you'll let me know when you're ready. I'd better have a word with the Hilarys. They seem to have paid a heavy price for your interference.'

'There is no need to worry about them. Gubbie is going to find them another job, which will doubtless be far more congenial than this. Gemma asked him to do this before she left.'

'You know it all, don't you?'

'Gemma mentioned it to me in her note.'

'The one you can't find?'

'Yes. Before you go, I would like to ask one thing of you, Rex. I hope you'll write to Gemma kindly. She'll be happy with John. I have no doubt about that. But she was fond of you, and it will mean a lot to her to hear from you.'

'Of course I shall keep in touch with her. It's very likely that she'll need my help.'

'You over-estimate your usefulness, I fancy. That is what has stung your vanity so badly, hasn't it? The fact that your Gemma should have ignored you and escaped to happiness with a man you didn't even know, right under your nose. You still can't think that she won't turn to you now to get her out of trouble. You forget that she has put her life in John's hands now. He'll look after her well."

'Until he finds out that the Pendine money is not for her. The proceeds of the necklace won't last long.'

'What a foul mind you have, Rex, seeing money as the only motive behind people's actions!'

'Not the only motive,' he said deliberately, and the dagger went home where he intended it should.

Ann pushed her hair back from her forehead and said wearily,

'Let's not stand here hurting each other so cruelly. I've given you a true account of the part I played. It was a minor part, and I don't regret it. I would do it again in the same circumstances. I'm sorry if your hopes of marrying Gemma have been foiled by it. If, as I supposed, John had left her for good, I think Gemma might well have turned to you for comfort. You would probably have made her happy. I don't know. But I do know that she loves John Hilary with all her heart, and I think their future promising. That's my last word on the matter.'

At the door, he turned as though to say something, but Ann held up her hand and stopped him.

'No, Rex. I can't take any more. It will be a kindness if you will leave me, even though you think I deserve no kindness.'

He went then, without a word, and Ann sat on the bed and gave way to the tears which had threatened to overwhelm her as soon as her anger had died. She had never been quite sure of his love, but she had never imagined that he would become an enemy because he believed she had ruined Gemma's life.

Later, she told Mrs Vincent that she would have her dinner in her room but she left most of it, feeling that the food choked her. She managed, with difficulty, to carry her two suitcases a short way down the drive and left them under a tree while she went to the cottage to ask Hilary if he would carry them to the gates for her.

"They're too heavy for me, Hilary. Would you mind?'

"That's all right, Miss Forrester. Lot of packing up going on here tonight, isn't there? Well, I'll be glad to be away from the place now. A bit tired of hearing my son referred to as a criminal.'

'Yes. I've been given the same label, too, as a sympathizer, and I'm tired of it. John's a fine boy, Hilary. They'll be happy, and do well, I'm sure.'

'I hope so. You know, I've been here most of my life, and the thought of leaving was like an earthquake, but now we're going, I'm sort of relieved. I guess I've been too timid all my life.'

'Mr Rockford will see that you're all right. He has a lot of influence in your sphere of work.'

'Yes. He's quite famous in a way, you know. Funny, isn't it? He being such an odd gentleman. What about you, Miss Forrester?'

'Oh, I shall stay at a hotel in London and have a bit of holiday while I decide about a new job. A car is coming for me at nine, Hilary. If you'll bring the cases down to the gates, I'll be very grateful.'

'Leave it to me. Feels a bit like autumn tonight, doesn't it? One thing I'm not sorry to miss. Clearing up all the leaves this autumn. Some job, that. I reckon the place will get buried by the leaves one day.'

'I can't think it would be any loss. It seems an evil place to me.'

'Without Miss Gemma and John, it's certainly lost what life it had. You'll be glad to be gone too, miss.'

'Yes. There's nothing here for me any more.'

Madge was the only person Ann saw before she left. They met in the hall as Madge was about to take a hot drink up to Mrs Pendine.

'Goodbye, Madge,' said Ann firmly. 'I'm off now.'

'Already? I thought you were going on the midday train tomorrow.'

'No. I was lucky enough to get a sleeper for tonight.'

'Oh well, a pleasant journey. Rex has gone off in the car. Any message?'

'No message. Goodbye.'

It was nearly dark as she walked down the drive for the last time. The sky was shut out by the overhanging trees, but when she came to the clearing by the gates, she saw a silver sickle of a moon in a dark blue sky. The air was chilly and she shivered. Another chapter in her life had ended brutally and

left her desolate, she thought, and for a moment it was hard to
resist a rush of self-pity. Then she squared her shoulders as the
car drew up, and Hilary came out of the cottage to help her
with her cases.

CHAPTER XX

REX did not return to the house until late that night, so that he
did not learn of Ann's departure until breakfast the following
morning.

'She went on the night train,' said Madge, buttering her
toast. 'Left about nine, while you were out.'

'Good grief! I didn't expect her to go so fast.'

'Aunt Alice hadn't exactly encouraged her to linger. She's
done enough damage. Good riddance, I say. Getting quite a
small party here, aren't we?'

'Be smaller still very soon. I shall be off to London at the
end of August. I've made arrangements with my friends to
take over their flat then. I need a few weeks in London before
I open my office at the beginning of October. I've still another
staff appointment to make and a deuce of a lot of details to
see to.'

'All deserting the sinking ship,' said Madge gloomily.

'Poor old Madge. You seem to be stuck with it. But I've
been retired long enough. I'm itching to get back into my own
show.'

'I wouldn't say you've been exactly idle. When will your
book come out?'

'Not until the spring. I wonder how soon Cardew will get
down here. I hope he delays it a bit, to give Madrina time to
soften. She can't just wipe Gemma out of her life.'

'She's a very hard woman, Rex.'

'She's got worse during recent years. She can't stomach
anyone crossing her.'

'Don't I know it! You haven't eaten much breakfast.'

'Not hungry. How was the old lady this morning?'

'Brisk. But she looks ten years older.'

146

'It's bad business. I've some letters to get off, so if you'll excuse me, Madge.'

'Sure. Going to type them yoursef?'

'Have a shot at it, because I want copies. My two-finger style of typing isn't very rapid, though.'

'I'll send in extra strong coffee at eleven,' said Madge.

In the study, Rex sat at Ann's desk and eyed the typewriter grimly. The tapping of branches against the window irritated him. It was small wonder that the room was as dark as a cell, with trees growing up to the window and a great holly bush half way across the lower panes. Why it had never been cleared outside, he didn't know. His eyes travelled over the heavy leather chairs and came to rest on the delicate little vase in the shape of a white horn which stood on the bureau and which Ann had always kept full of flowers. He remembered her buying it and showing it to him. It had come from a church jumble sale and she had been delighted with it. Now, the pink roses had wilted and dropped their petals on top of the bureau. It was the only pleasing object in the room, he decided, its elegant fragility standing out like a lily in a gloomy forest. As he pushed open a drawer of the bureau for some notepaper, the last of the petals fell with a little rustle, and he picked some up and let them fall through his fingers. He supposed she had forgotten to pack the vase in her rush to get away.

He sat down at the desk again, and pushed his hands through his hair. He remembered how honest those brown eyes of hers had always looked. Brown with flecks of gold. And the sheen of sunshine always on the smooth hair that swung round her cheeks like a bell. And then Gemma's laughing little face came to his mind, and he remembered how enchanting she had looked in that filmy dress, the colour of those rose petals, with the diamond and sapphire necklace at her throat. How would she stand up to a tough life as a farmer's wife? Perhaps she was tougher than he thought. He was losing faith in his judgment. He had thought he knew Gemma as well as he would know his own child, but the most important decision of her life had come as a bombshell to him, and he had not even recognized that most easily diagnosed of complaints, a girl's first love affair. He thought he had learned all there was to know of Ann, and yet she had behaved in a manner quite contrary to his opinion of her. Somewhere, deep down, he felt uneasily that with Ann he had gone wrong, or was it that the facts painted a picture of her that he couldn't face? He would have sworn that she was a person of integrity.

Doggedly, shutting out both Ann and Gemma from his mind, he started to type.

Two days later, Mr Cardew arrived, and was closeted with Mrs Pendine for over an hour. Rex, who had fetched him from Truro early that morning, drove him back to the station after lunch.

'A long journey for you, Mr Cardew. Pity you couldn't stay the night,' said Rex.

'Yes. I can work on the train, though.'

What a dry stick he was! thought Rex. No feeling ever came through that thin, pale face of his, and the precise voice was devoid of expression, so that whether he was discussing the weather or sudden catastrophe, the tone was the same.

'I am sorry that Miss Forrester did not prove altogether satisfactory,' he said now. 'A nice young woman, I thought. Mrs Pendine is—er—perhaps a little stringent in her demands.'

'Yes. Age is beginning to tell on her, I'm afraid, and this latest blow is a very heavy one.'

'She mentioned it only in the briefest terms, but I fear it has struck very hard. Mrs Pendine is, however, made of stern stuff.'

'Yes. Quite frankly, I had hoped that she would wait before making any drastic alterations in her will. I would like to think that she might become reconciled to her grand-daughter in some measure, at least.'

'Mrs Pendine knows her own mind, Mr Vernon. What very pleasant weather we are having for the holiday season, are we not? Usually so disappointing.'

Rex grinned to himself and agreed with Mr Cardew that the weather was very pleasant. He was going to get no change there.

When he arrived back at Rosevean, Madge came down the drive to meet him.

'Find out anything from the old bird?' she enquired.

'About what?'

'Don't be so lofty. About the will, of course. What else?'

'If you think Cardew is the talkative type, you're a worse judge of people than I thought, Madge.'

'Has Aunt Alice told you anything?'

'Only that she intended to disinherit Gemma. That is what she has done, I'm afraid. I wish to goodness I'd been able to persuade her to wait a bit.'

'Can you imagine her softening?'

148

'Well, damn it, she must have a heart somewhere. She's always been kind to me.'

'You are her pet. A reminder of the days when she did have a heart. Funny to think of Aunt Alice ever being in love, isn't it?'

Rex was suddenly tired of Madge's eager, curious eyes and healthy face. They irritated him.

'I guess all people in love are pretty comic,' he said.

'You do sound blue. Poor old Rex. Deserted by his girls. Can I offer any consolation?'

'Don't be an ass, Madge. Anyway, you're the mainstay of Aunt Alice now.'

'Yes. Poor old girl. I feel a bit sorry for her, except when she makes me so livid that I could strangle her.'

'You're very patient with her. She'll not forget you, Madge. That I know.'

'Do you? Has she said anything specific?'

'No. Only that you have proved the only loyal member of her family, and she'll see that you are rewarded.'

'Oh, I've only done what any nurse would do for a difficult old lady. She's a marvel, you know, Rex. In spite of that heart of hers, she's as vigorous as a woman ten years her junior. She has enormous will-power, of course.'

'Yes. She'll reach a century, I dare say,' said Rex as he went in.

Madge pulled out her cigarettes and walked round to the terrace for a quiet smoke before tea. Another twenty years of servitude? Her spirit drooped at the prospect. She would never be able to stand that. She would be an old woman herself by then. No. she didn't think her aunt would last very much longer. This latest shock had not helped her. Madge recognized the signs, and did not think she would have long to wait. She would travel for a year or two, she thought. She had always wanted to see Paris, and the Swiss Alps, and the south of France. Then she'd settle down in a little house of her own on the outskirts of London, perhaps. She liked a bit of life. To be able to give orders instead of take them! To be free! Her childhood and schooldays had been spent on the fringe of poverty, for her father was a failure and her mother had worn herself out in the struggle to make ends meet. It had rankled them to have to accept Aunt Alice's charity in the way of holidays at Rosevean and the odd parcel of clothes and gifts of money to her mother, accompanied always by criticism of the foolish marriage she had made. Nursing had not brought Madge much money, either, for such hard work. Here at

Rosevean, the work had been lighter, but only Madge knew what she had borne in the way of humiliation. She had earned some reward by now, she thought bitterly. By heaven, she had! Gemma had always lived in luxury. Had everything she wished for. Now she had a good-looking young man for a husband. That, too, Madge knew would never be for her. Surely it was only justice that she should inherit her aunt's money? Surely some recompense for life's niggardly hand was due to her now?

It was a pity Rex was so set on reconciling Aunt Alice to Gemma. Not that he would succeed. Madge knew the old lady too well. Hard as stone. Her pride would never forgive Gemma. Still, it might be as well to keep a watch on the post. Rex had written to Gemma, she knew. She could rely on the kid to keep her word, but she did not want Rex nosing around for another guilty party if Gemma cleared Ann. Madge watched a smoke ring curling up above her head. She would need to keep that aspect in mind. Not that she was greatly worried. Nothing could be traced to her, and Rex would soon be immersed in his business. With Gemma married and so far away, that connection would soon wilt and the affair be dismissed. It had really all worked out very well, she thought, but she would still need to keep her head and take no chances. Aunt Alice would never forgive Gemma, but if she thought that Madge had helped Gemma to elope, Madge would be out, too, just as quickly as the Forrester girl. She couldn't see how Aunt Alice could ever find out, though. No, she was safe enough, she concluded, as she stubbed out her cigarette and went into the house.

When she took the tea-tray up to her aunt's room, she found her resting on the sofa, her book unopened in her lap. Madge drew up the low table beside her.

'Shall I pour your tea, Aunt Alice? You look tired. Mr Cardew's visit was a bit much for you, I guess.'

'Yes. There was a lot to arrange. We shall have to see if we can get a gardener from the village, Madge. The grounds aren't in good order, heaven knows, but we can't let them become a jungle. If we can get a man to tide us over for the autumn, I can take my time over appointing another couple. I suppose Mrs Vincent can get some casual help from the village to make up for Mrs Hilary.'

'Yes, I'll see to that. Don't you worry, Aunt Alice. Wait until you feel stronger.'

'I don't seem to have any interest left in the place now. Nobody cares for it but me, and I shan't be here much longer.'

'It's not like you to talk so pessimistically.'

'Merely facing facts, Madge dear,' said Mrs Pendine dryly.

'Well, drink your tea. Have you taken your tablets?'

'Yes. I'm full of tablets. I wonder I don't rattle.'

'That's better. Mr Cardew's enough to depress anyone. I suppose he is alive?'

'His brain is very much alive. I fancy that outside of his work, life has no meaning.'

'Nice for his family. Will he be coming down again?'

'No. He is drawing up my will according to my instructions, and will be sending it to me in due course. You will not have to worry about the future, Madge. You are the only person I have to provide for now. I appreciate the way you've carried out your duties here, and you will not find me ungrateful. Now leave me, dear. You can take the tray away. I shall only need this one cup of tea.'

The flesh seemed to have fallen away from her aunt's bones so much lately that her skin looked almost transparent, and Madge felt a genuine pang of pity for her as she took the tray away. Poor old woman! She was lonely and unloved, and didn't even know how to enjoy the money that could have consoled her. She would use it better. What was it for, if not to make your life more cheerful? This mausoleum would be put on the market joyfully as soon as it was hers, Madge decided, as she descended the wide staircase. Not that she thought anyone would want to buy it, unless the National Trust might regard it as a historic relic worthy of preserving. Personally, she thought it was the last word in gloom and discomfort. A nice little house, with central heating, close to a cinema and some decent shops: that would be her cup of tea. She would go to Madeira, perhaps, for the worst of the winter. Or that four-star hotel in Torquay where she had once stayed with her aunt for a few days would do very nicely. To be waited on and give the orders for a change. Happily, Madge allowed the dreams of her future to cast a rosy haze round the present.

A week later, the Lloyds were invited to dinner, ostensibly for social reasons, but actually, Madge confided to Rex, to witness Mrs Pendine's signature to her will. It was heavy going that evening in spite of everybody's efforts. There were too many ghosts about, thought Rex, as he tried to listen to Dr Lloyd's description of a climb in North Wales. They had imagined Gemma to be with the Lloyds on that holiday.

While Madge fetched coffee and the Lloyds and Mrs Pendine disappeared for a few minutes into the study, Rex played the piano, but here again ghosts haunted him as he remem-

bered Ann singing Greensleeves, and later she had leaned on
the piano while he played, her face thoughtful. He remembered every feature as distinctly as if she were there in front
of him now: the silk smooth hair in the lamp-light, the dark
eyes widely spaced, the oval symmetry of her face, the tender,
expressive mouth. Knowing how sensitive she was, had he been
too harsh with her in spite of her conduct? Whatever she had
done, he knew that emotional crises flayed her. And yet, for all
her sensibilities, she had urged a course of action on Gemma
which would probably hurt that child for the rest of her
life. Torn by conflicting feelings, Rex played on, hoping to
release the tension of his nerves.

At the end of the evening, when he was alone with Madge,
he said,

'Did Ann give any address when she left, Madge?'

'No. Don't think she knew where she'd be staying. Why?'

'She left that little flower-vase in the study. I thought we
might send it on.'

'Haven't a clue where she is. If you're wise, you'll not get
within range of her guns again, Rex. She was hunting you
down all right, at Gemma's expense.'

'I'll be relieved when I hear from Gemma. She'll just about
have arrived at the uncle's home by now, I guess. I might get
a letter in a week.'

'If young madam chooses to write. Depends if you chewed
her up when you wrote.'

'I let her down as lightly as I could. After all, the harm's
done now. Pretty ghastly, this evening, wasn't it?'

'Thought it would never end. Another couple of weeks,
and you'll be gone to more cheerful climes. Lucky dog!'

'Come to London when you can, Madge. It'll be pretty
bleak here for you without any young people around and
Madrina so broody. I'll lay something on for you.'

'O.K. I'll hold you to that, Rex. Lord, I'm tired. Think I'll
skip my evening constitutional. Must be getting old.'

'Don't exactly feel full of youthful verve myself,' said Rex.

CHAPTER XXI

THE days to Rex's departure crept slowly by. With much on his mind connected with the starting of his business, he did his best to comfort Mrs Pendine, who kept up a cool, controlled front which did not deceive him for a moment. His idle moments were filled with the ghosts of Ann and Gemma, and they haunted his restless nights. After one such night, he woke early and decided to go for a stroll before breakfast. It was a pearly grey morning, which might herald heat or rain.

Glad of the peace of the deserted lanes, he walked further than he intended, arriving back at Rosevean in time to meet the postman at the gates.

'Good morning, Jim.'

'Good morning, Mr Vernon. Just left a letter for you. From Canada. Hope it's good news from the young lady. We all miss her bright young face. Always did you good to see her smile.'

'So it did. I'll be glad to hear from her.'

'There was one for Mrs Pendine, too. Hope it will cheer her up, although Miss Trent said just now that she didn't think the old lady would read it.'

The whole village had soaked up the story of Gemma's elopement, and Rex knew that the grape vine along which news travelled kept them up to date. Gemma had been well-known and popular in the village, for she had no airs and graces and had been friendly with everybody.

'We'll have to try to persuade her,' said Rex, and nodded as he went on his way, anxious to get the letter.

There was only one letter on the hall table for him, from London. He picked it up and tapped his hand with it. That was odd. He threw it down unopened and went in search of Madge. He was wearing crêpe-soled sandals so that Madge did not hear him as he came into the kitchen. She was standing over a kettle of boiling water, steaming open an envelope.

'Hullo, Madge. What are you up to?'

She spun round guiltily and flushed crimson. Then she recovered herself quickly, and poked the letter into her overall pocket.

'Good morning, Rex. You made me jump. What brings you through the green baize door at this hour?'

'Postman said there was a letter for me from Canada. It wasn't on the hall table, so I came to look for it.'

'It wasn't for you. The postman must have been mistaken. It was for Aunt Alice and I've burned it.'

'What was the one you were steaming open just then?'

Madge laughed a little too casually.

'Oh, just getting the stamp off the envelope. Mrs Vincent's got a young nephew who collects them.'

'Why did you burn the letter for Madrina? I thought we'd decided to try to persuade her to read anything that came from Gemma.'

'More than my life's worth, Rex. I sounded her out about it a few days ago. Her instructions were explicit. I was to burn any letter that came.'

'You should have let me have a go at her.'

Madge shrugged her shoulders and went to the larder.

'I don't think you'd have budged her, Rex. Mrs Vincent's late with breakfast this morning. I'd better get it started.'

'Give me that letter in your pocket,' said Rex quietly.

'I've told you. It's only the envelope.'

'I collect stamps, too.' said Rex dryly, and caught her arm. 'Come on, Madge. I mean to have it.'

As she twisted out of his grasp with unexpected strength, Mrs Vincent appeared. Madge stood still when she saw the expression on the woman's face, and Rex nipped the letter out of her pocket. Mrs Vincent, with a face as white as chalk, gasped,

'It's the mistress. She's half out of bed, making the most horrible noises. I think she's had a stroke.'

As soon as Madge saw her aunt, she told Rex to telephone for the doctor, cut short Mrs Vincent's stammerings of distress at the grotesque spectacle on the bed and gave her precise instructions in a tone that permitted no hysteria. When Doctor Lloyd came, there was little he could do, and Mrs Pendine lay in a coma until the early afternoon, when she died without regaining consciousness.

Escaping from the house later that day, Rex walked down the twisting cliff path. The sun was hot, and the sea was hazy below him. She had little to live for, he reflected. Her life had been an unhappy one. She had married for money, and that was all that was left to her in the end. You reap what you sow, he thought, but somewhere his godmother had lost the key to living. She had not always been so hard and domineering. At some time, early on, she had taken the wrong path, opted for the wrong values. If she had married his father, she would, perhaps, have been a different woman. There had been potentialities of kindness and goodness there, he knew. It was the growth of that terrible possessiveness that had brought her ultimate loss. Left only with Gemma, she had tried to chain the girl to her, and that was the surest way of any to lose a person you loved.

He sat down just above the cove in the clearing where he had seen Ann taking her dress off on that hot Easter Saturday, which now seemed so long ago. She had been reluctant to take his advice against a swim, he remembered. Afterwards, he had lain on the bench and watched her paddling along the edge of the waves. Then she had gone to sleep with her head on his shoulder. It brought an ache now to think of it. She had been won over very reluctantly, her brown eyes wary of hurt. She had been right to be wary, for the hurt had come. Having read Gemma's letter, he wondered how much he had been to blame. He took the letter out of his pocket and read it again.

Dear, dear Rex,

You will never know how glad I was to find your letter waiting for me when I arrived, and to learn that you hadn't cast me into outer darkness for ever! But how gloomy you are about my future! It's never looked rosier, Rex darling, so cheer up.

I knew you would find it hard to understand, because you didn't think I was old enough to love anybody for keeps, but perhaps the Italian blood in me has made me mature earlier than you expected. Anyway, Rex, John and I are truly happy and the future looks good to me.

John's uncle is a dear and gave us such a warm welcome. He is going to help us look for a home not far from him, and is going to put up half the money for the land John wants to buy. We can manage the rest.

I am terribly sorry that Grandma has taken it so hard. I knew she would. I can only hope that when she hears how well John is doing as a fruit farmer, and I know he will do well, she will be reconciled. I did feel badly about her, in spite of the fact that she deceived me into believing that John had deserted me, which was a cruel thing to do, you must admit.

I had a lovely letter from Ann. She told me that she was

leaving Rosevean as her job had come to an end there. I hope there wasn't any trouble for her because of what I did. She didn't say so, but Grandma meant her to keep an eye on me, you know. But Ann had nothing to do with my elopement, although she knew John and I wanted to be married some day. I purposely stopped myself from telling her because of what you once told me about not involving her in trouble with Grandma. You see, I am not entirely irresponsible, as you hint!

Do you think you will ever be able to come to British Columbia? It would be so lovely to see you and I would like you to reassure yourself that I am not living in abject poverty, tied to a callous husband. How sweet and old-fashioned you are, Rex dear! That's why I couldn't confide in you, though I wanted to, and tried to once, but you didn't take me seriously. But always you will be my dearest friend, and I hope you'll say the same next time you write.

No more room. Air mail letters are too small. Please write and tell me about your business in London. And try to make Grandma see reason. I have written to her, but without much hope. Lots of love.

Gemma.

An odd little smile played about Rex's mouth as he scanned it. Sweet and old-fashioned, indeed! That came as a bit of a jab. Made him feel very ancient. It was a reassuring letter, though, and he had felt vastly relieved when he first read it. Young Hilary seemed to know what he was about, and Gemma was plainly happy at present. Ann had been sure that the match would turn out well. Had he misjudged the boy? Taken too materialistic a view of the whole affair? The one thing he had not credited was that Gemma really loved John Hilary, that it was not an immature infatuation. Now, he was not so sure. In any case, you could not run other people's lives for them. He should have known that. His picture of himself as guide and counsellor to young Gemma had certainly been sweet and old-fashioned. Ann was right. The rôle had appealed to his vanity.

And now he would have to write to tell Gemma of the death of her grandmother. A sense of failure gripped him as he sat there. He had been no use to Gemma, he had messed up his friendship with Ann, and had been of little help to his godmother, who had shut herself up with her own bitter thoughts during these last weeks. Now, he supposed, Rosevean would be sold, if anybody would buy it. Madge wouldn't keep it. And what she had been up to, steaming open his letter, he didn't know. He would have shown it to her, if she wanted to know how Gemma was getting on. Something odd there. He was willing to bet that she had read Gemma's letter to her grandmother before burning it. He would tackle her about it again some time, when the shock of her aunt's sudden death had passed.

As he climbed up the path again, he felt glad that he would soon be leaving Rosevean and its failures behind. It had been an uneasy summer. He would be thankful when the funeral and the formalities were over, and he could escape. The flat was empty now, and waiting for him. And somehow, he must find Ann again.

During the days following Mrs Pendine's death, Madge displayed unusual signs of tension, and Rex said nothing to her about the episode of the letter. There was a queer excitement throttled back there, he felt, due presumably to the prospect of inheriting her aunt's fortune. Not surprising, really. She had never had anything of her own. If anybody had earned it, he supposed Madge had. He hoped it would bring her more happiness than it had brought her aunt.

Mr Cardew came down to Rosevean for the funeral and brought the will with him. There were few mourners at the ceremony, which took place on a grey, humid day, which Rex found trying. When Mr Cardew read out the contents of the will to them afterwards, Rex noticed Madge's hands shaking, and gave her a cigarette which she had some difficulty in lighting.

It was, in effect, a simple document. Mr Cardew and an accountant were appointed executors. After leaving Mrs Vincent five hundred pounds, Rex certain shares, and Madge an income of three hundred pounds a year for the rest of her life, Mrs Pendine had bequeathed the remainder of the Pendine fortune, representing the bulk of it, to three charities. There was silence for a moment after Mr Cardew finished. So the old girl had given the Pendine fortune away, after all, thought Rex, but before he could speak, Madge burst out with,

'No! She couldn't do this me. It can't be true!'

Mrs Vincent stood up nervously, and said,

'Well, if you'll excuse me, I'll go and see to the tea. I'm sure I'm very grateful to the poor mistress,' she added formally.

'Did you say three hundred a year for me, Mr Cardew?' demanded Madge.

'That is correct, Miss Trent. That will be the income from certain specified securities.'

'What about the securities? Will they be mine to cash if I choose?'

'No, Miss Trent. It's quite clearly stated here. You will be entitled to the interest only; the securities themselves will be sold and the proceeds divided between the same three charities on your death. A generous margin has been left to ensure that your income will not fall below three hundred pounds a year.'

'And won't it ever be more? Share dividends go up, don't they?'

'That is the specified sum, Miss Trent. Any surplus will accrue and ultimately be divided between the said three charities.'

And suddenly Madge lost control of herself, and shocked both Rex and Mr Cardew with a tirade of abuse of her aunt. She thumped on the table with her clenched fists as she used words which Rex would have supposed outside her ken and which Mr Cardew, to judge by his face, had never heard uttered before. It was an ugly scene, and the solicitor lowered his eyes and studied his papers until Rex said sharply,

'That's enough, Madge. What's done is done.'

'You! You don't know what it's like to be dependent on an old tyrant like that. All these years I've borne her insults and slights, waited on her, run like a cowed dog at her bidding, and now she leaves me this pittance out of a fortune of hundreds of thousands. How much was she worth? Not far short of a million, I guess.'

'Not far short, Miss Trent,' said Mr Cardew coldly. 'The Pendine money had been wisely invested.'

'Oh, it's wicked, it's wicked,' moaned Madge, and got up and rushed out of the room, leaving the two men looking at each other.

She did not appear at dinner, and Rex drove Mr Cardew to the station directly afterwards, for the solicitor was travelling back to London by the night train. It was on his way back to Rosevean that Rex saw daylight, and realized who had encouraged Gemma to elope. Of course, he thought. There was the motive, right under his nose, and he had never seen it. The most powerful motive of all. Money. He drove through the dark twisting lanes faster than he should, his face grim.

He tracked her down in the kitchen as soon as he arrived back. She was standing by the stove, heating some milk. Her eyes were red and swollen, but she was in command of herself again.

'It was you who told Gemma what happened while we were away in London, wasn't it?' he asked, then went on

158

impatiently as she said nothing, 'Come on, you might as well put the cards on the table now. It won't alter anything. It was you, wasn't it?'

'Yes.'

'How did you know what happened? Madrina didn't tell anybody.'

'I overheard what she was up to. A typical piece of scheming. Managing other people's lives as though they were puppets and she their manipulator.'

'And you encouraged Gemma to elope on the strength of it?'

'She didn't want much encouragement.'

'Perhaps not, but she wouldn't have run away if you hadn't told her what Madrina had done with John.'

'Have it your own way,' said Madge, shrugging her shoulders, and pouring the milk into a glass.

'Wait a minute. Sit there and drink your milk while we have a little chat, my dear. You broke Madrina's heart, encouraged that child to make a disastrous runaway match that disinherited her, did all you could to put the blame on to Ann Forrester, all to get hold of the Pendine money yourself.'

'And all for nothing,' said Madge bitterly. 'All for nothing, or next to nothing.'

'Don't expect any sympathy from me.'

'I don't. After all, I sent away your little *protégée* who made such a hero of you and who would probably have brought you the Pendine fortune in due course, and I also helped to despatch the pretty little piece you enjoyed flirting with. I'd be a fool if I thought you'd be anything but hopping mad about it.'

'I never had any designs on the Pendine money, Madge. I was fond of Gemma. I've been desperately anxious about her. If this marriage doesn't turn out to be the most ghastly calamity that could befall an inexperienced young girl, it will be no thanks to you.'

'She'll have a man. That's more than I've ever had, or shall have. She's always had everything she wanted. I've had nothing. Worked hard all my life, at other people's beck and call. I'm big and plain and I'm forty-two now, and I've never had any fun or enjoyment in my life yet. Why shouldn't I expect to do well out of a rich aunt I've served like a dog? Three hundred a year. A pittance compared with what she might have left me. I'll have to go on working, and live a dull, narrow life. Be given the orders, and never give any. What do you think it's like for a woman of forty-two who's unattractive and alone in the world to face the years to come? Good old Madge. So cheerful and willing. Cheerful! I could have put my head in the gas oven sometimes, with all the bullying and patronizing I've had to put up with. And for what? A miserable little pension. And middle age on me now. What have I to look forward to?'

And at that, Madge put her head down on the table and cried, her big shoulders heaving, sobbing convulsively like a child. Rex looked down at her and was moved to pity. Compassion, he thought. We all need it, poor devils that we are.

'Well, three hundred a year is better than nothing.'

'But it's so unfair. I am her niece.'

'Gemma was her grand-daughter, and got nothing,' said Rex dryly.

'She's young and pretty and attractive. Everybody likes her. I've got nothing. I suppose Aunt Alice thought three hundred a year was all my type needed. The daughter of that common man her foolish sister married. No refinement. Coarse, like her father. The times I've had that aspect presented to me in her cold, polite voice. Ghastly old snob.'

'Let it rest, Madge. She's gone now. If she knew what you'd done, you would never have got a penny. You knew that, of course.'

'It was worth the risk. Or so I thought.'

'What were you opening my letter for? To see if Gemma might have given the game away to me?'

'She gave me her promise, and I thought I was pretty safe to rely on it, but you never know. She might have given you a hint without realizing it. Even that went wrong. I needn't have bothered since Aunt Alice was beyond learning anything more, and now I've made you hostile. We've always got on pretty well, too.'

'You can't expect me to approve of what you've done. If Gemma's marriage turns out a failure, I'll never forgive you.'

'Oh, bosh. You're silly about that kid. She'll be all right. Couldn't see much wrong with young Hilary myself, but then I'm not a snob.'

'And what about Ann?'

'She'd have left this job when you went, anyway. She was nuts about you, of course, but she'll get over it.'

'And what about me? Don't my feelings come into it?'

'You were only amusing yourself, weren't you?'

'No.'

'Well, if you whistle, I'm sure she'll come back. Honestly,

though Rex, I didn't think you were serious. I thought you'd booked Gemma.'

'That idea was absurd. She was a child to me. And if you think Ann Forrester is the sort of girl who can be whistled back, you're mistaken. She feels things too deeply. Her parents' death put walls between her and the world which needed dynamite to break down. She won't come within miles of me again in a hurry.'

'Try that fascinating husky voice of yours,' said Madge sardonically. 'Don't tell me you're losing your confidence.'

'Shut up, Madge. I may be as vain as a peacock, but there's nothing superficial about Ann. You've botched everything beautifully, I must say. I'm as much to blame as you, though, where Ann's concerned.'

'Well, my fibres being as coarse as coconut matting, or so Aunt Alice once told me, I think you're making a fuss about nothing. But that, of course, is me. No sensitive feelings, just a clumsy clot.'

'Well, let's not go on indulging in self-pity. I'm going to get a drink. I'll be leaving here tomorrow, Madge. What are your plans?'

'To get away from this dump as fast as possible. I can't see any further than that at present,' said Madge dejectedly, leaning her head on her hand.

'Well, if you want any help, I'll do anything I can,' said Rex briskly, and left her.

Madge sat on at the kitchen table, fingering the empty milk-obscured glass, thinking of the dreams she had been indulging in for the past weeks. Fool. She might have known that Aunt Alice would never leave the Pendine fortune to someone she despised. Paid off like a faithful servant. No more. Oh well, she'd survive all right. She'd been up against it all her life. She was used to it. Just at present, though, the crashing of her dreams had buried her under the débris, and she hadn't the heart yet to begin to climb out.

CHAPTER XXII

REX left Rosevean on a still, hazy September morning. The
leaves on the trees overhanging the drive were beginning to
turn colour, and one or two drifted down in front of him
as he walked to the car. Madge and Mrs Vincent were leaving
in a few days. The cottage was empty, and even the stable flat
was deserted, for Barnabas Rockford, with the unexpectedness
which had always characterized his actions, had gone on a
plant-hunting expedition to Portugal immediately after his
sister's funeral, having seen Hilary and his wife installed in a
cottage attached to a National Trust garden where their services were needed. And so, by the end of the week, Rosevean
would be left silent and alone with its dark river and its trees.
How suddenly the end had come, thought Rex, as he pressed
the starter of the car. They had all been shut up in this place
like dice in a box, and now the owner of the box was dead and
they had been thrown out to make new lives: Gemma, the
Hilarys, Madge, Ann and himself, all on their own now, and
the dice box empty, for sale. But he was still not free of what
had happened here. With only a few weeks to go before he
started his new business, and much still to organize, the
dominant thought in his mind was Ann; how he could find her,
how put things right between them.

All his efforts to trace her, however, came up against a
blank wall. Mr Cardew did not know her address, and could
offer no suggestions.

'She had very few relatives, and those were out of touch
with her, I gathered. When her parents died, she was to all
intents and purposes left quite alone,' said Cardew's precise
voice over the telephone.

'If she should get in touch with you, Mr Cardew, I'd be glad
if you'd let me know. I've one or two things of hers which she
left at Rosevean.'

'Very well, Mr Vernon. But I doubt if I shall hear from
her. Goodbye.'

There seemed nothing for it but to wait until he heard from

Gemma, but that meant another ten days at least, and he was in no mood to wait that long. He tried Ann's old firm, thinking that she would have had to give them as a reference for any future job, but he drew a blank there, too. Confound the girl, he thought, running his hand through his hair after this last frustration, why did she have to run out of Rosevean like a scalded cat and leave no trace? They had quarrelled, but not as finally as that, surely. When he thought of their last interview, though, his heart told him why she had wanted to put a large space between them as quickly as possible.

When Gemma's letter came, it brought little help. She had heard again from Ann, but only from the hotel where she was staying temporarily until she found somewhere more suitable. She gave him the address of the hotel, however. The rest of the letter was again reassuring. Much as she grieved over the death of her grandmother, she wrote, she would never regret her flight from Rosevean. She gave him details of the little house which went with the land John had bought for his fruit farm. Until this land was productive, he was working on his uncle's farm as well, to earn their keep, and Gemma was helping and thought it was all very splendid and exciting. The proceeds of the necklace had been put to good use, anyway, thought Rex, as he smiled at Gemma's naïve enthusiasm and put the letter aside to telephone the hotel where Ann had stayed. Yes, they remembered the young lady quite well. She had left three weeks ago, but they had no knowledge of her present whereabouts.

That evening, Rex was gloomily casting his eye over the *Radio Times* when his attention was caught by the programme of a promenade concert at the Albert Hall. It included Beethoven's Choral symphony, and he remembered Ann saying that she went to hear it whenever she could. It was on that Easter Saturday; he remembered distinctly. There were all sorts of little incidents that he remembered distinctly from the past summer, and they were all to do with Ann. The harder it became to find her, the more urgent was his need. The concert was on the following Friday. He decided to buy a ticket and take a hundred to one chance of seeing her there.

He arrived early, and as he viewed the vast rotundity of the hall with a sinking heart, he reflected that there could be no building in the whole world where it would be more difficult to spot anybody. There were so many entrances all round that he would need to circle it like an electric hare to watch them all. Whichever section he chose to patrol, there would be entrances out of his view. The sun was setting as he began his patrol, and it was growing dark when he went in, a few minutes before the concert was due to start, having scanned the crowds in vain. He had bought a seat at the side of the hall, close to the stage, from which he could look round at most of the house. It was crowded, and the sea of faces looked as numerous as the grains of sand on a beach, and just about as distinguishable, he thought. And then, just as a scatter of applause greeted the leader of the orchestra, he thought he saw her on the opposite side of the hall, just below the B.B.C. commentator's box. His heart thumped as he screwed up his eyes. Smooth fair hair, grey coat. She was reading the programme. As she looked up and clapped for the conductor, he knew that it was Ann. Happily, her seat was easy to fix in his mind. He heard little of the Wagnerian prelude that started the concert, and even the Choral symphony which followed held only half his attention. Before it finished, he was seized with a sudden fear that she would find the second half of the programme an anti-climax after the grandeur of Beethoven and leave at the interval before he could get to her. The contemporary music in the second half of the programme was not all that tempting. As the applause at the end of the symphony broke out, he left his seat and ran up the stairs. His sprint along the perimeter corridor of the hall would have done credit to an Olympic runner and caused an official to gaze after him in astonishment. His intuition had been correct. He met her face to face in the exit at the top of the stairs. Her brown eyes widened at the sight of him, gasping in front of her, and her amazed expression made him say, with difficulty,

'It's all right. . . . I'm not a ghost. . . . Out of breath. . . . I've just run the full stretch round the hall to catch you.'

'We're blocking the exit,' said Ann, and only the slightest tremor in her voice betrayed her.

'Are you going for coffee?'

'No. I'm leaving now.'

'Me, too. Anything that comes after the Choral is an anti-climax. Ann, I've got to talk to you.'

'I'm sorry, Rex, but I've got nothing to say to you, and I don't want to see you again. Good-bye.'

'No, you don't,' he said, catching her arm. 'I've been trying to track you down for the past three weeks, and I'm not letting you go now. Come and have coffee at a little place I know only a few minutes' walk away.'

In spite of her efforts to free herself, he held her arm in a firm grip.

164

'Don't make it a fight. You can at least spare me half an hour before you shake me off for good.'

She said nothing, but ceased active resistance under the curious stares of a party approaching them. Outside, she tried to free herself again, but Rex kept hold of her as he said,

'Promise to have coffee with me, and I'll let you go.'

'Why should I?'

'Because I want to say I'm sorry.'

She said no more, but he felt the resistance go out of her, and he left her free. They walked in silence to the little restaurant, and Rex installed her in an alcove while he exchanged greetings with the proprietor.

'Anything to eat, Ann?' he asked.

'No, thank you.'

With two cups of coffee in front of them, Rex studied her. She looked pale and was thinner. Black shadows lay under her eyes like bruises, and her eyes and mouth wore the old wary look.

'You've been very difficult to trace. Where have you been since you ran off?'

'I stayed in a hotel near Victoria for a few weeks, and now I'm in a residential hotel in the suburbs, which is cheaper and near my job.'

'Which is?'

'In the music department of a big store.'

'Like it?'

'I've only been there two weeks. It seems all right. Have you started your business yet?'

'No. The week after next. Ann, Mrs Pendine died at the end of last month. She had a stroke.'

Ann was silent for a few moments as she studied her coffee. Then she said,

'Did she write to Gemma before she died?'

'No.'

'Have you heard from Gemma?'

'Yes. She sounds very happy. Mrs Pendine disinherited her. Most of the Pendine money was left to charities.'

'I want to forget all about Rosevean, Rex. Please don't tell me about it.'

'And me, too?'

'Yes. It hurt too much. I don't want to feel any more, I want to stay away from trouble.'

'I know,' he said gently. 'You went through it all before, and I persuaded you to come out from behind the walls, and then I hurt you again. Won't you let me try to make amends?'

'Isn't it rather late?'

'Not, perhaps, too late. Listen, Ann. Give me a chance to explain. We can't talk here. Will you have dinner with me tomorrow evening and come round to the flat afterwards? I promise you that if you still feel you would rather be rid of me after we've talked, I'll not trouble you again. Will you?'

She hesitated, and he said,

'You can dismiss me just as well tomorrow as now, and I would like to square one or two things.'

'Very well.'

They arranged a meeting place, and then she slipped away, elusive, detached. Rex decided to walk back to the flat, which was not far away, for the night was fine and his mind troubled. She had gone into retreat this time, with a vengeance. He would have felt happier if she had shown anger.

At dinner the next evening, they talked politely together, like acquaintances. She wore a black silk dress, trimmed with velvet, which emphasized her pallor and made her look older than her years. It was not until they went back to the flat that reality broke in.

'I asked my daily treasure to lay the fire this morning, as it seemed chilly. If you'd like to put a match to it, Ann, I'll make some more coffee. My one culinary skill,' said Rex with a cheerful air which masked his anxiety.

'This is a very comfortable flat. Did you inherit the treasure too?'

'Yes. With stern instructions about treating her with every consideration, and a penalty cause inserted in case I should cause her to give in notice. I'm afraid to open my mouth, I can tell you. Be with you in a shake.'

Seated in armchairs on either side of the fire, the coffee on a low table between them, they must present a truly domestic picture, thought Ann wryly. He had organized it very nicely even to the flowers on the bookcase.

'Rex, before you start tactics to get round me again, may I state my case? I've thought it out carefully over the past weeks. Nothing will make me change it.'

'Go on.'

'Rosevean stands for something evil in my life. I've known unhappiness before, but not cruelty and greed and tyranny. I felt it when I first went there, and experience confirmed it. Money was the God in that house. Nothing else counted. And you were part of it. I want to put it behind me. Blot it out. All of it.'

'I'm sorry if you think that money is my God, too.'

166

'It governed everybody's outlook, except Gemma's. Mrs Pendine wanted to make sure that her money would be looked after by the right husband for Gemma, which was you. Madge hung on there, obedient and servile to Mrs Pendine's tyranny, for the sake of the money she might inherit one day. You condemned John Hilary out of hand because he had no money, because you were sure he was after Gemma's money. You were all tainted with it. Nothing else counted. I'm thankful that Gemma escaped. And now I've escaped, and I'm not picking up any connecting threads.'

'You've escaped to what?'

'At present, loneliness. But I've faced that before.'

'I see. Well, let me put my case now. I admit, in the light of Gemma's letters, that I may have been wrong about young Hilary. I was wrong, too, in thinking of Gemma as a child, not old enough to know what love and marriage meant. Was it such a crime to be angry because what I thought was a tragedy for a child I was very fond of was precipitated by your actions? I was wrong about that, and I apologize most sincerely for ever thinking it, but the facts were against you, and in those circumstances, was it such a crime to behave as I did? A crime you can't forgive?'

'It wasn't only that. It was taking your stand with them, with their way of thinking. I shall find it hard to forget how you stood with your back to me while Mrs Pendine said those cruel things. You lined yourself up with them, and I thought I had a right to your loyalty.'

'I was out of my mind with worry about Gemma.'

'Then why are you bothering about me now? Am I for your spare time amusement?'

Rex put his cup down and studied his hands as he said quietly,

'Yes, I suppose I deserve that. She was a child, Ann. You were an adult.'

'But I feel, as Gemma feels. Being older doesn't make cruelty hurt any less.'

'No. You are very vulnerable. I know that. It's what I find hard to forgive myself for. I hoped you would be more generous. I meant to be a kind tiger, and clawed you like the rest. Don't think I'm pleased with myself over this, Ann, or expect you to forgive easily. It opened my eyes to several aspects of myself that I'm not proud of, I assure you. I was vain and stupid about it. I saw myself as Gemma's hero and guide. I saw myself as a wise friend to you, helping you over the unhappiness of your parents' sudden death. When you both behaved as though I didn't exist, as though I was the last person in the world you'd confide in, my vanity received a clout that made me angry. Gemma had deceived me, you had deceived me, and I thought I was so important to you both. If you hadn't shot off so quickly from Rosevean, I might by the next day have been a little more civilized. I don't know. I'm trying to be completely honest.'

It was the one thing she had not expected from him, humility. Always, somewhere at the back of her mind, his arrogance and self-assurance had jarred a little. Now, she found herself warmed a little by the change.

'You were important to both of us, Rex, but not so important to Gemma as the man she loved. She wanted to turn to you, but she felt you wouldn't understand, that you would take the same view as her grandmother, which you did.'

'Yes. I suppose as you get older, worldliness increases and idealism dims. I was taking too practical a view perhaps. But it could so easily have been a fortune-hunter taking advantage of Gemma's youth and inexperience. You must admit that, Ann.'

'I made it my business to get to know John. It didn't take long to realize that he was sincere in his love.'

'And you doubt my sincerity?'

Again she hesitated, and he waited.

'Your words have so often said one thing, and your actions another, Rex. When it came to the test, your concern was all for Gemma, and I was an enemy for hurting her.'

'That would have passed if you'd given me time. It was Madge who was at the bottom of it, you know.' Ann looked surprised, and he told her of Madge's part in it.

'I expect it was Madge, then, who took Gemma's letter,' said Ann thoughtfully. 'The one I couldn't produce for you. I never found it.'

'Most likely.'

'How cruel of her! Money again. It was always the driving force there.'

'Yes. She botched it all, of course. Nearly threw a fit when she discovered that Madrina had only left her a small annuity. Yet somehow, when we had it out, I felt sorry for her. Perhaps because I, too, had botched it all. I'm sorry, Ann. I love you. I think I only realized how much after you'd gone. Whatever you may think of me, please don't ever say that I used you for a diversion. It was never that. Not right from the first, when I wanted to help you. I haven't deserved to have that said of me.'

168

'You never committed yourself, Rex. Not in words. What was I to believe? Madge and Mrs Pendine both took pains to point out to me that you liked your fun and that I was making a fool of myself if I took your attentions seriously.'

'Did they? Well, what did they know of what had passed between us? Did I ever treat you as a little bit of fun?'

'No. Oh, that whole place was poisonous. It would have undermined any trust.'

'Do you believe me now?'

His eyes held hers and of his seriousness there could be no doubt.

'Yes, Rex, I believe you.'

'It wasn't easy for me there, Ann. Madrina was an old lady to whom I owed affection and loyalty. She had been very good to me. There were family ties. And apart from that, my own position was in a state of flux. I didn't feel able to commit myself until I'd got my career on a firm basis. Gemma told me in a letter that I was sweet and old-fashioned. That shook me a bit, too. But I suppose I am old-fashioned in that I wouldn't propose marriage until I felt myself in a position to maintain a decent home for my wife. I wasn't worried. But it seemed neither the time nor the place to commit myself. I said to you once that time was on our side. I believed that. I thought you cared enough for me to wait. I was pretty sure of you. My vanity again?'

She shook her head, and now she was smiling, and Rex felt a wave of relief wash over him as she said,

'No. I cared enough, but I wasn't sure of you. Perhaps, anywhere else but at Rosevean, I should have been sure.'

'But if it hadn't been for Rosevean, we shouldn't have met. Do you wish we hadn't?'

'No, though I can still feel the bruises.'

'Come here and let me comfort them.'

In his arms, she said shakily,

'Don't rush me, Rex. After the past weeks, my legs are still shaky. I'm not absolutely sure of my ground.'

He put her head on his shoulder and kissed her forehead gently.

'I won't rush you. I don't know how I'm going to make out as a consulting engineer, but as you seem to condemn worldliness with such severity, I won't harp on that. If I can make the ground firm under your feet again during the coming months, will you marry me in the spring?'

'I think so,' she said, smiling with a tenderness which caught at his heart.

They paid one more visit to Rosevean on their way home from their honeymoon in the Isles of Scilly the following April. It was Rex who suggested it on the boat as it neared Penzance, where they were picking up the car.

'Let's-go and lay the ghosts. It won't be far out of our way, darling, and we've plenty of time as we're breaking our journey somewhere tonight.'

'All right, Rex. I wonder if it's been sold yet.'

'Not as far as I know.'

They were standing at the prow of the boat as it nosed its way into Mounts Bay. The crossing had bene choppy but they were both good sailors, and had enjoyed the trip. As they leaned on the rail in the spring sunshine and watched the harbour approach, Rex put his hand on Ann's and said,

'Enjoyed your honeymoon?'

'You don't really need to ask, do you?'

'Not everybody does, I'm told.'

'It's been wonderful, Rex. I've never been so happy before.'

'Nor me. I'm quite looking forward to life in the small house at Kew, too,' he added, with the droll smile she loved.

'I still can't quite believe it, you know,' she said.

'Believe what?'

'That I'm Mrs Rex Vernon.'

'Some people take a lot of convincing,' said Rex, amused. 'I don't find it a bit hard to believe. Perhaps you'll feel it's really happened when you're at the gas cooker presiding over our dinner.'

Ann shot him a sidelong glance, her eyes mischievous, but her voice was serious as she said,

'A pity you don't like the idea of a career wife. I think Gemma's way is a good one, helping her husband in his business.'

'For a career that meant a lot to you, I'd give a reluctant yes. For some job that has no meaning apart from pocket money, no. I'll provide that.'

'So sweet and old-fashioned, darling,' murmured Ann.

'I thought we'd agreed about that,' said Rex, then caught the twitch at the corner of her mouth and shook his head at her. 'I see. Getting at me, are you? All right, I'll admit it. I consider that I'm a full-time career for you. If that hasn't become apparent so far, it will.'

'Yes, dear,' said Ann demurely.

'You know, you're not nearly as submissive as you look,

170

with those big brown eyes. You have an insidious way of undermining my authority. I shall have to deal with you at a more suitable time,' he added as the engines stopped and the gangway was run down from the harbour wall to the dock.

The hedges were showing their first green leaves along the lanes to Rosevean that afternoon. Ann's thoughts went back to the morning she had first driven along them with Hilary. So much had happened to change her life since then. She looked at Rex beside her, driving easily, as he always did, and remembered the first time she had seen that swarthy face with the dark, probing eyes, and the first words she had heard in that deep, slightly husky voice. Mia Gemma. Thinking of them, she said now,

'Do you know Italy well, Rex?'

'Yes. I used to spend all my holidays there. Florence is my favourite city. I'll take you there. I promised Gemma I'd take her for her twenty-first birthday present.'

'A lovely one. Do you miss her, Rex?'

'My life is too full of you to miss her, but I should very much like to see her. We'll have to find time to go over there for a holiday. No prospects of it at present, though. Far too busy.'

'She's a good correspondent, anyway. I'm glad that everything has turned out so well for her. She has a great zest for living, though. She takes her happiness with her.'

'M'm. What put Italy into your mind?'

'Thinking of the first time I met you, and how you often used Italian phrases with Gemma.'

'It pleased her. She never forgot that her mother was Italian, even though her grandmother never talked about it.'

It was little more than a year since that first meeting, Ann thought, and now Rex was her husband, and she could not envisage life without him. The months before their marriage had been enormously reassuring. He had shed the lazy arrogance that had often pricked her in the past, and had taken every care to build up her confidence in him and their future. Before, she had felt that he took her for granted, but whatever else those last calamitous weeks at Rosevean had done, they had destroyed Rex's complacence. He could still be autocratic in his charming, unhurried way, and she teased him for it, but she knew now that his love was as deep as hers, and that it was based on a marriage of minds that brought enjoyment at all levels. She looked at his hands on the wheel of the car: lean, brown, musician's hands, strong but capable of a delicacy of touch that had surprised as much as it had delighted her.

To have given her life into those hands without any doubts whatever seemed remarkable, as she looked back, for she had found life threatening and happiness a world away after the accident which had destroyed her old sheltered life.

As they approached Rosevean, they saw the boards on either side of the gates. "For Sale".

'Shall we leave the car inside the gates and walk up the drive, out of respect for the old lady's memory, whatever her sins?' asked Rex.

'Yes. This gives me an uncanny Through-the-Looking-Glass feeling.'

Arm in arm, they walked up the drive to the house, which looked even more gaunt and desolate than before, with its lawn uncut and bushes overgrown. Branches were strewn across the terrace, legacy of winter's gales.

'Spring and Rosevean don't seem to go together,' said Ann. 'I think a wet November day, with dripping trees and fallen, sodden leaves, would be more in tune.'

'And yet when I was a kid, I loved the place. It was exciting and mysterious and there was no end to the discoveries you could make.'

They peered in through the dusty windows at empty rooms, and Ann could imagine she saw Mrs Pendine's erect figure, hear the tap of her stick as she walked slowly across the floor. She shivered and held Rex's arm more tightly as she said,

'Who will buy a place like this?'

'Lord knows. Not even suitable for a hotel. I'm rather glad Gubbie's decided to give up the stable flat. Too morbid, living here on his own. He seems to like Portugal.'

'Yes. I wonder when he'll come home again.'

'When he's exhausted the flora out there, perhaps. At his age, that might well mean we never see him again.'

'I hope we do. I like Gubbie.'

They walked beside the river where it flowed past the turret wall, its dark, slow course winding smoothly like a snake through the woods ahead.

'Shall we go down to the cove?' asked Rex. 'It'll be warm down there. These trees make everything so dark.'

The little cove lay warm and peaceful at the foot of the cliff, its sand untrodden. A calm sea produced only a ripple of waves that scarcely had strength enough to break. Rex put his arm round Ann's waist.

'Remember that Easter Saturday?'

'Yes. I remember so much. I keep expecting to see Gemma flashing down the path, and hear her laugh. She always moved

172

so quickly, as light and graceful as a fawn. There's something melancholy about coming back to a place, Rex, don't you think? Too many ghosts to remind you of change and the passing of time and the frailty of our hopes and dreams. The sea and the trees never change, but they seem to mock our busy little lives.'

Rex took off his jacket and spread it on the grassy clearing above the beach.

'I know. There's something about the time theory which is always disconcerting. Come and be reminded of the present. You are my wife. Remember?'

'Really? Can't be. You're a ghost, like the others,' said Ann lightly, trying to throw off Rosevean's melancholy spell.

'We'll see about that. You were challenging my old-fashioned conceit this morning, I fancy, madam.'

'Surely not, my lord,' replied Ann gravely, and as his eyes moved over her, she felt the ghosts of Rosevean recede.

In his arms, the tremor that went through her brought a gleam of triumph to his eyes. That victory she would never be able to deny him, she thought. He laid her on the grass and leaned over her, cupping her face between his hands.

'I think you shall justify my old-fashioned conceit and at the same time be reassured that I'm not a ghost. Love me?'

'Fathoms deep in love. With my husband, too. Isn't it absurd?'

'Crazy, but convenient. We'll lay those old ghosts here and now. I'll give you a brand-new, much jollier ghost to remember if you ever come back here again.'

But in a few moments, ghosts of both past and future melted away, and only the here and now existed for them.

ALL FOR LOVE

A love story by Ethel Hamill

Jill Gaylord was in love with one brother and engaged to another. Torn between loyalty and love, she faced a choice that would affect the lives of three people. Would she make the right decision?

Paperback Library Romance #3

52-855, 50¢

LOVE IS FOREVER

A love story by W. E. D. Ross

Was beautiful Edna Blandish still in love with her old flame, Tom Haines? Dare she jeopardize her engagement to another by taking one last fling in order to find out?

Paperback Library Romance #4

52-856, 50¢
